The Horse
with the Golden Mane

STORIES OF ADVENTURE, MYSTERY AND ROMANCE

RUSSELL A. VASSALLO

Danville, KY

ISBN: 9780977673919
Library of Congress Control Number: 2007901338

Published by
Krazy Duck Productions
P.O. Box Box 105
Danville, KY 40422

www.krazyduck.com
Email: KrazyduckProductions@msn.com
Order Fax: 606-787-8207

Contact the author at: Russ@krazyduck.com

Cover Photo of Red Leader, Courtesy of the Author
Book Design: Janice Phelps, www.janicephelps.com

PRINTED IN THE UNITED STATES OF AMERICA

To the woman who drove me to my fate.

Alison Colleen

Russell C. Vassallo

To my wife, Virginia, for her tireless work in reading, editing, discussing, encouraging and marketing my work and for showing me what lay beyond the end. To my step-daughter, Heather, for teaching me to blog. To Lucky Press, and my editor Janice M. Phelps, for kindness, patience and advice. To my good friend and supporter and the best racing partner a man ever had, Kathy Cook. To the Eastridge family that has plied me with suggestions on how to market my writing.

To all those who encourage and befriend me, because they are too numerous to mention. To all who trusted me enough to purchase my book. And finally, to all my readers, wherever you are, I thank you for your wonderful support. A man does not know how many friends he has until he writes a book.

Russell A. Vassallo
February 2007

WHEN WE ARE DOWN

It was so vulnerable as though life had placed it in harm's way and left me to rescue it. I saw it as I asthmatically wheezed my way up the long, steep driveway to my home. The bird was nestled against the foot of St. Francis in the rock garden beneath my porch. I glanced upward at the elevated porch and then again at the tiny animal, its head tucked against its breast, its eyes closed as if sleeping or awaiting death. From the high perch of its nest, an overanxious mother had booted it out of the nest and now, it lay there dozing in the morning sun. What would the fate of this tiny creature be? What had been the fate of its predecessors?

Each year they came, building their nests in the receptacles of my outside lights. I plugged the openings with plastic because the heat of the lights might harm them and then, after a monstrous rat snake slithered up to the high lights and consumed a nest of baby birds, the war intensified. It was no longer a matter of animals nesting and soiling my garden and my concrete. No! It was a matter of a screaming wife, awakening me with shouts of "There's a snake in the light!" I recall that day because sleepily I looked at my bedroom lamp and observed: "Honey, there's no snake in the light."

But there was indeed a snake in the light, overhanging the wrought iron picnic table on our front porch. It was coiled round and round, as snakes will coil, full from its evening meal of tiny birds and sleeping atop their nest. It hissed and growled as I tried jarring it from its perch. And it was a task to dislodge it. Rat snakes are known to return so I herded it into a garbage can, stuck on the lid and drove the reptile miles away. *He can eat someone else's bird*, I thought.

After that, each spring, when birds attempted to build, I clambered up a six-foot ladder, stuffed towels or paper or plastic into the spaces about the lights and shooed them away. Later, when the spring wars were over, I observed them sitting on the telephone wires, scolding me for having interrupted nature. The eastern phoebe comes in early spring and builds its nest on joists or beams. At least I think it is an eastern phoebe. I am often at a loss to identify birds. I cannot yet identify poison ivy after fifteen years on a farm, let alone identify birds.

All this is germane to the story because there was this little bird, stuffed against the foot of St. Francis, sighing great, sleepy breaths as it recovered from the stressful ordeal of flying twelve feet to the ground.

Should I leave him in his chosen repose? Simply let the fates decide whether or not he lived? And yet, he seemed so vulnerable, so helpless, I could not turn away from him any more than I had from two foster horses, a worthless, ugly dog, and three useless barn cats that played with the mice rather than devoured them.

High up on the porch was the nest where hours earlier, he had been secure. His mother flitted around the nest, chirping, then listening, then chirping, hoping to help her errant child. But he was dozing, oblivious that life was unfolding around him, oblivious to the danger lurking in the corners of the garden. And why not be oblivious? It was a pleasant garden, framed by flat rocks forming a linear circle, egg-shaped, yellow stone filling in the rest, and two fountains, one at either end, gurgling happily as if cheering the day. We were quite proud of that accomplishment as for years that stretch of yard lay droll and weed-driven. Each year we grumbled at having to yank out the weedy growth and fill plastic bags with the destruction. Each year we complained as we pulled unidentified plants from the clay soil until there was nothing but earth there. We left it to the grass that never seemed to grow and each year we complained and, as we complained, I fought the birds that sought refuge in the light receptacles under my porch.

But now, one had outflanked me. It had built its nest while I tarried with farm work. Before I knew it there were the familiar droppings and the mud nest. Worse, one of its denizens had escaped the nest and visited St. Francis. What better protector could he have?

I knew if I touched the bird the scent would drive his mother off and she'd not care for him. Gingerly I shoveled him onto a piece of cardboard and pushed him into a small bucket. He startled awake, as if jolted from the revelry of bird-dreams, shocked by the world that suddenly roused him. Then he chirped and looked up at me, and I knew he was in my charge because he was my subject and I was his God.

The nest was on the upper porch. I knew it was there but ignored it. One can fight a war only for so long and then one tires of invention and ingenuity. They had come on the first level and I displaced them. And the birds had moved to the upper lights and I displaced them again. They built along the rafters, again and again, though I destroyed their nests. They came, intent on doing what nature best suited them to do. At least they had a purpose. I did not. So I tired of the battle and accepted a truce. They seemed not to dirty my porch with their droppings and I, in turn, left them undisturbed. It was a convenient truce because the birds were winning anyway. At least, until the snake came. Then I knew that other snakes would come and all of them might not submit to transportation in a garbage can.

The nest was a perfect bird's nest, round, toughly constructed, with down clinging to the bottom and no other fledgling in sight. The bird must have glided down to the porch beneath. From there, through open wooden rails, it again balanced on the edge and coasted down. When it reached St. Francis, it tired and, hence, slept against his foot. And indeed, the animal-loving saint must have been protecting that tiny creature. Did he not send me up the driveway at that particular moment to locate this lost soul? Did he not keep the dog away until I rescued the small creature? And, somehow, as I slid it into the bucket, had not the fountains gurgled even more happily? *One is nearer God's heart in a garden, than anywhere else on earth.*

I returned to my work—the work of retirement—the work of finding things to do with oneself when age has rendered us useless. A patch of weed to kill in the hay field, a broken board on the fencing, the placing of deer licks, the spraying of mud wasps building too near the house, grooming and tending the horses, feeding the barn cats, all this assumes an importance life never connoted to such things. And to what purpose? Perhaps some, in retirement, fish or hunt or ride or travel, but others need to find their way. We are lost. We have been active our whole lives and now, the pendulum has stopped and we are idle. And idle hands are the food of depression and self-hurt.

The day I found that tiny bird passed as others have passed. We mark our lives in seconds passed. Seconds into minutes into hours and suddenly years. A tiny bird enters our lives and we are aware then of how much time has passed and how little time remains. We think of infinity, of the earth's beginnings, we think of Christ and the hereafter and we wonder if all these things exist—and if they do not, we wonder then how it all began if not for God. How did the earth come from nothing? How did the animals come from a dead sperm? How did man—so complex in his construction—so infinite in his anatomy—come to be if not for some higher power? What are we doing here? Why? How can I be of use to an infinite power so great it has created all living things? As surely as I thought these things, that tiny bird must have wondered at the meaning of the awesome and vast space around him. Did he ask the same questions? Think the same thoughts?

My day passed. I gloried in having saved that little bird as if, in saving him, a part of me had also been salvaged. But on the morrow, I noted the absence of his mother and the bucket was empty. Down below, near the water fountain, my black, pit bull/shar pei, Spunky, was staring at the stones. My breath froze as if a cold wind besieged it. I saw the object of his quest. There, at the end of that black, flat snout was the tiny bird. It had again floated out of its nest and found its way to the ground. I did not hope for its fate to be anything other than a sudden death. And yet, Spunky merely sniffed it, startled as it hopped toward him, fluttering its diminutive wings.

Spunky is not brave nor is he courageous. In a fight, he'd side with the attacker rather than the assaulted. He chases deer across the field only to turn and flee when the deer stop to peer at him. He is more a danger in his clumsy maneuvering than in anything deliberate. I did not fear he would snap the bird in two. I feared he would accidentally trample him with his weakened front legs. For he was a young dog when taken from his dam and sold to a hapless woman who thought a six-week-old puppy would guard her home. She went off to work for days and left the animal alone and uncared for until the county took him away. Even then his fate was no better as the rescue people did not think anyone foolish enough to adopt him. They were mistaken. There *was* someone foolish enough to adopt an ugly, misshapen, bow-legged dog with an exuberant attitude and a need for affection and love that paralleled my own.

The spell was shattered with a single chirp. It was like a warning shot to the puzzled dog. He watched its wings flutter as it charged straight into his face. Spunky sounded the retreat. He raised his head, emitted a puzzled bark, and slowly, slowly backed away. Then he glanced at me, at the bird, at me again and awaited my command. In truth, if I had told him to *sic him,* he would have pretended he did not understand. If I commanded him to *run,* he would have happily obliged.

I sighed with relief for the little fellow. I admired his spirit. His life was but beginning and he was anxious to be on with it. But neither his wings nor his strength were commensurate with his anxiety and he fluttered about, tiring himself until his head dropped and turned into his fluffy breast. He nodded off to sleep. I could not help but admire his tenacity nor could I ignore his digressions into oblivion. The outside world was new to him. To me, it was a cruel world, filled with dangerous people and dangerous things. But to that tiny bird, so filled with the fury of life, it was a mysterious place filled with fresh sounds and changing sights, and he struggled to take his place within that world.

The sea of life was once too full, so said the poet in Dover Beach.

The poet saw it as a world of conflict where mysterious forces clashed. But to that tiny creature, the world was new and fresh and vibrant and there were neither dark forces nor any dangers. It simply wanted to fly, to assert itself, to take place in that strange new dimension. Who was I to ignore it? My own battle with cancer carried with it all the depression, anger, dismay and faithlessness that all people suffer in the face of grave illness. When I became ill, I was ignorant of the forces that struck me. I did not care to live because the depression had numbed me the way a wood tick numbs its host.

Now, having survived, I wondered if I had been like that tiny bird, spreading my wings, perched on a porch railing, ready to venture into the netherworld. Yet, I had been spared...and others, more worthy, had trekked beyond the shadow and into the light. Why, then, was I saved? Was it to tell others that illness and depression weaken the fighting soul? Was I nominated to inform the world, the ill, the dying, the aged, the infirm, that there is hope beyond the horizon because it is only the horizon which changes? If we lose faith...if we lose hope...we are doomed, not only in this life but in the afterlife—was that my message?

Who I was to ignore this tiny creature? He so wanted to take his place in the world, but his tiny wings were futile against the air that would not support him. I could feel his panic as the wings failed to lift him. He glided momentarily, then plunged to the earth, tumbled head over feet. I could sense his frustration at having tried so many times and failed. It did not deter him. He found the nest again, because I put him there, and he tried again to find his place in the world. He poised on the porch, then cast himself forward, flapped his wings until they weakened. And so he lay in my garden, exhausted from his continuing effort to experience the living world.

Was I alone in this sense of desperation? Were there others who felt despair, depression? Were there others who surrendered before the battle ever began? Were they swept up in the "confused alarms of struggle and flight" and then, having weakened and tired, simply gave up and tip-toed into death?

I scooped him into the bucket again and returned him to his perch. His mother flashed down from the rafters, ignoring me and depositing food into the fledgling's mouth. He chirped hello and she chirped an admonishment not to leave the nest again. Respecting their reunion, I moved away. There was work to be done. Hay to be harvested. Animals to be fed and groomed. Water to be brought.

I did my work and, as I plied my chores, I thought about the eastern phoebe, flailing its wings against the air, trying to meet its destiny. The little downy titan brought to my mind a thought, a thought about my friend, Millard Allen, no longer young but humbled by pain and illness, suffering the indignity of medical probing, enduring surgery, laying alone at night, coping with all the unanswered questions.

Yet, each Sunday, he arises from his pew in church, shuffles forward encumbered by stiff and arthritic legs. On good days, he abandons his cane and draws himself nearly straight. His steps are more certain, even a bit of spring as he strides forward. On those days, he passes the collection plate and journeys to the altar where he deposits the collection. And though his steps be sometimes awkward, there is nothing awkward about the man. His spirit is measured and resolute. Like that little bird brawling with the elements and its own frailty, he does not falter. Courage drives him on. Faith sustains him.

This is what I recalled as I did my chores and searched to see if the little bird had again deserted its nest. So each day passed and each day I protected the little bird. Time and again, I replaced that little bird within its nest. Time and again, I found it somewhere on the front lawn. Several times in the garden; several times in the path of my mower; countless times in the driveway itself. Once on the head of St. Francis, teetering as if about to fall. No matter how often I rescued it, it was determined to fly and it deserted its nest for the promise of freedom upon the wind. And each time, it flew a little further.

We became such friends that it no longer started when I scooped it into the bucket. It knew that I was a friend, trying to help it survive, to grow, to meet its destiny. When he was awake he tried desperately to gain the air. I marveled as he flitted across the lawn, exuding the will to endure. I searched for the mother. Sometimes she was stationed on the high telephone wire above me. She did not seem troubled by my actions. I wondered if she understood. Understood that life means enduring, surviving, giving our best effort so that when we come to judgment, we may say: *Lord, these are the talents you have given me and this is what I have done with them.*

My greatest fear for the little phoebe was that Spunky would inadvertently harm it. His great jaws had snapped two skunks in half. He seemed to delight in this even though he never ate anything he killed. It was ludicrous to see him carrying a full-grown possum in his jaws, depositing it on the front porch with a satisfied smile of triumph. The possum never moved. But in the morning, it was gone. On occasion he brought home a mole, which never brought any shrieks of elation. But he presided respectfully alongside as I scooped the mole into the garbage and spoke a few words of passing.

On the day I missed the phoebe, searching in the usual places where it had landed, I sighted Spunky staring down at the ground. The sight I might see would end all the rescues I had performed. And what could I say to the dog? That he had done what nature intended for him to do? "Bad dog! Very bad dog! Killer."

No, I could not say those things because they would not be true. It is not within him to harm anything deliberately. My tread was slow. I needed to see without alarming him. I stalked the scene as one stalks an animal in the woods. He emitted a low growl. He had never growled at me before except in play. But this was not play. He was protecting something. Was it the dead body of his little friend? Had its daring finally destroyed it?

I approached another step. He growled again. I tried to calm him but he did not calm. I put steel into my command and he slunk to the side. Then the victim chirped and the bird flew a few steps. Spunky chased it, barking as he did. When the phoebe landed, Spunky again stood guard. He waited a moment more then nudged it again. It flew again. So the game went on until the poor creature tired and when nudged, pecked Spunky lightly on the nose. There was a look of dismay on the dog's face as I took his playmate away.

I thought of the little bird just before I slept that night. If only those who suffered pain, depression, indecision could learn from the tenacious determination of that tiny bird. If only they could seek their own purpose as diligently as did that small creature. How those who traipse the halls of dismal reflection would suddenly rise up and smile. How those in pain might find renewed strength. How those who fail and fail to rise again might find new hope and courage to step into another future day. How those who cannot live at all, could live again just for the moment, no matter how short the flight.

All this I thought of and then I put my pen to paper. I put to paper all the stories of a lifetime. Stories of human strength and forgiveness and courage. I found in that a new purpose—one filled with hope—one in which that hope could be distributed to others.

What of the tiny phoebe who gave me all this kind reflection?

I searched for him one day. He was not there. The nest was barren. No amount of seeking could find him. But on the high wire were two birds, one smaller than the other. The larger flew with certainty—the assured flight of one who has flown before, but the other flew with determination and purpose. And when it settled, it looked down upon me with recognition and gratitude. So are we all a part of his flight...into new and distant lands...the lands of each new day...of each new hope...of each new faith...all borne higher and higher on the simple flutter of a tiny bird's wings...as we pass from one horizon into another.

What has all this to do with the stories in my book?

It is how they came to be. It is what motivated me, what drove me, what inspired me. From that little bird struggling to take flight, did I learn determination. What did it matter if my books sold or made money? What did it matter if most people never read my work? As long as I stood on the precipice, looking down at the faraway world...as long as I flapped my wings and strained to be heard...as long as I launched myself into the land where I wished to be, as long as one person read my book and benefited...took heart, gained hope, it did not matter if the book sold a million copies. Only that one copy would be important because only that one person was important.

In turning the pages of my book, if that one person regained his spirit, found his strength, launched himself into the world of hope, if only he or she did that, my work was a success...my book a rousing best seller. And when that final accounting comes and I am asked what I did with my talents, I can bring forth my work and respectfully offer it for review: *This, kind Lord, is what I did with the talents you gave me. I dispensed hope when they were in despair. I meted out love when they were alone. I infused them with courage when they were afraid of a new horizon.*

I taught them to fly.

ERIC

He knew little of the man who befriended him. Only that he was an old man who was kind to him and who had known hunger and desperation. He did not even know how incongruous it was for such a man to befriend the very breed of dog that once hunted him for Nazi persecutors. Yes, Eric saw the tiny blue marks on the man's arm, but he did not know who put them there or that the man once waited in a crowded ship to be admitted to the newly formed State of Israel. Nor would he have cared about these things if he had known.

Eric only knew that when he passed before the clouded mirror in the man's store the reflection that stared back at him was black and tan, short-haired and muscular, with a narrow snout accentuated by black and tan streaks and short cropped ears. He was larger than the average Doberman.

Eric had once been sheltered by other people, for no one can truly own a Doberman. To be precise, he had been harbored by a young husband, his wife and their two pesky, noisy children who insisted on turning Eric into a play horse rather than a guard dog. And to be exact, Eric often wished he were elsewhere with voices not quite so shrieking or so loud that they hurt his ears. How he came to be the friend of the old Jew is not a matter of conjecture. He appeared in the old man's back alley soon after a fatal auto accident that happened near Sol's shop. It was thought he may well have been the sole survivor of that accident, for no one ever came looking for him.

Sol did not know where Eric came from. The man only knew that he was a lonely man. He only knew that the dog was abandoned. One summer evening as he emptied his garbage in the alleyway behind his store, he startled at seeing Eric lying near the cans, blood streaked across his muzzle. He felt no fear at seeing the dog and even when Eric emitted a low growl, daring Sol to come nearer, the old man went about his business as if the dog did not exist. Sol knew better than to approach. He'd seen Eric's breed in Germany and knew well enough to keep his distance. Handled kindly, the Doberman can be a staunch and loyal ally. But with attack training or mishandling, the same breed can be a lethal weapon. Eric knew nothing of this. He only knew he was hurting, hungry and frightened. He did not know that Sol had once watched German soldiers attack train shepherds and Doberman pinschers using Sol's bunkmates as quarry. But something about Eric seemed more frightened and wary than vicious, so Sol plied the animal with quiet words and slow, careful movements.

"So, vas is?" he cooed lightly, lifting the lid and slowly dumping the refuse into it. "Ve got neighborhood dawks, ach, I know dem all und dey are mutts. You got class, breeding. I know your kind. So, from vhere did you cum, ah? Maybe, I call you dawk until you haf a name. Is goot?"

Eric did not move but neither did he growl again. His eyes showed interest in the refuse being dumped in the trash; an interest Sol noted as he calmed the animal. There was something about the old Jew he liked, something that told him this man had been lost and hungry, too. His eyes never left Sol though. Wariness and suspicion were part of his breeding, and despite his injuries, he'd defend even the small piece of territory he now claimed. But Sol made no threatening move or gesture, and Eric felt himself relaxing.

The old man disappeared into the door only to reappear a moment later. He scooped a can of dog food into a round, small plate and pushed it slowly forward with his foot. He stopped when the dish was three feet from the dog. Though Eric had not eaten for two days, he did not rush to accept the offering. Instead, he crawled slowly forward as though stalking the dish, stopped to eye Sol, then inched forward. Only when he reached the bowl did he eat voraciously, stopping occasionally to eye the old man and take note of his position. The old man sat on the doorway step, unmoving, speaking calmly to the dog.

"I'm alone here. Ve could use a goot guard dawk. Mein store is vorthless. Still dere are men who vould steal from me. Ida, mein vife, is dead. Dey separate us in Germany. I tink I never see her again. Den, I go to Israel und dey find her for me. Vent to Israel und I tought ve haf a goot life. Den dey put a bomb in the place vhere she eats lunch und she is dead. Tventy-years gone mitt von bomb yah? Und I am not vit her vhen she dies. Such a voman dat Ida. So I leave Israel. I cum here. No more bombs. No more vife. Now, I jus' live alone, yah? A bomb snuffs out so many tings? So vhat is vun vife vhen so many udders are dying? So," he drew out the words, "from vhere do you come?"

The dog still made no moves but neither did he growl again. The old man's voice seemed to reassure him.

"I don't get company. Und friends, I got none. Dead or in Israel. The Promised Land, ach. So I got nobody und you got nobody. Maybe ve stay togedder. You trust me. I trust you und ve stay. You tink about it. In der morning, if you are here, I feed you."

And then he rose and entered the building again because he slept in the tiny back room of that ramshackle place. He left the door open, something he never did. He hoped Dog—for that is what he named him—might trust him enough to make it his home.

In the morning, he placed a food dish and water near the rear step and went about readying the store for the morning crowd. Newspapers had to be opened and put out for sale. He reheated yesterday's coffee and placed fresh buns and rolls in the glass case that separated the front from the rear. The first morning customers liked their newspaper and their coffee. Some purchased hard rolls with chunks of butter in them. Others just took a donut or two, paid and left. No one tarried in the musty store with faded wooden floor boards encrusted with soot. And they ignored the walls with their peeling wallpaper and "Drink Coke" signs. Few even bothered to note the antique cash register perched at the start of the glass case. Even fewer bothered to note its contents, boxes of Dutch Master, Corona-Corona, Panatela cigars, packs of cheap cigarettes. Behind the counter lay shelves with straws, misted glasses, spoons, forks and other utensils. It was not much of a confectionery store, but it kept Sol alive and he enjoyed the few customers willing to tarry for conversation.

And he knew them all. The mechanic from down the street whose uniform never changed, the prostitutes chasing the evening hangover with cups of coffee and sugared donuts, the delivery man catching a quick break, the little kid who chose to spend his dime on something sweet rather than donating it to the Catholic Missions. They were part of his day, part of his existence.

Eric sniffed at the door. The smell of hot coffee melded with the odor of canned dog food wafting from the stairs. He was thirsty more than hungry so he finished the bowl of water, then ate. There was dried blood on his chest though he was not wounded. The blood dried and stiffened even though he cleaned himself. The old man stepped through the curtain that divided the storefront from his sleeping quarters in the rear, saw Eric standing over his food dish and slowed his movements somewhat. He wanted to do nothing to alarm the animal.

"Gooten tog, mein friend. Did you haf a goot sleep? Ach but you finish your vater. I get you zum."

He approached the dish carefully as Eric studied him. He remained stone-like, observing Sol with deep, black eyes that pierced the man's every move. Sol filled the dish and the dog obediently drank from it as if wishing to reward the old man's efforts. What Eric saw smiling at him was a slightly-built old man, erect in stature, with thinning gray hair that flopped down over his ears and curled across his forehead. There was something almost boyish about the man as if he had once been young. Eric stared at the blue numbers on the man's arm as if he recognized them or knew their significance but he did not. He studied the worn shelves that lined the back room, dusty, unused shelves, yellow with age and dirt. A bed, a small round table with a single chair, a plastic tablecloth. Tucked in the corner, an old gas stove, buttressed by a small, rusty sink. Here and there, a glass or two, some cups, loose utensils completed the embellishments. The floor was faded linoleum with loose tiles that skidded across the floor if the old man didn't lift his feet high enough. It held the aroma of mold and mildew, stuffy and choking to the dog's sensitive nostrils, but he tolerated it. Somehow the claustrophobic room seemed little used except when the old man ate or slept there. But it was home.

A bell tinkled from the storefront signaling that a customer had entered and, before Sol could move, the dog strolled confidently toward the entrance. Sol experienced a tinge of fear that the customer might be in for a nasty shock, but Eric merely positioned himself by the cash register and sat. And so it was throughout the day. When customers came in, Eric stationed himself behind the counter. If they approached too near the cash register, he raised himself to full height and blocked their path. If nothing else, the dog's presence encouraged more conversation from customers than usual. The old man reveled in his new-found friend.

He marveled at the dog's protectiveness, too; and he was proud of his newly-acquired guard dog. Eric was beautiful, lithe and slender, his coat clean except for the dried blood. During lulls in business, Sol fed the dog tidbits from his own lunch and at closing time, he sat on the floor near the dog and softly groomed him with his hand.

"Vell, mein friend. Do I haf a beautiful dawk? Ve need to clean der blood, yah? Nicely, I do it. Sol has experience mit cleaning blood. I tell you sometime."

He fetched a warm bowl of water, soaped it with gentle dishwashing liquid and soaked a cloth. Moving slowly, he held out the cloth, then made a slow swiping motion in front of Eric, barely touching him. When the dog made no movement, he soaked the stiffened hair and gently rubbed away the crusts of dried blood, stroking the nap forward and back until the coat lay bloodless. If Sol's supposition about the accident were correct, no one would come to claim this animal. They were all dead. Still, where had the dog been since the accident?

He removed the dog's damaged collar. A metal name-plate affixed to the leather read Eric. *Yes, Eric.* He liked the name. He repeated it softly as he cleansed the dog's wounds. "Ach, tomorrow ve get you a collar und leash. Den ve valk at night by der railroad. Der Meadows is a goot place und der valk vill do us good, yah."

Unexpectedly, the dog poked his snout into Sol's armpit and sniffed. Sol felt reassured by the animal's confidence. He knew that the Doberman did this to gain the scent of a friend. When the dog licked his hand, he knew he was gaining its confidence. He rubbed until the blood gave way to the dirt beneath and finally the dog was clean.

Sol always closed the store at seven. There was little point staying open beyond that. Tired from the long day, he settled into the small bunk and lay there looking at the grease on the ceiling. His hand drifted down and found the dog lying next to him, and gently, Sol stroked the bristly hair until he drifted into sleep.

The old man's slumber was never restful for the dream was always the same. He is hiding in a dark corner, near the fencing. The Nazi patrol is searching for him. Suddenly, a light flashes on him. He is discovered. They butt him with their rifles. Then the dogs are loosed. They savagely attack. One is tearing at his throat as he desperately struggles to protect the soft skin. In a blinding panic, he awakens. He is saturated with perspiration. The room is dark and quiet. No Nazi troopers. No attacking shepherds. Just an ominous din.

Sol remembers when he was a trustee in the camp. He ladled soup to the prisoners, soup that was watery and contained little nutrient. It was not the bountiful soup the kitchen trustees ate. Nor was the quantity the same. He saw the faces of his friends, pleading eyes, pleading for a drop more of soup, a larger hunk of bread. But he could give them nothing more than the command instructed him to give. So each night he saw their faces. Faces that remained only for a time and then were gone. Some lasted longer than others. None lasted forever. One awoke with the uncommon knowledge that he might be awakening to his very last day.

To have a friend now, one that could not be taken away, overjoyed the old man, whose heart was heavily burdened with guilt. All Sol had wanted to do was help his friends, help his wife. Life decreed that he do neither. He focused on the dog because the dog was his final hope.

"I jus' vant to help. In camp I try to help mein friends, der prisoners. I am only an inmate dere. I cannot help. All doz lonely faces. Dey haunt me. Und now I haf a friend. I help you und you help me."

Sol bought Eric a bright orange collar to accent his short, black coat. He did not trust the smaller retractable leashes so he purchased one heavy enough to control a full-grown horse. That would give Eric twenty feet to roam. When the dog was better trained, Sol would release him at the meadowlands.

After closing, they emerged from the store for their evening walk. Sol locked the front door and turned to face the deserted streets. Newark, after working hours, loomed ominous and silent as if a huge cloth descended over the town and smothered all signs of life. The smell of burning rubber and sea wind blended together in a strange friendship. To the east lay the metropolis itself, stone buildings blotting out the sky, empty and forlorn now that people were gone. People worked in Newark, but most of them did not live there. It was no longer a city of mixed origins and social strata but a ghost town that sprang to life only with the daylight.

The store Sol owned was harbored in a huge, old apartment complex, twenty-four dwellings massed one upon the other and enveloped in a dark hallway that led to every apartment except Sol's store. Other buildings appeared much the same, drab and dingy, smothered with smut and pollution. To the south lay the industrial businesses, chemical factories such as Dooner-Smith, the East District fire station, Sherwin-Williams paint factory, Wilson pallets, then small, dark, faceless residences with stone stoops and lightless windows from behind which furtive shadows peered out into the empty streets.

To the west lay the highway out of Newark, heading toward Port Newark. A few blocks from Sol's store, the road swept sharply right, crossed the entrance to a highway ramp, then curved to the left. It was in the vicinity of the ramp that Sol walked in the evenings. He made the sharp right turn along with the road, crossed the street to the ramp. Directly before him was an elevated roadway that rose up over the swamps and meadows. Beneath the highway, to his right, was abandoned land. It was useless land. Made so by the highway that passed over it and by heavy rains and flooding that made it mostly swamp, but the area directly beneath the highway was kept clear and firm by the road department. But that was important only because it was where Sol walked, down near the roadway where the meadow began and sank into the tall, covering grass and mushy wet grounds. Occasionally young people ventured into the swamp roads to make love. Occasionally someone walked into the swamp never to retreat. But Sol found it quiet and comforting. He carried a heavy walking stick with a brass lion's head, so he felt well protected.

And it was only three blocks from the store, not far enough to drive. Even if he had done so there was no safe place to park. Drunks often swept wide on the curve, missed the ramp entrance, steered right and skidded into the marshy swamps where Sol walked. Two months before a pedestrian had been killed right at the crosswalk. It was where the accident of Eric's former owners occurred as well. People complained, but the city did nothing. What could it do? Drunks are drunks and drunks drive. So Sol kept his vehicle safely tucked in front of his store.

He pointed Eric in the direction of the open lands and, for the first time in a very long time, he felt proud. Proud to have the magnificent animal next to him. Secure for the first time that he had a friend. Eric maintained a steady pace beside the old man, stopping to stare into the dark alleys that lined the path to the highway. When they arrived, Eric studied the configuration of the land, eyed the tall grass and weeds that formed a small lake to the right, noted pockets of water scattered between islands of grass and debris. Unlike his human counterpart, Eric could sense and could smell. He tested the air and on it came the smell of rats, raccoons, possums, snakes, coyotes, even other dogs. They scurried in the grass like vermin fading before the light.

It was five miles to Port Newark. A break in the overgrowth provided a passable path so one could walk. Even on a humid, summer's eve the sea breeze wafted across the grasslands and the path beneath the ramp that led to Newark Bay. But no one ever walked there, and Sol never walked very far. He wanted just enough exercise to keep him fit. He did not venture beyond safe boundaries. With Eric, he walked a bit further than usual, happy for the dog's company. At first Sol did not release Eric when they reached the outer edge of the city. He let the leash out to its end, then summoned the dog, rewarding him with a treat each time he returned. In time he'd let Eric run free, but only when certain he'd return.

So they walked in the evenings, listening to the wind whoosh through the cattails and wild reeds. They halted when something slithered into the high grass and disappeared. Sol was not afraid of rats. He'd seen too many. Seen too often when rats were the only food for desperate men. They had no weapons so they stoned them, lifting rocks in feeble and trembling hands to cripple them. He recalled men fighting over dead rats, watching them torn apart. It repulsed him now to think that he had been reduced to eating rats, to fighting with fellow prisoners for a piece of leg, stomach, anything that would keep him from cramping. And he'd seen guards turning their dogs on living beings just for the sport of watching them ripped apart.

But that was before he became a trustee. After his assignment, he enjoyed more scraps from the kitchen. Often they had whole potatoes and even some meat. The Germans were not inclined to mistreat the trustees as they didn't care to do the work themselves. So he enjoyed the benefits of his work while other men starved and died. But it troubled him deeply for Sol wanted only to help. Yet, the same guards who granted him privileges turned on him when he attempted sharing small favors with other prisoners.

Why had men done this to other men? He often thought of the *Merchant of Venice—The Quality of Mercy is not strained.* And yet it was. There was no mercy. Men died upon whim. Upon quotas. Men too weak to live had to die. It was ordained. But he always wondered why. And the dream was always the same, men in black, in brown, in gray—boys, hovering over fallen men, whopping them with truncheons, lashing them with whips and leaving them dead in the streets.

But Eric knew none of this, and would not have cared if he had. He had his own history. He was the largest of his litter, big-boned and brawny, too large for show, and thus he'd been given to a local family on condition that he not be credited to the breeder. In terms of dogs, Eric was a misfit. He did not even have registration papers. He was massive. His thick, long legs made him appear much taller than he was, and he had the rapier, sleek lines of a greyhound. For the most part, he was quiet except when he rumbled that low, threatening growl that displayed a pearly row of jagged teeth.

And Sol was proud of his new friend. He sensed in Eric a power he had never possessed. Certainly not while Nazis swept Jew after Jew out of homes and hiding places, crammed them into trucks and trains and delivered them to waiting deaths. Sometimes in the dream he saw their faces, haunted, frightened, questioning. He saw their bodies shoved with bulldozers into waiting pits while the gas showers pumped more death into humanity. But now he was safe in America, safe with a fine friend.

When they returned from their evening walks, Sol made himself a cup of tea and read the *Newark Evening News* while Eric laid alongside him. He shared a few cookies with the dog and rested his hand on the animal's back, stroking lightly until, being an old man, he tired and drifted to sleep. Somehow, with the dog lying next to him, he slept more peacefully, but it was never completely restful. Sometimes, in the darkness, he woke suddenly and let his hand search for the dog. Finding him still beside him, Sol patted Eric gratefully and slipped again into slumber.

Sometimes, he remained awake long enough to read the newspaper to Eric, telling him about the day's events. Other times he told him how the German government promised a better way of life. Changes were so subtle. First, the designation of all persons of non-German origin and Jews to be marked with a star so they could be identified. Then, the registration of guns and soon after, the confiscation of all weapons for the safety of the state. Without them, the Jews were helpless when Germans arrested them. How much resistance would they have given? Sol didn't know. He had always been a peaceful man. He knew that Jews fought in Warsaw. He heard some survived too. Others were driven into open fields where they were machine-gunned. He had wanted to help his fellow prisoners. Yet, he was helpless. It was the way of war. People die.

In this new land, this America, there were places where a man could still carry a weapon, but not in New Jersey. In his state, a man could only carry a walking stick or a cane, something with which to defend himself. He could not carry a gun. And so, Eric was doubly reassuring to the old man.

Eric knew none of this though. He only knew that when he settled near the old man he felt a strange surge of security, a sense that he was home. He pushed his snout under the old man's hand, stained with liver spots and stiff with age, and he was content. Occasionally wind rattled the front door and Eric went to investigate, his feet tapping rhythmically on the linoleum floor. The sound reminded Sol of German officers tapping windows with their riding crops as they inspected the darkened rows of barracks. And then they would decide who might live and who might die. In the end, most would die unless they were able to work. Sol was assigned to work as a cook and then to ladle food to the inmates.

The old man rubbed Eric's head until sleep overcame him and when the hand went limp and did not respond to Eric's urging the dog took his evening turn around the store, drank a little water and settled into sleep beside his friend. Thus man and dog bonded as friends rather than as those owned or possessed. The dog vigorously protected the old man as friends might do. People who came into the store feared Eric and gave Sol deference. If they approached him too closely or ventured too near the cash register, Eric warned them away. Otherwise, he sat obediently in his station, watching, waiting.

Winter slipped into spring and then spring into the long days of light and warm evenings. The sea wind rippled through the high grass of the meadows. Sol and Eric walked there each night to enjoy the freedom and the quiet. Crickets chirruping in the darkness. Katydids buzzing like chain saws in the far swamps. Often the sea wind smelled of salt air and brought to Sol's recollection the smell of wave and wind as he waited to enter the Promised Land of Israel. But it did not remind Eric of anything in particular because he scented the wind but also the stench of decaying vegetation and dead animals. The wind kept the insects from annoying attacks on man and beast, and thus they welcomed the freshness of its glow upon them.

As they strolled along the high grass, the old man spoke, more to himself than to Eric.

"Vhat I belief is dat ve all going to be togedder in der next life. Yah, I belief dat. You und me und Ida. Ve all going to meet. Und ve can help people because ve vill be spirits und spirits can do anyting, yah."

But the dog only sniffed the ground, marked his territory and kept near to the old man. Although the old man allowed Eric to run loose, he experienced a tinge of fear when the dog did not immediately return when called. And when the animal returned, Sol felt a confidence and command he had never before enjoyed.

But fate has a way of intervening and changing things, and so it was that on a breezy July night, when the moon illuminated the earth, Eric did not venture far from Sol. Instead Eric paused frequently, peering into the darkness at the swamp's edge, alerting at every slight sound. His staring unnerved Sol. Then the old man spoke to him as much to quiet his own nerves as that of his dog. "Ach Sol, you're gedding old. Und Eric, you seeing tings vot isn't dere. Vot is, mein friend? Dere is nothing dere except der rats. Ve see dem every night. Ve hear dem. Rats. Cum now, Eric. Ve valk a little more und den ve go home." And Sol was happy to turn around.

He was hoping the dog would signal that all was safe. But Eric did not. It unnerved Sol to see the dog so apprehensive. From the gloom, he saw the uniformed guards, stepping into the light, punching and trouncing men. He saw them barging through flimsy doors, grasping men and hauling them into the compounds where prisoners screamed in agony. The voices, he heard those voices, hundreds of times, in his waking dreams. And now, he saw the guards again, moving from the shadows of the meadows and rushing toward him. He heard Eric growl. Saw the animal hunch. But it was not men plunging headlong from the tall grass. It was animals. Sol gripped his walking stick in his right hand, prepared to defend his dog and himself.

The high grass split apart and four distinct forms emerged into the clearing, single file, moving quickly. At first, Sol thought them coyotes, for he'd heard that coyotes inhabited the swamp as did other animals. The moon was bright enough to discern the shapes and sizes and they were not coyotes but wild dogs. He saw an immense German shepherd leading the pack, its silver, black coat glistening in the moonlight. Next came an animal that resembled a coyote, a small dog with a linear face and hair the color of wheat. The third dog was box-faced, bulky and long haired with a jagged scar across his snout, and finally, a black, massive animal resembling a pit bull with a flat head, short-cropped ears and a wrinkled face. They were wild and fierce. They hunted quarry. To them, Eric and Sol were food. To Eric, it was if they had been enemies for life. For the laws of the jungle were as sinister in the swamps of Newark as they are in any African jungle and the quarry is just as vulnerable.

They didn't circle as wild dogs are apt to do. They had killed before and thus had no need to circle. So they charged at Sol, three of them attacking Sol, one lying behind to guard their rear. Eric intervened and smashed into the shepherd. They clashed with bared teeth, snarling and growling ominously. They leaped into an arc and heaved against each other in combat. The coyote-like dog attacked Sol, grabbing him by the lower leg and wrestling the old man off balance. Eric broke off the siege with the shepherd and plunged into Sol's attacker, grasping him by the hind leg and snapping his jaws shut. The dog yelped its dismay. It moved in behind the pack. Then "Scar" and the pit bull divided their efforts, "Scar" menacing Sol, while the bull-like dog joined the shepherd in his attack on Eric. The three dogs rolled over and over and over. Eric seized one by the leg. Sol could not tell which one. "Coyote" renewed his attack on the old man. Scar nipped at his arms while Coyote gnawed at his leg.

Then Eric was pinned under the shepherd and pit bull. Both animals were tenacious in their grasps. "Shepherd" went for Eric's throat, missed and then grasped the flesh around his neck. "Bull" ripped at Eric's stomach going for the throat, trying to tear a hole in the soft underbelly. Suddenly the shepherd snapped and in his frenzy savaged the pit bull by mistake. Eric was free and resumed the battle.

Scar attacked again, leaping for Sol's face while Coyote nipped at his legs. If he bent to swing, Scar leaped for his throat. Both dogs bit deeply into Sol, ramming against him with enormous force. Scar sank his fangs into Sol's right hand, tearing flesh and drawing blood. He felt himself toppling. Feeling himself doomed if he fell, he swung the heavy stick as he fell. He rapped the brass end on Coyote's jaw. He saw blood and spittle slew from the coyote's mouth, saw the neck snap around, watched as the yellow dog rolled over and curled into a defensive ball. Scar did not relent. He savaged Sol's arms. He bit wherever he could get a hold. Sol pounded the scarred animal like one brushing off a leech. The pain was incredible, but he'd known pain all his life. German tormentors pummeled and beat victims often with the hatred bred of propaganda. Sol had been one of them. He had been younger then but the beatings extracted no less a toll. Dogs or Germans, what did it matter? Death was death. Winded, he swung the cane again and again, some blows meaningless to the powerful animal; others causing the dog to interrupt his attack. When he saw the coyote move, he scurried to the fallen animal and smashed his head with his cane. Scar rushed to the scene as well. He jolted Sol until he fell. The animal leapt upon him, sunk his teeth into Sol's face. Eric broke off his fight and bowled the scarred dog over. Sol hurried to his feet. He slammed the brass knob down against Coyote's jaw, saw its head careen around.

Eric clashed with the shepherd and pit bull again. "Shepherd" struck hard, using his brawn and nearly toppling Eric. But Eric knew that going down was death. He regained his balance and renewed his defense against the massive animal. Tooth and fang bared and savaged. Paws clawed. They fought with feral snarls and yelps. They fought on hind legs, rolling in the marsh, spinning and twisting to gain advantage. They plunged, shoved and butted against each other. Brute strength and fear clashed against the other. With brute vigor, each struck. Oftimes it was impossible for Sol to distinguish between one dog and the other. While the shepherd engaged Eric full on, the pit bull savaged Eric's legs. The pit bull attacked from behind, driving his teeth into Eric's leg with a crushing grip. It was enough distraction for Eric to turn and strike at him. As he did so, the shepherd clamped down on Eric's left eye, sinking his teeth into the soft orb. The eye shattered. Fluid gushed out. Eric yelped loudly and pulled away. He was clearly in trouble.

While Eric clashed with the others, Scar ravaged Sol. Fear stabbed at Sol as it had not for many years. There was no one near enough to help. No one near enough to hear the commotion. This was abandoned land, desolate and uninhabited except by animals and foolish men. But Sol was tenacious and he was fighting, not just for himself, but for his friend.

The bull-like dog grasped Eric from behind again, seizing his leg, chomping on it as if it were food. Sol saw blood and spit splattering all around him and felt helpless. He dragged Scar toward Eric, fighting the dog's dead weight. With the desperation of a panicked man, he swung the walking stick down, down, down against the bulky head of the bullish animal. He heard the dog yelp and realized it had been hurt. Its flat head was solid and the first blow was ineffective. Sol hammered again. He heard it shriek and snarl, rolling to escape the blows. Sol was slowed by his wounds. He dragged his leg but could not hurry. He was carrying the weight of Scar as well as himself. In the midst of his own pursuit he saw two dogs, one Eric, the other the shepherd, jabbing bloodied fangs into one another. Coyote still lay motionless. The pit bull, now recovered from Sol's blows, made the fatal error of charging Eric head on. Instantly, the Doberman seized the animal in his gargantuan mouth, crushed down upon its head. The shrieks rang in Sol's ears. Eric tossed the animal aside, watching it roll to a stop several feet away. Flowing blood blinded the pit bull. He rubbed his head and eyes against the ground seeking to clear them. Sol willed himself closer to the injured animal. He swung the weighted stick like a sledge and struck the blinded dog between the eyes. The sound reverberated up the long stick. Sol saw the animal go limp. Shepherd sought Eric's throat again but fastened on his neck. The teeth drew blood and Eric growled, wrenching himself free.

Sol directed his attack at Scar who tried to evade the blows. He raised the stick again and again. Brought it down, feeling the pendulum gain momentum on the downswing. Scar sunk his teeth into Sol's ankle. Blood seeped from Sol's wounds. He continued swinging. He feared the stick might break and he'd be helpless, but he swung again and again. The scarred dog twisted and snarled at each blow. It moved beyond Sol's reach to renew its attack. But Sol was on the animal again. And he did not see a dog but men, huddled over other men, pounding them with clubs and truncheons. He heard the crack of skulls as blows landed and saw the lifeless bodies hurled into street gutters like limp rags. Then anger seized him. He struck again. At dogs. At Nazis. The brass knob smacked the bulky dog between the eyes. He saw an eye explode and squirt liquid into the air. The dog stood motionless as if assessing the damage it sustained. Sol aimed a crucial crack right between the animal's eyes. Scar yielded under the whack, again stood disoriented. Then, with its last breath, it lay down, its paws straight out in submission and rolled slowly over to expose its belly. But Sol did not see it. With the anger accumulated through years of helplessness, he struck hard, relentlessly again, and again, and again until the skull shattered like porcelain. Now revived, he carried his anger to the shepherd that was savaging Eric who had fallen and was writhing on the ground. The shepherd attacked Eric again and was shaking him. Sol struck the shepherd full, swinging the stick like a golf club. Heard the brass peal as it struck bone. "Again. Again." He heard himself saying: "Again, again, killers, monsters. Innocent people. Vhat harm did dey do? You kill dem for no reason. No reason." And the words were in cadence with each blow he struck.

The black shepherd turned his attack toward Sol. It was no longer fighting for food but for its life. It charged Sol and caught him on the upper leg. His savage jaws bit deep into the man. Eric staggered to his feet and charged the shepherd. It was enough to deter the dog. Sol struck it as the animal was going away from him. The force of the blow propelled the animal into a roll.

In that moment Sol was not a Jew but a German beating the life out of moving forms. He hated the vision, hated himself, but his friend, his poor friend, was torn to pieces. So he became one of them. He smashed Shepherd across the eyes, along his jaw, on top of his head. He clipped at the eyes, the teeth. He struck with a fury borne of anger and hate. He struck and struck again. His blows dented the massive dog's head. He saw an eye burst, blood and fluid squirting from the wound. Blood spurted from the animal's nose and mouth. Shepherd stayed down now, its bloodied sinister face amassed with welts and broken bones. It did not rise but lay there, panting hard, beaten, dying.

Sol stood erect. He was breathing hard as dizziness overtook him. For a moment he felt he would pass out but when he looked around for his dog, what he saw propelled him to action.

Eric lay beaten, but breathing. The old man could not see the injuries, but he felt the torn flesh and smelled the flowing blood. He knew his friend was dying. There was no time to return to the store for help. If he left Eric there in that condition, something else from the swamps would get him. He had to get help for his fallen friend. He had to get to the store. Once there, he could transport the animal in his car. Somewhere. Anywhere. Get help. It was all he could envision. Get help. Not even for him. For his friend.

And who would help anyway? Who helped the Jews when Hitler exterminated them like insects? He thought of putting his friend out of his misery, but should such a loyal friend die out of kindness? What if he were wrong? What if the animal could live? He stroked Eric with caressing hands, then struggled to lift him without causing further pain.

The dog was dead weight. Still, Sol hefted him into his arms and rose. He heard a frail cry, a sad, pained whimper, and he knew his friend was hurt so desperately that he could not even snarl at the pain.

He straightened himself, sagging slightly under the weight of the dying dog. The ground yielded to his steps as he moved the dog nearer to the street. Step by step, he moved the dog down to the street. When he tired, he leaned against any wall that would support him, but he dared not put the dog down. He would not be able to lift Eric again. Step by miserable step, he carried the animal. Each stoop became a resting place. Each wall another support. Nightmares seldom end abruptly and Sol's did not either. But if he died, if he died carrying his friend, if his heart gave out and he fell beside his noble friend, wasn't that still better than the gas chamber or starving to death?

He reached the car and gently laid Eric on the rear seat. He would never recall how he did so or how he found a vet who would attend him. Later, he would recall the vet recommending that Eric be put to sleep. He would recall the "Nein, nein, nein," he heard himself repeating. No one had the right to condemn another. No one had the right to inflict the death sentence. He remembered expressing those same thoughts to other prisoners as the Reich herded them into prisons. And so he expressed the same thoughts to the vet, with tears flowing down a face that had failed to see tears when living people died. Tears did not come then because there had been so many deaths one could not cry for them all. He did not recall if he had cried for Ida. He recalled only the numbness that followed her death. And thus the tears went inward until Sol pleaded to save his dog's life.

The vet examined the bloodied dog, shook his head and dropped the stethoscope onto the table.

"Mister, this dog is dead. He's not even breathing."

Sol shoved the man out of the way. "Nein, nein, he isss not dead! Look, his chest moves. You make him well. I pay you. I pay you goot."

The vet stretched the limp animal on his metal table and listened for a heart beat.

"Nothing. I don't hear a thing."

"Yah, yah, I tell you Eric is alife. He don't die." Sol fondled the dog's head, kissing the animal between the eyes, eyes that were tightly closed and motionless, one with fluid dripping down along the snout.

"Vake now mein friend. Herr doctor haf vork to do, yah?" He stared at the vet for a long time. The man wilted under the innocence of his stare. Slowly, methodically, with the skill of one who has many times performed the same task, the man positioned the stethoscope on the dog's body. He listened and then seized a syringe and loaded it with liquid.

"Yah, yah, I tell you right. Eric isss alife. I know dis. He lives because he is mein friend." There was a triumphant smile on Sol's face, not the leering glance of a man boasting but a man's self-doubts resolved.

"I'm not promising anything, understand? I'm not sure if I hear a beat or not, but I'll assume he's alive. But sir, this dog will never be right. He'll always be in pain. Even if I can save him, that right eye is gone for good." He removed the instrument from the dog and turned to Sol again.

"Look! I know he's your friend. You love him. I wish I could save him." His eyes narrowed and pierced the hope in Sol's eyes. *God damn it,* the vet thought, *this man has such faith, such hope. He believes in miracles. And I'm no miracle man. How many times have I seen this same hope, this same faith? They think I'm God. They grovel, thinking I have some special power. Hell, I'm just a man who treats animals and hopes he's right.* The vet emitted a sigh. "Sometimes loving means letting go. Sometimes, it's the kindest thing." But he knew he'd lost the argument somewhere between his thoughts and Sol's innocence.

Sol raised his head and faced the vet. "You tink Sol doesn't know about letting go? I know about letting go. In mein life I haf let go many times. Family. Friends. Men I share der bunker mit. Mein vife." There was an unfathomable sorrow in his eyes, a sorrow that dug deep into the vet's soul, a sorrow that he could not add to, nor one he could ignore.

"All right," he submitted. "You'll have to help."

"Yah, yah, ve make Eric vell." Then all was silent as the vet pointed to various instruments, chemicals, swabs and medications.

David Dunn, DVM, was a man just a shade beyond fifty, sandy-colored hair, grey eyes lined with furrows that sunk deep into his forehead. His cheeks were ruddy and weathered, as if he spent his time sailing or wind surfing, but he had a thick moustache that covered his upper lip and hid a poker face. Sol studied every grimace, every twitch the vet made, but he could read nothing in the man's face.

Dunn thrust a mirror beneath the dog's nose, more to prove to Sol that the dog was dead. To his utter shock, the mirror fogged. Not much, but enough to savor that tiny spark of celestial life to which Eric still clung. He had been so positive the dog was beyond saving. Now, his own faith began to escalate.

Hour after hour, the vet worked, not knowing where to begin or when to end, where to stitch, where to drain; where to disinfect. In thirty years of practice, he'd not seen an animal so thoroughly wounded. Nor seen a human so totally dependent on a dog's existence. He inserted an intravenous needle into the dog's forepaw, hung the bag on a tall stand, and then the bag, thus suspended, swung back and forth like the pendulum of a giant clock, ticking away the hours, ticking away the life. When the bag was empty, he replaced it. Into the bag he injected another chemical. Still, the dog did not move, but his heart did not cease either. The beats resounded methodically. Kerthump! Silence! Kerthump. Silence. Kerthump, kerthump. Silence. Silence. Silence. Ker...silence. Twitch. Kerthump, kerthump, kerthump, uniformly, steadily, one beat upon another cascading into the next.

"I don't know," the vet commented. "It could be the drug."

Sol bolstered the vet when doubts weakened his resolve. He watched as the right eye was removed and the cavity sewn shut. Watched as the vet began stitching the wounds along the stomach. Braced as the vet taped the broken leg. Helped apply the disinfectant to the tears along the snout. He watched the dog breathe, each quiver shocking him into the reality that at any moment Eric might simply stop living. But at each hesitation, Sol rallied the dog with his soft voice. Although the dog could not consciously hear him, he did not stop breathing either. So Sol watched. He waited. The vet picked out bone fragments from the dog's nostrils. He could not even say if they belonged to Eric. From time to time, he shook his head in exasperation. Sol urged him on.

"Please, Herr Doctor, I have no udder friend. I haf been alone so very long, since Ida vas killed. Please, you can save him. He vants to live. He vants to come home. Please."

Through fourteen hours, Sol watched the vet ply his skills. For fourteen hours, Sol stayed with his friend. He refused to leave, to seek medical attention for himself. In desperation, Dunn sutured his wounds and injected antibiotics, declaring Sol the most stubborn man he'd ever known, though his eyes acknowledged a curious admiration born of Sol's unselfish devotion to his animal.

Days Sol spent at his shop making frequent telephone calls to Dunn's office. Evenings he spent at the vet's, laboring with him to nurse the wounded dog with nourishment. Two months later, Sol brought him home. Eric paused at the threshold, as if he had never been home before. Then, his toenails tapping as he traced across the linoleum floor, he settled next to Sol's bed and curled into a tight ring. Exhausted himself, the old man settled on his cot and quickly dozed.

When he slept, Eric's light whimper aroused him. It was not a whimper of pain but the will of an animal wanting to be with his friend. In the ensuing days, Sol plied the dog with favorite foods. Food to build his strength. The same hope that kept men alive behind concentration walls. Often, the food contained medication: antibiotics, vitamins, even herbs to aid the animal in his recovery. He made the tiny meatballs Eric loved and laced them with pills. He studied his friend as the wounds healed into scars, watched as the animal adjusted his depth perception to a single eye.

Eric was no longer beautiful, no longer handsome, but to Sol it mattered little. His friend was alive. Sol would limp from his wounds. The scars would not heal. And he would always feel pain where the predators had bitten him. But in the evenings when he slipped into dream, his hand still rested on a living creature and he was no longer alone.

WHEN I MET ERIC, HE WAS NOT SEEMLY TO LOOK UPON. He was a large-boned dog, with jagged scars running along his chest and snout. One eye was sewn shut and part of the massive head seemed uneven and misshapen. Though he limped when he walked, he was still an awesome animal. It was then Sol told me the story, how the animal that could have run from danger, stood and defended him.

At what cost, I wondered?

Although I had only seen the old man sporadically, I admired him and his dog for their courageous fight. The old man wove such stories of his youth, it was as though I had lived in Europe myself. When he and I spoke, it was apparent his sole interest was in being a benefactor to the less fortunate. Despite his experiences in a German concentration camp, he considered himself lucky. In time, too, Eric accepted my friendship and in later years I owned several Dobes of my own.

I had not known Sol very long when he invited me to dinner.

"You are a nize young man," he said. "You cum! I make you zum nize zoup."

"Jewish soup?" I asked.

"Nein, nein! I make der minestrone. Yah. I haf mein friend. He is Eytalian. Und he make der minestrone. He teach me, und I learn goot. I make for you."

So I accepted his invitation on a Sunday when there was no work and no school. We sat in the small back room that was his home. There were pictures on the wall but he would not discuss them. The memories were too painful. Clearly one photo showed him and Ida with a distinguished gentleman in glittering uniform, but there were others. Solemn-faced images of stone, photographed when camera speeds were far slower and thus, they stood as if frozen. The men wore fedoras and long, camel-haired winter coats. The women wrapped themselves in sheer cashmere coats, ludicrous looking hats, black leather gloves. Their lips were thin and their faces white, marking the solemnity of the occasions. Some even wore veils, as if hiding their sallow countenances from the camera's truth.

"Dey are from an udder time. A goot time. Before the Nazi cum. See, Ida und me mit der Vice Chancellor. Ya, ve know him. I go back to my house und I find dem in ze ruins. But dat is gone. My home, gone. All gone." He appeared wistful and forlorn when he said this.

"You know, I vork in concentration camp. Dey make me cook und gif der food to prisoners." He bowed his head and looked away. "It vas hard to see dem starving. Skin und bones. I cannot gif dem even vun scoop too much or der guards thump me mitt der clubs."

Sol ambled to an old victrola. He lifted the top and wound the handle. Gently, he placed an old record on the turnstile and moved a latch to start it. Strains of Strauss scratched their way into the air. He spoke of the old Germany and the old customs. They were all German citizens then. They danced to the music of Strauss and marched to the music of Wagner. Band concerts wove a magic spell over them on summer nights. In winter, they drove carts and wagons across the frozen lake and shared hot cocoa as they ice skated. He spoke of the old ways and the old mores. He spoke of holiday customs, Christian and Jew alike. He spoke of marching soldiers, goose-stepping down the main streets and brown-shirted thugs pounding their rivals into submission. Suddenly, an entire country had gone mad. Neighbors defiled and scorned other neighbors. Children spied on their parents and reported them to block captains who reported to the Gestapo.

He spoke for hours and I found myself a frequent visitor with Sol, the magician, casting a spell. I was mesmerized by his stories, by his life. I gazed at the pictures. Photos of him, relatives, friends, his wife, Ida. Photos of himself as a young man. His wedding photograph. His parents. His sister. When I edged toward the door to say good night, he always had some excuse to bring me back. In time, I found it more and more difficult to leave.

"Vait, vait! I haf zum Bach," he would say. "I show you pictures of Israel. Or ve haf a little schnapps before you go, yah?" And invariably he addressed the dog as if forgetting he was entertaining a human guest. "Yah, Eric, ve haf zum schnapps," he repeated. He would reach a shaking hand into an old, dust laden china cabinet and produce a bottle that was equally dusty. The faded label read Aqua Aquavit but the liquid was crystal clear and tasted like molten lava. The schnapps was always good for another half hour of conversation and company. Still, I enjoyed learning from him, listening to him. I had never traveled anywhere, and he painted such vivid pictures of Europe and, in particular, Germany and Bavaria that I was seldom bored.

I enjoyed the old man's company, but there was something strange, something ethereal about him that struck a little fear into my thoughts. Times, for instance, when I stopped in for cigarettes and coffee, I found him searching the rooms; when I asked him what he was looking for, he scratched his thinning hair and told me he couldn't find Eric. He had searched the entire store, all five rooms, and he could not find his dog.

I stepped outside and looked up and down the block. The rear door had been locked so there was no opportunity for Eric to escape. And why would the dog escape when he never left the old man's side?

I pulled the aged door ajar and stepped in. The old man was talking to the dog. "Cum in from der back room. But I look der and der vas no Eric." Then, he addressed the dog again.

"Und Eric, vere vas you? You hide on old Sol and make der joke?" He stroked the dog's head with soft, loving hands, hands that had seen days before they became stiff and gnarled, spotted with liver spots and veins that bursts through the skin. "He vas hiding somevhere. Ach, dis dawk. Vere can he go in zuch a small blace?" But Sol never knew that, nor did Eric reveal his whereabouts.

Then, as suddenly as it began, the old man was gone. I visited some relatives in Louisiana and was absent for several weeks. When I returned, I was commencing my final semester in school. I saw Eric and Sol periodically. Over the months Eric mellowed and was as kind to me as the old man. Yet, he had a strange feel to him, as if he'd been struck by lightening and sparkled with electricity. I did not always patronize the store though. It was in a long-forgotten portion of the city, not always easy to park, not always safe to walk. My work schedule changed to the midnight shift, and thus it was a long time before I passed the store again. When I did, the front window was dingy and abandoned. There was a sign, and then just the empty darkness of something forsaken. For a second I thought I saw Eric pass by the window, but the store was deserted and he could not have been there.

"Closed for death in the family," it read. I heard from neighbors the old man suffered a heart attack and died. Eric guarded the body and refused to let anyone near it. In the end, the vet who struggled so long to save his life was summoned to tranquilize the dog so the body could be removed. The dog did not resist nor did he menace the vet. The dart struck him in the chest but the animal did not wince. He simply lay down and went to sleep. When the vet tried to revive Eric, he was lifeless.

From that time on, whenever I passed the store, I couldn't help but gaze into that darkened window, hoping to see the pair of them. But they were never there. Several years later the building was razed by fire and completely destroyed. Thereafter, the rubble was removed and there was nothing but an empty space where a building and the lives within had dwelled. I never drove around the curve in that road that I did not peek down along the highway ramp and view the place where Sol and Eric had walked. The place remained much the same through the years and would have been of no particular interest to me except for a single evening when events defied explanation. As in all things, we whip through life on a familiar course until the unexplainable happens and our lives are changed forever. My life changed that night.

It was a sultry evening when I punched out from work. The sea breeze was just wafting in from Newark Bay and, as it often did, brought a refreshing mist along with it. The mist was always heavier near the meadows where Sol and Eric had walked and it was difficult to see as I drove the deserted streets. Because of the fog, I moved slowly around the curve. As always I glanced to my right along the highway ramp. For some reason, I felt there was something to see and I found myself studying the area. I didn't understand this since I seldom gave it more than a hopeful glance. It was as though something were summoning me. I peered through the haze and caught a glimpse of red. It was not clear, at first, so I braked and stared into the marsh.

Taillights. There were taillights peering back at me. *What would anyone be doing in that god-awful swamp?* A cold premonition snaked up my back. I moved off the road and down into the darkness along the ramp. The sea breeze swirled the mist in wispy circles and, through the strands of fog, the outline of a car appeared. I pulled in behind it. An attractive woman in her forties, wind-blown, auburn hair, distressed and frightened, darted from the car, waving frantically at me.

"Hello," she shouted. "Please, can you help me?" She seemed alarmed and desperate.

"What's wrong?" I asked, noting the motor on her car was still running.

"I missed the road in the fog. I think I jumped the curb and damaged something. It won't go into gear."

I slipped behind the wheel of her car. In moments I confirmed that she had damaged the transmission linkage and some minor repair would be needed.

"It can be fixed in the daytime. It's too dark to work on it now. And, believe me, this is not the place to work on it at night."

"Can I get a taxi?" she asked, frowning but trying to appear confident.

"This time of night? Here? Not likely. It's all right though. I can drive you home. Where do you live?" I was tired but my sense of chivalry prevailed.

"Linden. Right off the highway. I was on my way home when I missed the curve."

She got into my car. I tried to assure her I would get her home safely and without incident, but she was clearly nervous at being with a stranger. I spoke about myself, telling her I was coming home from work, attended Seton Hall University, was in my senior year and worked full time. With each passing revelation, she calmed a little more until we were making polite conversation. I also kept full distance between us.

"Do you pass by there every night?" she inquired.

"Every night I work. I was on the midnight shift but in summers when school is out, I work four to midnight."

"What made you look in that direction? It's such an awful place."

"Intuition, I guess. I just had a strong feeling I should pay more attention than usual. I'm not sure I really know why. I had a friend who used to walk there. I guess I'm still looking for him, but it's not a good place to be, day or night."

She remained silent although pensive.

"Perhaps he was the man who came."

"The man?"

"A man came while I was stranded there. He told me not to worry. He had sent for help and someone would be coming. Such an odd-looking man."

"What did he look like?"

"It was difficult to see in the fog. Older. Short, thin. Very ordinary really. I suppose I should have been frightened but he was so kind, I felt reassured. He said he just wanted to help."

"Can you tell me anything more?"

"Not much. I don't even know where...now that I think of it, he really came from nowhere. Oh, yes. It was difficult to understand him. He spoke with some kind of accent. Couldn't say his w's. I was happy to have the company. At first I thought there might be a woman with him but I was so frightened, I really didn't want to look beyond him. That place is really scary." She hesitated for a moment. "Do you know him?"

"What happened to him? I mean where did he go?" I asked, my spine turning shivery again.

"I don't know. One moment he was there telling me you were on your way. As soon as I saw your light, he disappeared, though I don't know where he could have gone except back into the high grass."

The hair crawled up the back of my neck. All along I'd felt as if someone were summoning me, directing me to that lonesome place in the marsh. And now, this woman was telling me she had been helped by someone who disappeared into the high grass. Only death awaited in the tall grass. No one in his right mind would go in there. A long silence ensued between us. I searched for the address she had given me and pulled to a stop in front of her home.

"Well, here you are, safe and sound." I turned to face her.

She thanked me with a warm handshake that told me I'd won her confidence. "I can't thank you enough, sir. Can I pay you something for driving me?" She opened a worn leather purse.

"No, ma'am, it was my pleasure, but I appreciate the offer."

She closed her purse and turned as if to leave, then faced me again. "If you see that old man, please thank him for helping. He really made a difference."

"Yes," I muttered, not quite knowing what to say and not wanting to tell her my suspicions. "Yes, he always wanted to make a difference. I guess he finally did."

"You knew him then?"

"In a way," I answered.

"Then what kind of animal was that? It was the ugliest thing I have ever seen. It looked like a dog but it was awfully scarred," she interjected while opening the car door.

"Dog? He had a dog with him?" My gut turned queasy.

"Yes, a large dog. It only had one eye. It must have been in a fire or a fight or something. It stayed pretty much with him. Every once in a while it went off until the man called it back."

"Yes, I think I do know him. He lived near me. Had a grocery and confectionary store. He always enjoyed helping people. I guess he'd once been in a position where his friends were in trouble and he couldn't help. He often regretted that. Felt guilty about it. Perhaps he finally found a way." My voice was shaking along with my hands. Could it really have been Sol who directed me to this woman? Had he finally found a way to help others and atone for his guilt? Was there another dimension in which spirits lived? *But it was too ridiculous*, I thought. *Someone walked by and just assured her. And yes, then walked off into the grassy swamp. Sure*, I told myself. *It's late. She's tired. I'm exhausted. I want to go home.*

"Yes," she said, "perhaps he was out walking his dog. Anyway I was happy to have company. I wasn't at all afraid after he came. But you said 'lived' around you, has he moved?" I smirked at the insinuation and ignored the question.

"Did the dog have a name?" I asked. "I mean, when he called the dog, did he mention his name?"

"Oh Lord," she answered. "It was a short name, funny name for a dog. It will come to me in a moment."

She swung the door open just a touch more, then her face brightened and she stared directly at me.

"Eric. That was it. He called the dog, Eric."

"Eric?"

"Yes, Eric," she repeated, moving like a ghost through the open car door. And then, like the old man and his dog, she was gone.

TAJ

Taj stood in the corner of his stall, his head hung low, his muscular body amassed with dejection and humility. When I squeezed through the partially open door, not knowing what to expect from this massive animal, he shot me a bored glance. *"What do you want now? Why don't you leave me alone?"* I heard the words as clearly as I write them now.

I had never seen an animal so depressed or unhappy. Yet he was magnificent, full of presence and personality. He had kind eyes and, though huge, stepped carefully when around people. He was a light-colored bay, sixty-eight-inches tall, marked by a large head with a white snip. Taj was a racehorse, a standardbred, but he had not panned out for his owners. So they were culling their stables, unloading the misfits and the injured. Racing is all about profit, for the glory is little enough. A horse is only as good as his last race and, if he does not race well, he has no tomorrow.

His trainer, Digger McCue, spewed hype about each horse for sale, but the gargantuan man of six-eight, with a wizened face that had tolerated frost in winters and searing summer heat, and hands that the weather had beaten into a hard framework of wrinkles and creases, hesitated when he came to the stall of Taj Mahal. Softness crept into his pale, blue eyes and the unmistakable look of love flickered there. He spoke from the side of his mouth as if his lips were too lazy to move in tandem with the words. I saw a glint in those tired eyes, something that told me he felt something more for Taj than for other horses.

I did not know this trainer. Like weeds in a field, so many of them spring up through the racing ground and flourish. Some remain and others are cut down by failure. Worse yet, some remain mediocre all their lives, never knowing fame. But he was employed by a wealthy owner who spoke in his favor, and he had survived longer than most.

He rubbed the horse affectionately. "Taj was a ninety-thousand-dollar purchase. Nice horse, do anything you ask. A little lazy. I always thought I could get him going, but he just never worked out. Won a couple in the beginning, then something went wrong."

"Checked him over for injuries?" I asked, playing the role of an interested buyer though I knew little about racehorses.

"He's sound as a dollar, better maybe, the way the dollar goes these days. It's his attitude, not his health. He's big, powerful, and he's fast when he wants to be. Just doesn't want to race."

"How old?" I remained safely against the far wall.

"Four. Bred in California. Never develops much of a coat in winter. The breeder's wife thought he reminded her of the Taj Mahal at sunset. Taj Mahal..." he reverenced the name and stared at the horse, his eyes still a bit teary.

"He looks cow kneed," I commented, noting the knees bent inward.

"He's big and solid, paces well. He paddles out a little, but he doesn't interfere with himself. Has a big stride when he's full out."

I clucked to the great horse once or twice, trying to catch his attention, but he slung his head low again and ignored me.

"What are they asking?" I asked, trying to sound disinterested. I edged cautiously nearer the huge horse. He didn't seem spooky, just bored. No, I was the one afraid. I seldom walked into stalls or near horses, but I had to appear knowledgeable if I was going to whittle the price down. I couldn't let the trainer know I had just entered the harness racing game.

"They're asking thirty thousand," he replied, not flinching but staring me in the eyes.

This trainer must play a good hand of poker, I thought. "Hmmmm," I purred, "high for this kind of horse. His race record doesn't show much."

"They paid ninety thousand at sale. His sire earned almost two million in purses. I can show you the records." He was defensive, almost argumentative.

"That was before they raced him," I said, even to myself sounding smug and overconfident. I felt the bargaining instinct rising up in me. "Now, they know what he can do and it isn't much."

Taj turned and glared at me. I swear that horse read my mind or, at least, understood the words. I shuffled closer; the acrid smell of fresh cedar shavings rose up as I disturbed the bedding. It was a beautiful stall in a beautiful barn. The stall grates were black, heavy steel, the kind one sees on million-dollar farms. The interior was redwood, with ceiling fan above, lights high up on the walls and an automatic waterer alongside the feed bucket. It smelled aromatic and felt cushy as I stepped into it.

Hay was stuffed into a corner rack. It was green and fresh and up from it wafted the aroma of new grass. I moved another step toward Taj but he remained stone still. He simply was not interested, not in Digger, not in me, not in his surroundings. Feeling more confident, I moved closer. He could have been a mastodon, so tall was he next to my diminutive stature and, being a short man, I was even more in awe of this gentle giant.

"Okay, big fella, I just need a closer look at you." He turned to gaze at me. There was something deep and loving in his eyes. It was as if he were fathoming me as a person, an individual. *Who is he? What is he doing here? What does he want of me? What do I want of him? Why doesn't he just go away and leave me in misery?* Suddenly Taj twisted toward me, stuck his face into my beard and began nuzzling me. He blew gently into my face, stared as the hairs on my face swayed with his breath. He blew again and nuzzled again and I knew then, he had taken a liking to me. Perhaps, in me, he saw some faint expectation, some slight hope that the future might gift him with people who cared.

Before I knew it I was standing alongside the huge animal, running my hand lovingly over his withers. He faced me and I reached up and scratched the white snip in the center of his head.

Careful now, I thought, *don't show too much interest. Can't negotiate a price if they think you really want the horse. God, he's huge but there's something kind about him.* Before I knew it the gentle animal placed his chin on top of my head. It could have been a bird so light was his weight. He nickered as if to say "*Hi, Shorty!*" I snaked my arm around his neck and rubbed my beard across his nose. Taj turned full around and faced me then.

Digger continued his dialogue. "He likes you, Mr. Larsen."

"Just call me Grant," I countered. "No formality."

"Taj has potential for the right guy. He needs someone to motivate him. He'll never reach his potential here because they ignore him. He's one of two hundred ten horses. I've got seventy horses in this barn alone. They either pan out or they go. Doctor's orders." He was referring to the owner who was a surgeon.

"What's his fastest time?" I asked.

"He's won in 1:58.2 Not very fast on a mile track but he's got more in him. He's just never showed it."

I feigned surprise. "1:58? They're racing in 1:55 in the non-winners classes. Meadowlands Stakes Races have been going in 1:53.1." I reached down and handled each leg. The great horse resisted on the first leg, and I did considerable tugging until he lifted it. Like most horses he didn't appreciate standing on three legs. It didn't matter what I discovered because my vet would examine him and make the final determination. I glanced at Digger and motioned to take the horse into the center aisle. He snapped on the lead and walked him outside. Down the long blacktop hallways, lined with red cedar and black iron grates and the perennial water hose lying across the aisle, half-filled buckets along the sides, we ambled slowly toward the doors. He moved Taj out of the barn and into the light. His coat blazed in the morning sun, but his eyes were somber and lifeless. He moved like a huge bulldozer clearing land, plowing through living brush, iron and steel and smashing everything in his path. Taj seemed capable of doing that.

Smashing things. Hurting people. And yet, for a large horse, he had a docile, knowing glint in his eye.

I stood before him and moved closer. They had groomed him until his bay coat radiated with a warm glow. The hooves had been glossed with lacquer, and he had been newly shod. His flanks rippled and glistened with a lustrous conditioner. I inspected his legs again. The muscles were massive, as if he had been lifting weights. I could not put my hand around them they were so thick at the joints.

Someone called Digger away, and he signaled he'd be back. I stood studying that fine animal, wondering why with all his mass and speed, he didn't have the attitude to go with it. But things are seldom in tandem in life. Those with intelligence seldom control their emotions. So it was not incongruous that so fine an animal did not have the will to compete and win. It is one of life's imbalances that those with talent often suffer for want of those with faith in their ability.

What's the key? I wondered, as I stood looking at him. It took Digger longer to return than I thought it would. I walked the horse around in a circle, feeling very smug that I controlled him so well. He turned well and handled smoothly. As we made each turn, he lifted his head so as not to collide with mine. My being short, it was easy enough for Taj to raise his head and avoid hitting me.

When I tired of walking him, I held the lead and stood facing him. Taj raised his head and lightly placed it on top of my own. He seemed to take delight in doing this. I glanced into his eyes. He was smiling. I was smiling too.

"I'm not supposed to allow you to do that," I whispered, "but I don't think you're being assertive. No, my guess is that you're a very kind and forgiving horse, and it's just your way of saying hello. " Taj moved his lips and placed his nose directly in my face. I blew into his nostrils because this was a sign of one horse greeting another. His lips quivered when I did this and he kept his face there for a very long time. He nickered softly as if to say: "I like you. I think we can be friends."

"I like you too, Taj. Can we work together?" I loosened my grip on the lead shank and let him graze. He clipped each blade with precision and care and respected my space.

Digger returned. "So, what do you think of him?"

"As a horse, I like him. As a thirty thousand dollar purchase for racing…uh, I don't know."

"Grant, I'll level with you. I like Taj. He's always been a favorite. There's a way to reach through that thick skull of his and make him race well, but they won't let me go on with him. The Doc hates him. Every time he and his wife have a battle, he wants this horse off the farm because he knows it will irritate her. If you buy this horse and find the key, you'll have a hell of a horse."

"I believe you. I just don't know about spending that kind of money."

"Have your vet examine him. He's sound. "

"What's rock bottom price?" I was not convinced this was a horse I wanted to buy. I liked him as a pet, as a trail horse, but I wasn't there for that purpose.

McCue bent down and whispered, "Buy Taj and I'll get them to accept twenty thousand. I'll even tip you on how to get him going." There was something sincere about his manner and I considered his words for a moment.

"You really like this horse, don't you?" I asked.

"Yeah, I do. He's lazy and he hasn't made his mind up if he wants to race, but he's a pure spirit. He'll do right by you." His eyes sparkled with the oncoming dew of sorrow. There are those who care nothing for the horse and still others who love them deeply. Digger was such a man. He trained, not for the money, but because horses were all that he held dear in life. That one horse, that one winner, that one dream of riches and fame, drove him as it drove owners and drivers and stable hands. Though horses came and went in his life, occasionally one touched his heart. He fell in love. He fell in love with Taj.

As a small child I had a circus pony. I was not permitted to speak to adults. For "children were to be seen and not heard," but I could talk to Lucky and he conversed with me. Animals speak. They speak from the heart rather than the mouth. Those who love animals understand the language. They speak from the heart as well.

"I'll take a chance. Not on the horse. I'll take a chance on you."

"It's a deal?" he exhaled and seized my hand to pump it vigorously.

"Done, provided you give me that help you promised and my vet gives him a clean bill of health."

We walked the horse back into the barn while Digger lifted a telephone and called the front office to report the sale.

"Taj needs purpose and he needs confidence. They kept dropping him in class until he had no spirit left. If he were mine, I'd take him up to the Islands. Nova Scotia, Prince Edward Island, some place where the tracks are racing cheap horses. You race him against the nags and done-fors. He wins. You keep racing him against inferior company. Building his confidence. Making him feel something for himself.

"That's the key. When he's ready you put him in the Gold Cup Trials on PEI. If he wins, it's ten thousand in purse money, and he qualifies to race in the Gold Cup. That's fifty thousand smackers. If he loses, he races in the consolation race for five thousand. And training is cheap up there too."

With that, we concluded the deal. I returned to my law office. It was a busy afternoon with several appointments and two walk-in clients. In between the hectic activity, the vet's office called and delivered a message that Taj was sound but with some minor cartilage problems in the left front foot. I got through the vet's message and the no-appointment clients without kicking a single piece of furniture. Walk-in clients always ticked me off because it disrupted my schedule, and my patience level was dipping below zero when the phone rang.

"Mr. Larsen speaking," I answered. Being a sole practitioner I did not employ a secretary but farmed out work to family members and used an answering service when I was away.

"Hi, Dad, it's Mary Beth."

"My daughter? Mary Beth? The one I haven't heard from in three or four years?" Sparring with the voice on the phone, I commented, "What's the occasion?"

In truth I had not heard from her in four years. When my first wife and I separated, my daughter entered her rebellious stage. She was a freshman in college and dating a custodian at a local high school. It was not just his lack of credentials that irked me but a couple of drunk driving convictions that set me on edge. Our parting had not been a good one. She came home one evening and told me she wanted to talk. We walked as we usually did when such conversations occurred. She had been my confidant, my friend, as well as my daughter. At that point she was sabotaging all the emotions and love I had for her as a parent. She was confessing that she had bedded down with Bill and was no longer a virgin.

It was a revelation that shocked me. Mary Beth had always been an obsequious daughter. I suspect she had a crush on "Daddy." When her mother and I divorced, she undertook the household management. I was free to practice law, invest in stocks and earn money. She ran the house. No secrets between us.

When she issued her defiant challenge about sleeping with Bill, she stunned me with the reality that she was fully grown. She did not approve of the woman I was dating and her action was calculated to hurt. Out of anger, I committed the cardinal sin of giving her two weeks to get out. Only later did I realize that she calculated exactly what I would do. When the college tuition bill came in, I forwarded it to her with a note:

Hi! I guess good old Bill should be paying this tuition. He's the man of the hour.

I was angry. I was hurt. I didn't care if she finished college or not. She betrayed me, abandoned me. After all, I raised her even after her mother deserted and stranded us. There was no justice in what my daughter had done.

Mary Beth continued, her tone more subdued, "No occasion, Dad. I missed you. I've wanted to call, but didn't know how you'd take it."

"Take it? Take what? A simple phone call? Maybe a Father's Day card or a Christmas wish, something to recognize I'm alive."

"Dad, you're yelling at me again. You always yell at me. Can't we ever talk without the yelling, the anger? I just wanted to say hello and maybe begin some kind of dialogue." She hesitated, as if waiting for a reply, but I gave her none. No quarter asked. No quarter given. After all, pride is pride. I'm her father. Entitled to respect. I didn't deserve the cut she gave me.

Then she went on, "I thought...well, Dad, I know I handled things badly, but you were pretty hard-nosed too. It wasn't that I objected to Saundra. She's really nice. But I couldn't visit Mom, couldn't leave the house without accounting for everything I did. I wanted a relationship with both you and Mom. I didn't want to be in the middle. Every time I saw Mom, your feelings were hurt. If I didn't call or visit Mom, her feelings were hurt."

"So what are you trying to say, Mary Beth? I botched the job as your father?"

"No," she whimpered, "Dad, there you go again. I'm trying to say I'm sorry—"

I cut her off before she finished.

"Mary Beth, I don't know what you want of me. I did the best job, as a parent, I knew how. Your sainted mother took off to California and rifled my bank accounts. I was in a hole and worked my tail off to make up the loss. I relied on you, and you dumped me like a lame horse."

"I know you had a hard time, Dad. I know I didn't make it any easier. That's why I'm trying to say I'm sorry. I miss you."

"Well, okay, you said it. Where do we go from here?"

"I don't know, Dad. I thought you might have some...some...ideas."

"Sorry," I hesitated, nearly softening my tone, "I'm fresh out of ideas today. Now, I'm busy so is there anything else you need to say?"

I acted badly. I knew she was reaching out, trying to mend fences, but I wasn't having any. She did me wrong and I wasn't going to forget it. Besides, how can you trust someone who ditches you the way she did? Like mother, like daughter. Still, I wished things had gone better.

"There was something else I wanted to tell you..." her voice buoyed a little. "Something special."

"I'm waiting. And I don't have time for guessing games."

I could hear her spirits deflating over the telephone. Whatever she wanted to tell me was important to her...but not to me.

"It's not important, Dad. I mean, it's not as important as I thought it was." Her voice softened into silence.

"Come on now! You got me all hyped up and now you're not going to tell me?"

I was already regretting my caustic approach. Something in her weak dialogue incensed me even more. Anger had always motivated me and anger drove me into problems. "I guess if it's important to you, the least I can do is listen."

"It's not important. I just got a new job. I'm an insurance adjuster."

"Really? Did you do that because you wanted to or because dad had been an adjuster way back when?"

"No, it's something I wanted to do. I guess I should also tell you that Bill and I got married."

"That's fine. Thanks for the invitation." I feigned being busy but inwardly I was happy she was settled. She tried a few more openings but I was just as abrupt and curt.

It little mattered what approach she tried. I wasn't listening. As she spoke I doodled on a little pad, marking down all the smaller race tracks where Taj could race. I pretended not to be interested in her conversation, but I had to have my revenge. I didn't think I was *that* cruel. Does one ever think of themselves as cruel?

The conversation ended with a disappointed, "I love you." It was whispered in between tears. I hung up the phone, knowing full well I'd botched things again. On reflection I recognized my own fear, fear of admitting hurt, admitting vulnerability, fear my anger and sarcasm wouldn't be defense enough to shield my real feelings. It was fear that I'd love her again and be hurt again. Because I hated myself for my cruelty, my anger, I pushed my daughter from my thoughts and started making arrangements to transport Taj to Canada. A new interest would keep me safe from my own emotions.

Taj was trailered to a holding facility on the Canadian border. It was not an easy trip, Taj being in the trailer for thirty hours between traveling and waiting for a local vet to examine him and certify he was healthy and could be admitted into Canada. I felt totally helpless as I waited for the vet to appear. For his part he would hand me a certificate and a bill that was healthier than the horse but not until he relegated me to the most unimportant person on earth. Authority has a way of doing that, of saying: "I am the authority here. I can admit your horse or impound him in a sanctuary and all your rights won't protect you if I decide against you." So he studied, and prodded, took temperatures and hummmmed, checked teeth and gums and feet. As I waited, I answered the few questions he asked, holding my temper in check.

He jotted notes down on an official-looking form, said nothing to me and spoke directly to the immigration official who glanced at me from time to time as though I had some communicable disease or a criminal record. After hours of needless waiting and suspense the vet handed me his bill and awaited payment. Not a word did he say. Not a mention of the horse's condition. Not even a thank you when I handed him the cash.

I visualized a drunken man lying in the straw of a dilapidated barn, awakened by a groom who tells him he has an examination to perform. He arises slowly, brushes back his ruffled hair with his hand, splashes some water on his face and slowly motors off to see the equine patient. He sobers himself only enough to recognize that it is the horse he is to examine, not the person, and then submerges again into his stupor. He checks off the healthy block only because his eyes are too blurred to see the comment section about the animal's condition and, in that respect, I am fortunate that he is oblivious for I do not want him to know that my horse has developed shipping fever and will require antibiotics once he is safely in his Canadian stall.

As Taj and I entered New Brunswick, I stopped at a local farm and rented a large paddock for Taj to graze. It was cloudy with a headwind coming from the east and such winds always blew the smell of salt and sea air across the land, the heady aroma, full of life and vigor and history and one could almost see the tall-masted schooners slicing quietly through the inlet waters. Like most Canadians, the farmer hated Americans as a group but enjoyed meeting the individual Yank. He had served with some of them in the Second World War and forgave them their heritage. Besides, they were stout drinkers and after a bottle or two, nationalities meant little anyway.

Next morning, I waited for the fog to drift high enough to see the roads and headed up the coastal route to Amherst, Nova Scotia. Amherst is a border town and the only land entrance onto the province. So not only was it an important city, but it was not very far from Caribou Wharf and the Prince Edward Island ferry.

Tourists passed through Amherst on their way north to Cape Breton. A tourist bureau complete with piper and dancers greeted them as they entered. The town itself was fairly large, yet small and friendly enough. There was a small restaurant on a back road called the Drury Lane where I had enjoyed many a good meal. Because Taj had been in the trailer for a lengthy time, I stopped at a vet's farm near the border. I wanted a competent vet to examine and treat him.

Taj ambled out of the vehicle as if he had been inside for only a short time. The local vet was an amiable man with a solid knowledge of horses. Like many Canadians he had a slight inflection in his voice. His face was round and affable, but there was a note of sadness in his hazel eyes that shouted "I am lonely." He had a rugged, cratered nose the color of burnt sienna, and I surmised that he had a healthy affair with bottled-in-bond whiskey. The man was lean and hard and weathered from the climate, but his hands were steady and his handshake could have brought tears to the eyes of an ox. He injected Taj with an antibiotic, checked him thoroughly and gave me sufficient medication to treat him until he arrived in Charlottetown.

Nova Scotia was green and hilly, spotted with quaint harbors and coves and mountainous in the north and the vet's land was no different. There were points where the land stopped and the endless sea spread across the horizon like a wave, a vast, grey desert. It was a land consecrated with American lore and history. When the American Revolution erupted, many of King George's loyalists escaped into New Brunswick and Nova Scotia, some never returning to their native land.

The vet was full of such history, and he rambled on as he smoothed his hands over Taj's legs and haunches. Then he stood studying the horse, watching how he stood, moving to see how Taj shifted his weight.

"It's only a touch of shipping fever," he commented. "Probably could race right now, but I'd give him a day or two of rest before you train again. And I'd watch that left front leg. The cartilage is probably worn thin from racing on half-mile tracks. He's a big fellow. Shouldn't really be racing on small tracks."

"I appreciate your help. Can I still keep him here, Doc?"

"Shane Herban. The locals call me Schooner, but Shane will do." He glanced down at my owner's certificate. "And you're Grant Larsen."

"Yes, sir."

"Ya can board the big fellow nowhere but right here, Yank. I've plenty of room but little company. I need to hear what you crazy Americans are up to now. Turn your horse loose in that paddock by the hardwoods and come along for dinner. I've a tidy little guestroom, and you can stay there."

We dined in a small dining room with a bay window that displayed the fields and paddocks surrounding his home. Red-throated and green-breasted hummingbirds whizzed about his feeders like large bees battling over the red syrup. It was an old home, decored with dark oak and musty carpeted floors, a field stone fireplace that almost shouted to be lit, dim paintings hung aslant on the wall. It had the look of a bachelor's home and yet there was evidence that a woman had once lived there.

There is neither more succulent seafood than in Nova Scotia nor any beer as tasty as when downed with fried clams or haddock. He served thin fish chowder with an aroma that spurred my palate, then steamed clams covered with seaweed and Irish moss to keep them moist, some cold lobster and rich, buttery mashed potatoes. This we washed down with ale into which he poured a touch of rye whiskey until it bit the tongue.

"There is a river near Amherst," he muttered as we drank cold brew and cracked hot steamers to dip in melted butter. "It's called the Missiquash...and don't ask me to spell it, for I don't know. It was named after the governor's daughter but she ran off with a soldier she loved. The governor was so outraged that he changed the name of the river to the ugliest name he could conceive. Missiquash. Sounds like an Indian name, but it's not. He just thought it up, the old beggar."

I moved closer to him, half smashed from drink.

"Did she ever make amends?" I asked. Somehow the question seemed natural to a man who had disowned his own daughter.

"No, Yank! She did not." His eyes glittered with the mirth of one who has just sold a parcel of smelly fish. I suspected he had told the tale before and not been held to account.

"And that's the truth of it?" I asked, staring back into those laughing eyes.

"The truth, Yank. Ask anyone."

I shook my head and returned his smirk.

"I mean no offense for you have truly been kind to Taj and me, but I disagree with how the river got its name." His face registered interest.

"Missiquash was indeed an Indian name until it was corrupted by the French. It means Red Mud and, if you see the river when the tide is coming full, it's sullied with red mud and brown currents. Now, as to the family, it wasn't the governor but a prominent man who idolized his daughter. He named the river La Margueree. When his daughter ran off with a widower— not a solider—his fury was unbounded and he dubbed the river the Missiquash. It was the ugliest name he could think of."

I leaned back into my chair, sampling the ale again. "At least that's the way I heard it."

He dropped his jaw, shocked. "Good God, Yank, how the hell did ya know that?"

"I've traveled in Scotia. I have friends in Yarmouth and Pubnico." I dipped another clam in drawn butter and continued, "Like family. There isn't much of the province I haven't seen. Been on back roads no tourist ever sees. Had tea with game wardens. Fished for striped bass on the salt marshes. Shucked scallops off a lobster boat."

He thumped the table and stamped his foot in glee.

"I've been passing that story off for years. No one's ever called me on it until now. I'll be damned," he concluded, shoving the ale aside and pouring whiskey into two brandy snifters.

"Well, tell me Yank, how'd you hear the story?"

"I had the good fortune to meet historian Will R. Bird at the Drury Lane Restaurant near Amherst. He'd written two books on Nova Scotia, and I recognized him from the cover. I asked him about that story because he mentioned it in his book, *So This Is Nova Scotia*. Every summer for years, I traced one of the routes in his books. Took me all over the province. "

He leaned across the table which creaked as he did and motioned me with a crooked finger. The meal was ended and the hour drew late. I rose to help clear the table but he motioned me to sit.

"The housekeeper will be in tomorrow. She'll tend to the dishes."

"I can't thank you enough for all your kindness. You're not offended about the Missiquash?"

He shook his head and became serious. "I like you, Yank. You're straight enough, eh. Are ya thinkin' of racing that fine animal on the island?"

"That's my idea. Race him against cheaper horses, hyping up his self-confidence, then to the Gold Cup Trials and maybe the Cup itself."

He squeezed his eyes tightly and shook his head.

"They'll not let you get away with it, Yank. Sad to say but they're a dirty bunch so watch your back. And look to your horse if you enter him in anything worthwhile." He sat back in his chair and poured more rye into his glass. My own was still half full.

"One for a good night's sleep." Then he downed it in a gulp and repeated, "Mind your horse for they'll do him dirt if they can. I've seen 'em drive a nail into a horse's foot."

I surmised the warning was born of the bottle and I ignored it. Except for breeders bidding on their own horses to raise my own bid, the Canadians had always been honorable and courteous to me. Why would they sabotage Taj when his winning would be a question mark anyway? I wasn't even sure he could beat the cheaper horses or that he would race any better for me than he did for the other stable. But I assured Shane I'd be careful and the evening wound down to a final drink. With that I toasted his hospitality and bid him goodnight.

Shane and I had several more conversations before we parted, mostly concerning his practice, his background and the passing of his wife, several years earlier. They had a vacation home on Prince Edward Island and spent a good deal of time there but after her death, he sold it off and seldom visited. He had a penchant for the races though and some gambling blood in his veins. Beyond that he enjoyed fishing from his dinghy in the nearby bay.

Taj had enjoyed the walks along the beach and two days whizzed by. It was seldom Shane had time to walk with us because of his practice. It was rumored he could study a horse and determine the cause of lameness just by watching where he leaned his weight. In the short time I'd known him I became attached to the genial but lonely man. He was on an emergency call when I left in the morning, but I wrote a note praising his kindness and inviting him to visit me in the States.

When it was time to go, I loaded Taj into the trailer and drove to Caribou. We debarked for Woods Island, Prince Edward Island, and I deserted my beloved Nova Scotia, its mountains rising up out of the morning gloom and the tiny village of Caribou, evaporating like the mist as we plunged across the straits. For twenty-five years, I had vacationed in the province. I knew the land like I knew the roads that led there. I enjoyed its succulent seafood, relished the freedom and space, inhaled its brisk salt air, purchased rural land, fished from its wharves, purchased lobsters from poachers who hid in obscure, dilapidated shacks deep in the woods near the inlets, and fell in love with its people. And like all the others, I swatted mosquitoes and black flies, strained to see through the fog, suffered the biting wind and saddened at the sounds of the mournful fog horns. So I could not believe the islanders on PEI would do me any more harm than my friends in Nova Scotia.

The land drifted behind me as it had drifted out of my life. Time and distance took its toll. Business sang its death chant. My friends grew up there. They married. They had children. Education took some. The sea claimed others. I celebrated their weddings. I marked the passing of my life as measured by their children. I was part of their lives and they were part of mine. It was sad that I had to leave on business without stopping to see any of them. But it was, nevertheless, my beloved land because I purged myself of the stifling air of New Jersey and breathed free. I thought of the evenings I spent listening to Yvonne Le Blanc talk about her fear of the Nazi officers who came to her mother's salon in Belgium to have their hair curled. We spoke of those the sea cheated of their lives. We spoke to the Great Wars and the German submarines that plied off the Nova Scotian coast. We talked of the Russian and Japanese fishing vessels that sailed their waters and sucked up their fish in great, wide nets. I won the hearts of some Acadians who hated Americans, and I played soft music on their pianos to woo them because it was in my heart to do so. As I stood on the cold, damp deck of the ferry, all these thoughts rushed me like the swirling currents that played off the bow.

They were kind times, compassionate times. I shook off the hasty life style of a metropolitan area and delved into exhibitions and ox pulls, rock concerts, tuna festivals, lobster feasts and barbecues. I searched for the few places that were permitted to serve alcoholic beverages, and I plucked blackberries and blueberries from bushes alongside the roadway. I felt liberated and alive. I chilled wine in frozen streams and barbecued in provincial parks that were all but uninhabited. I sat mesmerized on summer days, staring into the quiet woods, tracing the splash of a lone trout, watching a hawk dive after its prey, inhaling the scent of pine and cedar, closing my eyes to the sights around me and yet, seeing all there was to see and feel.

All this I recalled as I drove onto the ferry and parked the car and trailer. I checked Taj and made certain he had hay and water. His shipping boots were still wrapped tightly around his legs and his spirits appeared strong. Then the ferry horn sounded. The great motors roared louder.

The ship chugged away from the slip as if destined to meet its fate somewhere out in the fog. There is an excitement that fills the breast of man as his ship motors off from home port. Perhaps it is the thrill of adventure. Perhaps the unknown exploration. Perhaps a man hears the Sea Wolf as it shushes through the windswept waves. The allure of travel, the exhilaration of new lands, did not lessen the sadness I felt at leaving Nova Scotia. The salty wind slashed at my face and my eyes teared from the sting of it. The fading bluffs slipped down beneath the mist line and my heart slipped with it. Its harbors became distant and indistinct. It was ever the land of enchantment and diversity, some of which had never been explored. And it was slipping fast away as Taj and I aimed for other destinies.

In contrast, Prince Edward Island was flat, nestled on the Gulf of St. Lawrence, with its high bluffs of red soil and long, green pastures. We crossed the Northumberland Straight and docked. At the entrance, I had to unload Taj because the government was spraying all vehicles entering the island to prevent a potato blight. Unlike Nova Scotia, I found the authorities there somewhat arbitrary and urban. They set up roadblocks and refused to explain the reasons. Where Nova Scotia was more rural, PEI bore the marks of tourism made apparent by the heavier intrusion of government authority.

Its people were friendly enough, at least the ones who didn't race horses. There was a healthy summer crowd there. The island was beset with artists, writers and even entertainers. It was replete with history including a quaint attraction called Woodleigh's Replicas where the owner had constructed scale models of famous buildings: Westminster Abbey, the Tower of London, London Bridge, the cottage of Robert Burns and others.

But the island also had its horse racing industry. Every islander, it seemed, owned a trotter or pacer. There were annual yearling sales as well as private sales from local farms. The island hosted two race tracks, the larger one at Charlottetown. It was a course laced with spires and gables in the land of Anne of Green Gables. The seats were plain but unsplintered and high atop, as with most racetracks, stood the announcer's booth and the clubhouse boxes and seats. The track was a half mile in length, decorated with lupines and tiger lilies in the infield, a small pond and an occasional duck or two. The tote board stood across from the bleachers.

Outside the track lay the antiquated barns with long, narrow corridors that passed through the entire building, wooden stables, pull-up windows crusted with cobwebs and dust. There is a sameness to any backstretch with its aged, pallid, ramshackle buildings spaced neatly apart, narrow roadways, an administration building hidden among the barns, a dingy cafeteria set off from the barns. The racetrack itself was apart from all these, decorated with an admission booth and several concession stands.

Horses entered and exited on their way to their morning jog for it was seldom there were no horses being trained and even more seldom there was no wind to stir the earthen aroma of manure, hay and grain. It was the place where Taj would begin his racing career under my ownership. It was the place where hopes began and dreams abounded. But it had been a tiring trip, for both horse and owner. Taj sat patiently in a makeshift stall. I examined him to satisfy myself and, when the examination was done, I closed the stall door and secured him for the evening. The next day I turned Taj out to pasture despite my trainer's desire to start working him immediately. I didn't have much experience, but I did have a plan on how to motivate Taj into racing, and I didn't want him going sour because he was fatigued.

The barn rats, the misfits who purchase cheap horses and think they will discover a latent million dollar winner, scoffed and laughed when I brought Taj into the barn. They thought it funny I spoke to him, lavished him with praise. They were men who dominated horses rather than loved them. Through their horses they lived the spirit of competition and the lure of the big dollar. They seldom made it. Their dreams often lay shattered on the rocks of life's reality. But they were there nonetheless and cruel in their derision.

"He's a big one, big as a house," one said.

"He can't get his legs out of the way," said another.

"Has he been pulling an Amish wagon or something?" said a rumpled, old sot at the end of the barn. "If it's the Cup yer after he'll have his work cut out fer him."

I didn't like the man. He had weasely eyes, a crooked mouth and grey stubble that made him appear darker than he was.

Even my trainer, Warren, was skeptical and asked. "What made you buy this one, eh? He paddles out. He'll rap his knees like a locomotive." He eyed the horse both front and rear, shaking his head in ridicule as he inspected him.

I did not hire Warren because he had any reputation as a trainer. He was inexpensive and took orders well. Whether he was trustworthy or not was something I would have to find out. But he had asked a question and deserved a response.

"I like him but I can't say why I bought him. Call it a hunch. Well, can you work with him or should I get someone else?"

Warren eyed me dirtily. Like most trainers, he appeared scruffy and disheveled, wore dirty, manure-stained boots, a checkered wool shirt, patched, denim jeans and the perennial belt buckle with its horse-head insignia. Warren always seemed to be smiling, even when he announced that a horse was lame and couldn't race. He wasn't a top trainer but he was cheaper than other trainers and, occasionally, he won. For someone only par-tially committed to standardbred racing, Warren was especially ideal because he had no preconceived ideas. He enjoyed what he did, wanted to do noth-ing else and succeeded only to the extent of his effort. It was not important that he exceed himself. He needed only to be equal to the task. That made it easy to orchestrate how he trained my horse, but it left me with questions about his integrity.

"As long as you pay the training bills, I'll work with him." He slapped the horse on his rump and Taj shot him a sullen glance.

"Well, for starters, I only want him jogged two days a week," I said, dropping the comment without warning.

He looked as if he'd been stung by a hot barb. "How am I going to work a horse up in two days a week, eh?" His Canadian accent got in the way. He was a muscular man, somewhat stooped at the shoulder. His waist had seen leaner days, which was not surprising considering his daily diet of fast foods. Still, he was active and physically able. He had an easy way of jogging hors-es, and he knew the techniques of racing.

"We'll jog him twice a week and swim him three days. Once a week we'll take him to the beach and work him in the deep sand. He gets Sundays off. It will put less strain on his legs. He's big and needs work but, with all that weight, too much on a half-mile track and he'll have leg problems."

He shook his head and coursed his hand over the horse's body. "Swim him? I'll not be responsible if he drowns, eh."

"Well, tomorrow we'll see if he can swim. Anyway, I've got my own ideas on how to work this horse," I finalized.

And we did exactly that. Warren and I took him down to the complex swimming pool, held him on a long lead, and walked him down the ramp until his feet no longer touched bottom. The great horse floated and began moving his legs. Then, slowly, he submerged to the bottom, remained there longer than was comfortable, then pushed off with his legs and floated to the surface again. Again, he sank to the bottom, remaining there long enough to frighten both Warren and me. But when he was ready he shoved off with his feet and bobbed like a cork. We worked him for an hour and brought him out. I recalled Digger McCue saying that he had swum the horse in the surf at the Jersey shore and Taj headed straight out to sea. They had to chase him with a small launch and turn him around. Somehow it seemed safer to have the horse training in a swimming pool than floating away in the Gulf of St. Lawrence. The human mind being what it is, I wondered just how smart Taj was. After all, where did he think he was going swimming out into shark-infested waters, heading to open sea? Was he oblivious or just plain dumb? When I witnessed him sinking to the pool bottom, I wondered if the pool was safe after all. Perhaps I'd made an error in judgment deciding to use water for training purposes.

The horse enjoyed the water. He pumped his huge legs and he returned to the surface, then relaxed and descended again. I breathed a sigh when it was time to remove him. We finished the session and returned Taj to the barn. Warren rubbed him down with towels and since the day was warm, we turned him out into a free paddock. The great horse rolled in the grass, almost as though frolicking with himself.

"Scared hell out of me," Warren commented.

"I thought he'd never come up," I added.

"Are you sure you want to keep this up, eh? I don't know what we'd have done if he didn't surface. I never had a horse do that before."

"Well, Taj is exceptional, I grant you that. I think he'll be all right." I tried to sound confident although I was alarmed too.

When Warren was gone, I ambled over to the fencing and studied the horse. He rolled again, then righted himself and trotted over to the fence where I rubbed his face and lavished him with praise.

"You are a fine horse, my friend. I'll just bet you can race. But what will it take to convince you?" He nickered as if to say: "*That's for you to find out.*" Taj was enormous. He had shimmering, muscular, fine lines. His hocks were large pistons capable of driving him at high speeds. Although his ankles were a bit narrow, his hooves were strong and solid. But he toed in at the knees. Without care, the cartilage in his legs might wear away, leaving bone rubbing on bone.

Yes, I concluded, it was safer to swim him than to train him on the hard track surfaces. Racetracks are a business like anything else. They turn a profit or they go under. In New Jersey, the advent of gambling in Atlantic City cut deep into the track receipts, and purses were slashed to compensate for the loss of revenue. In order to generate excitement, the tracks focused on speed records and fast winning times. To do this, they installed hard gravel on their tracks that would boost the "win" times, but the tracks were like concrete. It was not unusual to see ten or twelve horses per week going lame due to the unyielding surfaces. A hefty horse such as Taj Mahal pounding hard on those surfaces could easily go lame or, worse, wear down the cartilage in his legs until he couldn't race. Since I had not had him x-rayed, there was no baseline to determine how much damage had been done by racing him on half-mile tracks.

He was a friendly enough horse and his eyes seemed brighter when I spent time with him. I wondered if a horse felt loneliness or uselessness. I wondered if their confidence levels could be influenced by praise and love, by racing them against cheaper horses and building a mindset of winning rather than losing. I was still standing at the rail, conjuring up a plan for Taj when he lifted his head high over mine and placed his muzzle on top of my head. It was remarkable how gentle he was, how lightly he held his head there. In a moment, he removed it and rubbed his face on my beard as if he liked the scruffy feel.

"I like you too, big guy. But can we make a racehorse of you? Because all you need is someone to show you just how good you really are."

He set his large, brown eyes on me and they seemed to flicker with radiant comprehension. But did he really understand what I was saying? Or thinking? In some ways, Taj was clumsy and tangle-footed and, in others, he was amazingly bright. His tame behavior reminded me of Mary Beth and I found myself thinking of our last conversation. It had not been unlike all the others. She was always trying to mend fences, and I was making certain they stayed in disrepair, though why, I did not understand. My second wife, Saundra, pointed out on more than one occasion that I was an "angry" person. I didn't see myself as such. Frequently she and I argued so vehemently

I wondered who had more anger. But it was easy to lose myself between practicing law and tinkering with racehorses, so I didn't need to concern myself with anger issues or recalcitrant daughters. While Saundra handled my law practice—which waned in summer like the last leaf on a tree—I concentrated my efforts on Taj. Mary Beth was forgotten.

The training began in earnest. I visited his stall several times a day. Often, I walked him along the byways of the racetrack, talking to him as if he were a person.

"Look at this *big* horse," I would say. "You're awesome, big guy. You've got champion written all over you." And the big horse nickered and pushed his nose into my hair. As large as he was, that was the sum of his gentility. "You can't be a nice guy on the racetrack, Taj. Life isn't that way. A race isn't that way. Well, you've got to pace yourself but, when you pull up next to the leader, that's when you stare him in the eye and spit him out. You can do it, too. There isn't anything up here that can touch you for speed."

Often, I trailered him to the beach and walked him along the water's edge. Salt water was good for the muscles. It tightened them and healed the impact of racing. Taj was a good listener, too. So I spoke to him of Mary Beth and how she'd deserted the household. "I don't know what she wanted from me, Taj. I raised her. Loved her. Stuck by her through my divorce. I didn't just put a roof over her head. She lived in a swell home: plenty of food, good clothing." I stopped and eyed him squarely. "Kids! They don't appreciate anything you do for them. Went to bed with this janitor. Can you beat that, Taj? She went to bed with a mop head." I laughed at my own joke.

But Taj just stared out into the surf. Perhaps he was ignoring me. Perhaps it was his way of telling me the conversation bored him. Or, perhaps he saw something in the waves. He stuck to his training. He worked hard. I experimented with outlandish ideas on horse training. Each time Taj worked on the track, I had Warren race him against another horse. If Taj beat the other horse, he got a few carrots at the end of the session. If he lost, he got no reward. It didn't take him long to learn that being lazy in the stretch didn't pay. But once Taj had the idea that winning brought dividends, I seldom gave any instruction but to let him race. When he got into close competition with the other horse and stared him down, I knew he was ready for higher purses and the big time.

In time, Warren agreed Taj was ready. "He done the quarter in 30 and the mile in 1:59," he bragged.

"Is that good time up here?"

"They did the last Gold Cup in 1:58 and the record is 1:57.4."

"Put him in the lowest class." I said. I wanted Taj to compile a string of wins against cheaper horses. I didn't want him demoralized by racing against tougher competition until I saw him on the track.

"He's lazy though. I have to get after him in the stretch," Warren continued. He shook his head morosely as if he relished the notion of delivering bad news.

"He'll do fine when he races for money."

"The lowest class pays three hundred dollars, Canadian. That's two hundred U.S."

I shot back at him as if his defiance annoyed me. "I brought him up here to prep him for the Gold Cup and then to race at the Meadowlands. I'm not interested in purse money. I'm building his confidence."

"It's my job as trainer to tell you these things. Don't get sore, eh. I don't mean anything by it." Warren always backed down when I stood my ground. I settled a little and let my feathers calm. Warren was smart enough to change the topic.

"Good horses coming up in the yearling sale," he commented. "I think you could pick up some nice stakes prospects."

"I've been through that a couple of years ago. Came up here to bid. Found out the breeders were bidding against me. I guess they saw a pigeon from New Jersey and tried to cash in on it. I stung a couple of them by pulling out of the bidding just when they thought I'd keep going. One guy came crying to sell the horse to me at a discount off my last bid. But I wasn't interested in the horse. I just wanted to sting someone to let them know I'm no dummy."

He shrugged. "They can be a rough bunch up here. I'll register Taj for the three-hundred-dollar class." Warren and I got along if we took each other in small doses. I started my law practice later in life and had been in practice for ten years, and the stock market for fifteen. The first lesson I learned was to manage my own money. Pick my own stocks. Pick my own horses. Prep my own law cases. I didn't lose many cases. I prepared them and tried each one as if it were a Supreme Court case. If I didn't win at the trial level—which was rare—I won on appeal. I did the same with horses. I read. I tried odd-ball techniques. Twice a week I telephoned the office and spoke to Saundra. If I needed to contact a client, I telephoned from PEI. On two occasions Saundra related messages from Mary Beth.

"She misses her daddy," Saundra said. "Can't you put your pride aside and at least try?"

My response was pretty much standard: "I love you, but stay out of my family business."

"I thought I *was* family," she answered. She then retreated with hurt feelings and I hung up the phone with a sense of guilt. Within a day Mary Beth was forgotten and I focused on racing. Warren was cleaning mold off the leather harness when I saw him at the barn. He motioned me over.

"Taj has a race tomorrow afternoon. Next week they're racing in Moncton, New Brunswick. It's a class he can compete in, and I think he can win." I was mildly shocked to see he had changed from the plaid wool shirt to blue denim. "You changed your shirt," I smiled.

"I thought it would change my luck," he grinned.

"Your luck is tied to me, Warren. Me and Taj. If he does well, you and I are going to the Meadowlands."

"Give any more thought to that sale?" He averted his eyes because it was a delicate question. Trainers earn money in many ways. They earn a commission if they negotiate a sale on an experienced racehorse, and they can earn money from breeders if they produce an interested buyer. On one of my first purchases, the trainer bought the horse for twelve thousand and promptly told us he had paid twenty thousand for him. We never knew until years later.

"That's out!" I yelped. "But there's a horse racing here in stakes races. Solar Knight. I like her. I think she can race at Freehold or Yonkers. See if she's for sale."

"You got a plan, eh?" his voice lilted.

"I've had a chance to study some of the horses up here. Rather than risking time and money on unproven yearlings, I prefer buying a horse with a proven record. We—as in you and me—bring them down to the States. We race them in claimers. They win. We move them into higher classes. I can buy good horses here for four to five thousand Canadian which translates into twenty-five hundred to three thousand U.S. and see them claimed for twice that amount in the States. What do you think?"

He puzzled for a moment, scratched his head and sat down. From a small, black lunch box he produced an enormous sub sandwich and began munching thoughtfully as if digesting the concept as well as the sandwich. Then he broke into a big smile, still chewing and swallowing.

"I'd say you're a pretty smart Yank. I've seen Solar Knight. She's pretty solid. I think you can buy her. I'll talk to the owner. And sure, there's horses up here can race in the States."

I visited with Taj while Warren was still eating. He nickered when he saw me coming, probably because I always brought him carrots.

"Now, Taj, you're racing tomorrow. And you can beat anything on the track. Just don't get lazy in the stretch."

And he was perfect. He stayed back of the leaders for the first half of the race, his superior class showing against the home bred. At the stretch he was fifteen lengths to the good. A week later we raced him against a good class of horses in Moncton. It was a close race, with Taj racing against an old competitor, but he nosed him out at the wire in a finish that had me videotaping while screaming with excitement. I photographed more floor than horse race. And it was a special privilege to stand in the Winner's Circle with a tired, affectionate Taj.

Taj kept racing on the island. His list of wins was impressive. Six in a row, by huge leads. Before each race, I brought him carrots and pumped him up with confidence. The stable hands smiled knowingly, as if I was a fool, and I kept cashing winning tickets as if they understood nothing about horses. And again the unsavory man was there, smiling and watching as we hosed and groomed Taj Mahal. He made no derisive comments. He just stared with tapering, furtive eyes.

After the races, I rewarded Taj with more carrots and more praise. On only one occasion did I note him injured and that was a small cut on his right side where the whip missed the cart and stuck his flank. I touched the bloody wound and, suddenly, tears surge down my cheeks and my voice went hoarse. Taj looked around, saw the tears. He pressed his nose against my hand as if to tell me that it was all right, that it didn't hurt. I knew something then. I knew that when his racing days were done, Taj was coming home. Coming home to my farm where he would live in green pastures and beside quiet waters.

Several times a week, I telephoned Saundra, not only to discuss personal affairs and business but to recount the string of wins posted by Taj. Moncton was important because Taj was racing against top horses and Saundra was coming up for the Trials and the Gold Cup. It felt good to know I'd be seeing her. She rattled off the messages, told me she had notified clients the office would be closed for vacation, brought me up to date on office business and concluded with a conversation she'd had with Mary Beth. It was then I tuned her out. My response to her "I love you!" was cold and unconvincing...my way of warning her to avoid a sore topic.

On the evening of the Trials, Saundra was with me in the stands at Charlottetown. I suffered from overconfidence so it was the one night I had not visited Taj before the race. We were shocked when the announcer summoned us to the barn of Warren MacDonald. When we got there I gazed at Taj and saw a different horse. He was lathered and weary. His gums were pale. His eyes dull. Warren had been up with him all night. Taj had colicked and someone called and told Warren he had a sick horse on his hands.

"I thought he was going to die," he said. "He's been casting around in his stall. Doc gave him a shot for pain, eh. I just don't know what happened."

"You don't?" My tone was sarcastic and biting. And Shane's words came back to me. "Somebody figured to improve the odds on the Trials. They slipped him something."

He shook his head in disbelief. I continued berating the Canadians.

"Doc Shane told me they're a rough bunch up here. This was their way of telling me we don't walk away with their purse money."

"But the barn was locked. How could they get in?" Warren wailed.

I prodded him again. "Warren, what time did this horse colic?"

"My stable hand called me about two this morning. Said he checked the barn and heard the horse casting around."

"And you wait until just before the race to tell the owner that his horse is not fit to race? So what the hell were you thinking about?"

His eyes rose when I stung him with the remark.

"Are you saying I had something to do with this, eh?" His eyes squinted down with arrogance.

"You know these boys up here pretty well. Fellow Canadians and all that. So why didn't I get a call at the campground? You know where I'm staying."

"I was busy getting a vet to take care of *your* horse."

"So this is just coincidence, is that it? We've worked with this horse all summer. Has he ever been sick a single day?"

"No. He never was." He turned his eyes away, and I hated him for his lack of strength.

"So it's not such a mystery, then, is it?"

"You think I had something to do with it, eh?"

I hesitated and said nothing.

"If that's the way of it, we can part company here and now." He almost sounded Scottish when he mouthed the words.

"I don't know what to think. I guess you might have suspected something. After all, you live here. You train here. If this kind of thing happens in your barn..."

"It's my problem," he answered.

"Well, I thought we were a team. I guess it's *our* look-out, not just yours though. Sorry about what I said."

His eyes blurred a little as he coursed his hand over the ailing horse. "It's a damn shame. But up here we'll never know who done it. All we can do is make sure it don't happen before the Consolation Race, eh?"

"We'll make sure of that," I said. "Damn sure."

Saundra tried calming me, but even she agreed something had happened to Taj. Not having raced in the Trials, Taj was out of the Gold Cup.

Under ordinary circumstances, I would have raced him in the Gold Cup and win or lose, shipped him to the States to compete at a better racetrack. I decided to race him in the Consolation race. I had a score to settle. And Taj was eligible for the Consolation because he had qualified for the Trials and the Gold Cup. The Consolation was a smaller purse, but enough to cover entry fees and costs. And I intended making sure he got to that race.

On the night before the Consolation Race, Saundra dropped me off for a long vigil with Taj. The barn was locked at ten. I hid behind an adjoining barn and waited until Warren's car puttered through the exit gate. Then I climbed through an unlocked window, thinking that it had been conveniently left unsecured for an evening visitor. Once inside, I groped my way through the darkened barn to Taj's stall and slipped inside. I settled myself against the right side wall. The smell of fresh hay rose up and greeted my nostrils. I was concerned I'd sneeze and reveal my presence but, after a few moments, I relaxed and found a comfortable position.

Night, it seemed, settled all the woes of the day. The horses were bedded down and silent. Only an occasional mouse scurried through the aisles. Otherwise, it was quiet. Yet even in the stillness there is life. The moans of an aged building, discernable in the silence, clamor to be heard. So it is silence, a silence that lives, that breathes, that has mass and dimension. In such a silence a building acquires a life of its own. It speaks of ancient times and history. It speaks of fame and glory. It speaks of conspiracy and treachery. Its message is for the ear of the beholder only. To me, it spoke of anger and the long wait.

I set down the aluminum baseball bat I had purchased earlier in the day. I recalled the store clerk stoically asking if I was going to "hit a few."

"No," I answered, "just one." I made a motion with the bat and I certainly meant *one* if the saboteur showed up at the barn.

Taj was awake and nickered for his carrot. He must have thought it queer to have me as an overnight guest, but he tolerated my presence as he always did. I shuttled over to him and smoothed my hands along his muscular body, still awed by the sheer power of the beast. Then he settled into a far corner and I slumped down near his feed bucket. Alone with my thoughts I wondered if money were so important men would damage a fine animal.

Although I worried about dozing off, my anger jogged me to awareness. I was guarding Taj, doing the job I thought my trainer should have done. I wanted to smash the person who had harmed my horse. Not for the purse money, or for the pleasure or revenge of it but because someone had harmed my animal for doing nothing more than fulfilling his destiny. Such men are useless in a world of loving people. They have no purpose but to destroy and profit by the destruction. What had Taj done except to race and race well? Was that not what he was created for? Was it not wrong to impede his destiny?

I grew angrier as I doted on the wickedness of their conspiracy. I also stood poised on the brim of doubt. What if I belted the wrong person? What if the Canadian Mounties arrested me? In a foreign country, with Crown Justice, I might easily languish in an island jail. Once before I had nearly been arrested when some jokesters befriended me with a bottle of beer just as a Mountie was driving up. I can still hear him saying: "I hope that's not what I think it is."

But once he learned I was a tourist, he begged off and returned me to the racecourse. Thinking about it just made me angry again. So angry I almost did not hear the fumbling of the barn door lock. I riveted on the sound but it ceased. Was I imagining something? Or did I hear the large pad-lock rattling on the door? There came a silence and the silence was agitated by fear. The sound came again. It was the lock, I thought. Someone was entering...and he was using a key to admit himself.

Then all my doubts were resolved. Taj had been drugged and it was not my imagination. A circular light expunged the darkness. Its beam lit the assassin's way. *The Iceman Cometh,* I thought. Indeed *he* was coming. His steps fell carelessly on the wooden floor. He was no stranger to the barn, this man. He had been there before. But Warren would have used the lights. There would have been no reason for him to seek his prey in total darkness. The footsteps halted outside the stall door. I slid quietly up the wall and read-ied my weapon. If it were my trainer, he would receive just compensation for his works. *By their works shall ye know them.*

The stall door squeaked open. Enough light fell from the skylight to outline the figure of a short man. *Too short to be Warren*, I thought. He readied something in his hand. In the darkness, a hypodermic plunger swished with fluid drawn into its receptacle. So it wasn't food. They injected him with something. The figure took an abrupt step toward Taj. He whispered to the horse to steady the animal, and, in timing with his movement, I smashed the bat against him. The blow stunned him as the wind went out of him. He shrieked with pain. He must have thought he walked into something in the stall. I resolved his doubts. Again, my bat whooshed through the air. It slashed the assassin's chest with a dull whump that drove him back through the stall door. Shocked. Muddled. My blow had rattled more than just his body. Gathering his wits, he stumbled about in the dark. His breath was raspy. He was hyperventilating from the jolt. I felt no remorse for my act. And I vowed that if I saw anyone limping at the races later that day, I'd clobber him again. Even Taj approved, moving toward me and nuzzling me as if to say: *"Thanks, buddy. I really didn't want to feel sick again."*

The would-be assassin staggered and clanged his way out of the barn. I pursued him and struck him once more just as he reached the barn doors. The bat slipped from my grip and in the time I spent recovering it, I heard the gravel spewing as the intruder raced away. He must have been on foot for it was quiet and there was no motor, no sound of a vehicle driving off. I flicked on the light switch, hoping the man had dropped the hypodermic. Nothing. Apparently he had the presence of mind to take the evidence with him.

Exhausted, I stayed with Taj until Warren arrived in the morning. Although I was fatigued and sore from my encounter, I drove around the island. In every town there are those who are part of the accepted crowd and those who are not. It was always a struggle to gain a foothold and only money and power made the difference. I had come to PEI hoping to build the confidence of a depressed horse. And there were those who hated our successes and stooped to treachery to impose their will, to punish the outsider. I returned to the track and stayed with Taj until Warren began warming him up.

BEFORE TAJ LEFT, I RALLIED HIM AGAIN. "Taj, these horses are nothing compared to you. Pace yourself. Don't slack off in the stretch. Win this one and I promise you a bag of carrots. Show these bums what you're really like inside."

His eyes brightened. I swore he nodded his head. Taj Mahal went off at 12–1 odds. Apparently the crowd was in on the scheme to drug him. Their wagering was erratic, uncertain. Mine wasn't. Once I saw Taj on the racetrack, I knew he was going to win. It's that sureness that comes with intuition. He pulled himself up tall and straight. In his warm up, he eyed the other horses as he passed. I confess that I took full advantage of my knowledge and wagered heavily.

Taj pulled away from the gate and paced to the front. A horse on the rail has a distinct advantage because he runs the shorter distance. His first quarter equaled the track record. Then, as if remembering my instructions, he slowed and let the other horses catch him. One tried moving into the center of the track while a second went wide and for a time there were three horses stretched across the track, vying for first place. But Taj never relented. By the third quarter, he pulled ahead again, keeping a length ahead of the closest horse. In the stretch, he paced himself well enough to maintain his lead. It was as if he were toying with them, giving ground, then pulling away. He won by a half length. No photo in the winner's circle was ever more proudly relished by Saundra and me. Even Taj appeared proud. I glanced into the crowd and studied their faces. The man with the crooked mouth was absent. Perhaps he was tending a wound because I never saw him again. It made the victory even more agreeable.

But with that victory and our sad experience on the island, it was time to ship Taj to the States. Time to move back into familiar territory. There may be dishonesty in racing no matter what the venue but at least in the States, they didn't poison your horse. Saundra flew home while I trailered Taj.

There is both a dark side and an aristocratic side to horse racing. On the dark side are the misfits and dregs of racing society and on the bright side, vainglorious names of society's nobility. But there are also people watching. People who care about the honesty of racing and who understand that dishonesty aborts and deters the most loyal fan. Horse racing was under the gun because of scandal and corruption. The public could only tolerate so much race fixing. Occasionally the F.B.I. arrested drivers and trainers in some alleged conspiracy, but no convictions ever occurred. The public held its own trial, found the industry guilty and turned their dollars away. Primarily because a driver barred at one track could simply move to another state and race there. Where was the enforcement in that?

We came to New Jersey to compete against the finest animals in the nation. I came back to New Jersey to prove a theory about animals. I was happy to see Saundra. She was happy to see both me and Taj. I told her I had purchased Solar Knight and was having her shipped down. We spent the evening having dinner at the Seven Hills, a classy Italian trattoria with a fabulous bartender. Saundra waited until after-dinner drinks and updated me on the law business.

"Hector Tajeda has a problem," she said. "His girlfriend got picked up for pushing drugs. He's admitted to the police the drugs were his and that he was the one selling."

"What the hell did he do that for?"

"He has a noble streak in him, I guess. He knows he can do fifteen years in federal prison, but he's protecting his girlfriend. That's Hector, what can I say?"

"If he has done all that, what am I doing in the picture?"

She handed me a small, brown bag. "He doesn't want you to represent him. He's already worked out a deal with the prosecutor."

She shoved the bag across the table. Inside was thirty thousand in cash.

"He wants you to hold it for him. Just hold onto it until he's out of prison."

"Hold thirty thousand? That's what he wants? He's very trusting."

She shrugged. "That's what he said." I studied the gestures of her face. For the first time I noticed that everything was in exact proportion. Her eyes were neither narrow nor widely set. Her nose, neither too large nor too small and in perfect symmetry with her jaw. Her brown hair, fluffed and shining, was neither too light nor too dark. Her aquiline, sloping features could have belonged to a queen or a Roman Empress. Still, she was more attractive when she smiled than when she frowned, and there were times when she was quiet and sedate and times when her temper flared like a spoiled child having a tantrum. I recalled the first time I met her. She wore a cream-colored dress, with a light jacket, and she was bright of face and fresh like the Noxema she had used to smooth her features. There was both excitement and fright in her eyes and I noted, as she reached to shake hands, that her eyes vacillated between grey and green. She was attractive but not so much because of her features or her slender body but because she radiated from within, a warm and enticing glow.

I picked up the thread of our conversation.

I was used to odd requests from Hector. Having thirty thousand in my office safe was just another of those odd foibles in the life of the average lawyer. I dare not question where the money came from. "Anything else?"

"Mary Beth called. We had a very nice conversation. Do you want to hear about it?"

I winced before I answered. "I'm not sure."

She pouted a little. Saundra was a peacemaker.

"Okay, what did she say?" I relented.

"Well, she had something she wanted to tell you but apparently she was afraid. She said she didn't think the time or the mood was right."

I was getting impatient. "Will you just drop the damn bomb and get it over with?" My voice raised stares from the surrounding tables. I shot them a glance that told them to mind their own business.

"I'm sorry. I'm a little tired and uptight after everything that's happened. Tell me what she had to say. Please."

"You've been a grandfather for two and a half years." She halted, waiting to gauge my reaction. I was so stunned I did not reply. "She wanted to tell you long before, but your ex-wife told her you'd probably kill her husband if you discovered she was pregnant."

"Of course, she'd say something like that. And, of course, my daughter would believe her."

"You do have a temper." She was mocking me and I knew it, but I was too happy to start a fight.

"Is that it?" I asked.

"Pretty much. His name is Danny. She sent me a picture, if you're interested. And if you want my opinion, I think you at least ought to see him."

"See who?" I fired back at her.

"Your grandson. Who are we talking about here?"

"Off it, Love. I'm not into this grandfather bit. I wasn't much as a father either. I figure they let you off in twenty years for murder. But for being a father, you get a life sentence."

"I can't understand how you can be so good with animals and so terrible with family. How is that?"

"Look, it's my first night back. Let's not screw it up with an argument."

"Okay," she frowned, "I have just one thing more to say."

"One more thing…promise?" My eyes pleaded with her.

She assented. "You've always done things in anger and regretted your actions down the road. All I am asking is that you carefully consider your relationship with Mary Beth…and with your grandson. One day, he'll be asking why his grandfather wanted nothing to do with him. I don't want you hurting when that day comes. If you at least try to have a workable relationship with your daughter and things go wrong, you know that you tried. Is that unreasonable to ask?" Her eyes met mine and remained questioning.

"No. It's not. It's not unreasonable. I've just got issues with Mary Beth. I need time to work things out."

"Wasn't it your aunt who had a child out of wedlock?"

"Yup!" I flipped the answer like a steel barb.

"Your grandfather disowned her. Never saw his grandson. Went to his grave hating her, didn't he?"

"You know he did."

"Then be yourself. Don't ostracize her because it's what you grandfather would have done. Make up your own mind and follow your heart."

When I smiled, she knew she'd made her point.

"You're good for me," I whispered.

I started looking around the restaurant, hoping the music would begin so I could escape the topic with a dance. The musicians moseyed back to the podium and began playing. Saundra and I got up and danced. In moments we were discussing Taj and the upcoming races and I recounted my experience at the training track.

She was smiling again and I wanted to keep it so.

"I have to tell you a funny story," I said.

"I could use one," she responded, motioning for me to pour her more wine.

"You remember Island Jewel? We bought her at the Spring sale?"

"I remember Jewel. She fell in love with you. Kept making that gesture where she pulled her upper lip back over her teeth."

"Right! Flehmen gesture. Signifies mating. Well, I went to see her out at Norman's paddock. She wouldn't come near me. Absolutely refused. I held up some clover for her and she wouldn't take it unless…and get this… unless I was on one knee in front of her."

"I told you she was in love with you."

"Norman said she hasn't been any good on the racetrack since I left."

She laughed. "You broke her heart."

"Can you believe it? A horse, in love with me. She doesn't even have good taste."

"What did you do with her?"

"The only thing I could. I sold her to Norman for six month's board. He's a kind heart. He'll take care of her."

In moments, any discussion about Mary Beth passed as we fell in love all over again. Later we lay in bed, Saundra reading and me studying the race charts of Taj's competition. I planned on visiting the track in the morning and asked her to come. She accepted.

At eight we displayed our passes to the security guard and entered the backstretch. The Meadowlands was a mile track and embellished with elaborate seating, posh betting areas, restaurants, bars, televisions throughout the grandstand and club house. Since we were owners and held our own box seating, we received first-rate service. Shapely waitresses brought food and drink and even carried our bets to the windows, though for privacy purposes, I preferred to do my own wagering. The box owner's world was far different from the owner who entered the backstretch. Fellow owners collaborated on developments within the racing field. They discussed purses, stakes races, racing luck, good and bad, fast track times, and the high number of lame horses reported each week. They shared drinks. They bought dinner. They discussed potential winners in each race. A fellowship existed that hardly revealed the competitive nature of racing except they never divulged information of any kind.

But the world of the back stretch was another dimension. Owners spoke to trainers and drivers in hushed tones. The racing barns were solemn places, filled with whispered instructions and furtive glances. It was as though a religious air descended over the concrete halls and stalls and in that cathedral, no prayer, no plea rose above a murmur. The backstretch consisted of blacktop alleys and open barns. Horses clopped along the pathways on their way to race. Others stood in cross ties within the barns themselves. A hint of expectation filled the atmosphere as the competition intensified.

The barns were either neat and cleanly painted or they were ramshackle structures that had seen better days. Somewhere in the complex, there was an administration building which housed the race secretary, a medical facility, and various offices connected with horse racing. In another building, a fly-filled café housed insipid food and drink. Pale red hot dogs wilted from over-cooking. Soggy French fries oozed week old grease and stiffened as they cooled. Coffee sprang from week-old grinds. I never saw a cafeteria that seemed anything more than dismal or smelled of anything more than a mixture of stale food and Lysol disinfectant. It was a world far from the club-house and the owner's quarters.

We visited Taj in his stall. As always, he nickered because he knew his carrots were coming. And with the carrots, the praise, the gentle laying on of the hands, the words of encouragement that transformed him from a lazy lout into a formidable racing machine.

"This is your big chance, fella," I said, rubbing his withers with affection. "You're in a tough race tonight." The animal stood erect and snorted. He had the bridle in his mouth and the bit hung beneath his chin. He pulled his head high so the metal passed over my head without touching me. Then, he laid that beautiful, equine head on my shoulder, ever so lightly and I knew he loved me as I loved him.

"That horse loves you," Saundra said, pulling near to stroke his flanks. "A lot of people love you, but you can't accept it."

She smiled, and in that smile, I saw a hundred years of aristocracy that ventured into a new land, fought in its revolution, its Civil War, the Great War, as well as World War II. I saw in that smile a woman as comfortable with animals as I was but who treated people with equal love and patience. "He looks good. Talking to him seems to hype him up," she commented.

"I know he's in tough but I can't drop him into a claimer. Too many guys out there looking for good horses."

"He may win. Hard to say. At least we know one thing. He'll try his best for us," she concluded.

We returned to my law office and Saundra left for court. The remaining day we filled with the usual accident cases, another drug bust, and assorted Disorderly Person's cases. I did net one peeping Tom case and had to chuckle when the defendant told me he was merely using his binoculars to admire a bird sitting on the bathroom window sill.

Saundra and I arrived early at the racetrack and went directly to see Taj. We fed him a few carrots, stroked him with words. "Look at that big fella," I said. "He's just full of himself tonight. Taj, you are going to wipe out the field. Fast, yes sir, tonight will be your fastest night ever."

When I saw him on the track later that night, Taj exuded spirit and the will to win. He pranced through his warm-up and drew himself to his full height. Though he could not hear us, he knew we were watching. The odds board did not reflect that confidence. It pegged him at 22–1 odds. I wagered fifty dollars to win and returned to the box. But as I watched him, that great horse paced with stride and determination. He was full of himself and confident. He was making clean strokes with his legs and taking long strides. It was too much to ignore. I returned to the betting window and wagered another two-hundred dollars to win. Then, I wheeled him in an Exacta, selecting Taj as the winner in combination with several other horses I felt would be second.

This would be his retirement fund, if he won. But he was coming out of the eight-post position, which in standardbred racing is not an easy post.

The car-driven gate moved ahead of them. Taj was chafing to be free of the mechanical monster. He surged to the front, moving on an angle until he held the inside post position. When I saw his time for the first quarter, he had broken his own record and my heart fluttered to reality because it was not likely he could maintain that pace. By the half mark, he held a mere quarter-length lead. Shootin' Sam and He's A Bug moved wide, challenging him for the lead. The driver checked him a bit as they reached the final turn. Checking a pacer at this point would slow the race and cause the other horses to swing wider in order to pass.

At the top of the stretch, Shootin' Sam swung from behind Taj and chewed up center track. He's A Bug gave ground to Kelly's Love and dropped into fourth place. The horse was spent. In the long Meadowlands stretch, it was still an open race. The driver rated Taj carefully. Too much and he'd tire before the finish line. Too little, and the other horses would pass and break Taj's spirit.

The other horses moved alongside. For a time, Taj's fate hung in balance and I could not tell if he was toying with them or was tiring. With only two hundred feet to go, the racetrack looked like a small stampede of six horses all vying for the finish line. Shootin' Sam stayed the course, still trying to capture Taj. He's A Bug rallied and again moved toward the leader. Three other horses came abreast of He's A Bug and were gaining ground. But at the finish there was only one horse clearly ahead, and he was half a length ahead of his closest rival. As we entered the Winner's Circle for our photo and award, I planted a kiss on his nose. Taj's head shot up as if he was embarrassed by this public display, but his blood was up and his pride was riding high.

Taj won that night as he did on other nights, but his victories were short-lived. The racetrack betting handle was dropping. The track could no longer pay the high purses paid in the past. Taj began racing for half the money he had formerly raced for, but worse, the race secretary began eliminating open classes and horses were forced into claiming races. A horse moving from open classes to claiming could be purchased by any owner racing at the meet simply by posting a notice of claim and paying the claiming price. Taj was at risk of being claimed and the only way of avoiding a claim was to race him against the faster horses in the tougher classes. The level of each race was determined by the horse's fastest time and Taj was, at best, a thirty-thousand-dollar claimer. If I tried racing him in higher classes, he'd be racing against seventy-five-thousand-dollar claiming horses with much faster times. He would not win against that class of horse. In time, his losses would add up. His confidence would nosedive. No amount of sweet talk or pep talks could change the reality of the situation. A racehorse is limited by his own physical capacity. The will to win, the love to win, is not always enough when racing against the clock.

Before I had an opportunity to decide whether to race Taj at the Meadowlands or at some out-of-state track, I was summoned to Prince Edward Island. A question of ownership erupted over my purchase agreement for Solar Knight. Evidently she had raced in a Stakes race and won. The former owner was claiming the purse and the race secretary was contending that it belonged to our stable. They were taking testimony before the judges and I had to attend. Saundra had to visit Colorado to help her aging aunt adjust to the mountain climate. That left Warren pretty well on his own.

I was gone for several weeks, not only to settle the dispute but to watch other racehorses and purchase those with potential to race in New Jersey. As it turned out the islanders decided to skyrocket their prices when they learned of my interest so my time there was a wasted effort. I did take home the stakes money for Solar but found nothing worthy of purchasing. Saundra was still in Colorado as I drove the long miles home.

When I returned Warren met me at the security station. His face was grim and he'd a nervous twitch in his eye.

"I've got good news and bad news," he started. My eyes rolled upward. He hesitated, not wishing to continue. "They claimed Taj for thirty-five thousand." He had a half-smile on his face as if he was not certain how the news would be received. I answered his doubts immediately.

"Who claimed him? How the hell did he race in a claimer anyway?"

"The race secretary eliminated the open classes. He put him in a claimer so you made a fifteen-thousand-dollar profit on the horse plus the purse he won that night. The Hammond brothers claimed him. They were just waiting for the chance."

"So? We claim him back. What's he racing in?"

Warren paled and turned away.

"Well?" I urged

"They moved him. He's raced at Freehold, Delaware, Pocono Downs, Yonkers. They keep moving him around."

"Half-mile tracks? They'll kill his legs!" I complained.

Warren shrugged. He loved horses, but he didn't see them as friends or pets. No, he saw them as dollars, as profit. We'd had our disagreements about my motives for racing horses. I think he was elated he'd turned a profit for me whereas I fumed over the loss of my friend.

"I argued with the race secretary and told him it was a set up, eh? He suspended me for three days and threatened to bar me from the track. I think some funny business went on but I can't prove anything. The Hammond brothers are tight with the racing Administration. From what I hear, eh, there were six claims put in for Taj but only one claim slip came out of the box." He turned his head and stared at the wall. He was a discomforted man if I had ever seen one.

"Sure they set it up. This whole lousy business stinks. If we blow the whistle, they'll make sure we never race here again!" I shouted.

"I can get you a replacement horse, eh. Raced in Florida Stakes until his knee went bad. Out of Trim the Tree. Clocked fast in 1:55.2. Needs some rest and some healing but I can heal him and he'll earn his keep," inhaling as he muttered the last word.

I shook my head. "Not right now, Warren. Sooner or later that bad leg will break down. I'll track Taj until then and try to cut a deal with the owner when he's done racing. Besides, Solar Knight is on her way. She'll race at Freehold and Yonkers. Ted Krolik will be training and driving her. He's top with fillies and mares. I'm really not feeling good about this loss."

"So, I'm sacked, am I?"

His face drew taut enough to read the hurt in his eyes. In that hurt, I recognized my own fallibility, my own inability to forgive transgressions, my stubborn insistence that everyone be perfect. I had done it with Saundra, with Mary Beth and now with Warren. But the fault lay not with them, but in Grant Larsen. Had I *always* been an angry man? Did something happen in my childhood to make it so? As I stared back at Warren, I spanned the human relationships in my past, recognized a pattern of anger, of impatience, of demand for perfection. Was I trying to make up for my own deficiencies by requiring others to be faultless? I had always believed that all love is based upon self-love. If one cannot love himself he cannot love others. If he cannot esteem himself, he has no esteem. I saw all this in the hurt of that common man.

What wrong had he done? He labored at his trade in all weathers and under all conditions. He brought my horse to the Winner's Circle. He followed me from Canada to the United States, left his loved ones behind, his friends, his familiar haunts. He toiled long hours and pushed himself in furious heat or stifling cold. Through the long night-hours he nursed my horse back to health and transformed misfits into racing machines. He received little praise and money for his efforts and took guff from owners when things went awry. Like other men he held a dream…that one horse…that one champion…that one record-breaker that would establish him as a man who knew his trade. He struggled to be the best at what he did and what he loved. Had he deserved my anger? Something needed to change but it was not Warren or Mary Beth or Saundra. My thoughts returned to the anxious trainer.

I stared back into that weathered face, stared into those lucid, hurting eyes and my soul teemed with pity and remorse.

"No, Warren. I'm not sacking you. You'll train other horses for me. I just need time to recover from the shock. It's the last thing I expected." I gripped his shoulder and watched his face unwind. "I am planning a stable of twelve or thirteen horses that we buy at the four-year-old sale. By then, we know how well the horses have done and we just pick out the sound ones and buy them cheap. Promise."

Warren looked a little lost. He wasn't used to owners who fell in love with their animals. Nor was he one to quibble if an owner found another trainer, such was his stoical attitude. He brightened and the tension slipped from his face. I relaxed too because he believed me. After all, he'd done a good job with Taj. I needed to be a better man to understand that. With that, I rose, signaled goodbye and left. There was nothing left to do but return to my law practice.

Several months passed. From time to time, Warren telephoned to tell me where Taj was racing. Our conversations were cordial and we often discussed other racing ventures. Then, the phone calls stopped. I knew it was because Warren could no longer find information on Taj. He confirmed that when I spoke to him.

The race entries for every track in the area showed no entry of Taj in any race. It occurred to me that the cartilage in his leg had worn and he was lame. I waited another week, checking all entries. The U.S. Trotting Association showed no current race record. I obtained the name and address of the Hammond brothers and telephoned Mark. The person with whom I spoke identified himself as the office manager and apologized when the Hammonds were not available. I told him I was interested in having them train a horse for me. He suggested a casual appointment, that amounted to visiting the training stable around eight A.M. I was there at seven.

Like most training barns, the business office was a converted tack room which reeked of leather and sweat. A single window admitted faint rays of light and the dull overhead bulb did little to brighten the place. A scarred, oaken desk huddled against the far wall, with few papers on it and a single, worn desk chair that was leather, weary and faded lay near it. On the wall hung several photos of the Winner's Circle, stakes races mostly, in which Mark or Dan appeared. They bought, trained and drove all their own horses and were highly regarded, but that would not be known from the flavor of the office. The ash tray was stuffed with crusted cigarettes. The odor gave the room a stale aroma. The remnants of coffee cups and fast-food meals rimmed the waste basket and overflowed onto the floor.

I knew the Hammonds. Both were trainer–drivers and both had individual ideas on horses. Dan Hammond objected to claiming Taj. He didn't like the way he raced, thought he was lazy and indolent and was willing to sell him immediately or place him in another claiming race. Mark, on the other hand, believed he could push the horse to faster race times and higher earnings. Neither of them contemplated two things: First, Taj would not race for anyone other than Saundra or myself; second, Taj was not suited to half-mile tracks and, in Dan's effort to keep him from being reclaimed by me, they shoved him into offbeat half-mile tracks where he floundered.

What I learned from the Hammonds was that Taj was stationed on a local farm, waiting to be shipped to an owner in Maine who had purchased the horse for five hundred dollars. The amount shot through my brain like a hot spark. Five hundred dollars? I couldn't believe it. For Taj?

We continued discussing Taj, but Mark was reticent to part with information. There is an adage in racing that one does not give away information on a horse. Down the road, he may wish to purchase or claim that same horse. He wants to be the only trainer who knows how to get the horse going. So Mark's questions and his reluctance were natural instincts. Unlike thoroughbred jockeys, standardbred drivers came in all flavors. Tall, short, stout, razor thin. Mark was lanky, in his thirties, a life-long horse lover with a hatchet-like face.

"You want to race that horse?" he asked.

I shook my head. "He's through racing. But he's got a retirement fund from one of his last races, and I have him slated for a nice, green pasture and a lot of love and affection. Besides, he's the only one I can talk to who doesn't give me a hard time."

He laughed and spat his tobacco to his left. "In love with the big bugger?"

"He's done right by me."

"Dan hated him. Called him a lazy barrel." He leaned forward, perusing his Rolodex file.

"We all have our opinions," I was noncommittal but seething about the insult.

He nodded. "If he races in Maine, they'll drug him until he breaks down. Then it's off to the killers. They have no drug testing at any of those small tracks. The Canadians buy lame horses, send 'em west and slaughter them."

"I didn't know that. Tell me about the buyer."

"First tell me what you slipped that horse to make him race for you."

I hesitated, knowing he would not believe me. "It's called 'TLC' and it's not very expensive."

"TLC? Where'd you get it?"

"Tender, loving, care," I answered, pointing to my heart.

"Sure."

"I'm serious. All I ever did was praise him."

He stared and I saw the disbelief in his eyes. Mark was a man who had been around horses all his life. He believed they were dumb, had to be taught, to be trained, had their good days and their off days and understood nothing except a shout and a clout.

"You're not the first one to laugh. I believe that animals comprehend. Not the words. The thoughts, the vibes, whatever you want to call it."

Even if he did not believe me, he respected my faith and, for that, I liked him. Suddenly he was replete with information.

"Name's Arthur. He buys horses from us from time to time. Runs 'em up to Maine. Sometimes he races 'em himself. Sometimes he sells 'em for what he can get over his costs. And sometimes the horses are sold before they ever leave here. Made of dollar signs so don't let him know how you feel about the horse."

"I'll visit with Taj, see what kind of condition he's in and then call the owner and negotiate with him."

"Tell 'im Mark put you onto the horse. He may scalp you on the tab but at least you'll get him home." He slid a name, address and telephone across the desk. He walked me out to the parking lot, keeping pace with my small steps.

I returned to my office. It had been an exasperating day. The brandy I poured splashed and dribbled down the snifter. I tossed most telephone messages aside but one that flashed before me was from my daughter. It was Saundra's handwriting.

> *Your grandson is cutting teeth. If you would like to see him, Mary Beth would like that very much. Saw his picture. He's a doll. Bill said he'd like to get to know you and he'd like you to know he loves Mary Beth very much. And for my part, isn't it time you mended some human fences as well as equine?*

SAUNDRA ALWAYS HAD A SARCASTIC TONE when she was displeased with me. I pondered my daughter's situation, envisioned her living in squalid quarters, ragged clothing, filth rampant throughout their small apartment. I recalled the days after my ex-wife, Sally, left home. Mary Beth and I walked hand-in-hand, like school children, talking about the future. *Could we make it through the difficult times? Would I be able to earn enough to make up for the money stolen by her mother? Did she know why the woman to whom I gave everything, including my complete trust, had chosen to pilfer money and abscond? Did Sally have all the jewelry I had given her or had she pawned it? And what about the loans she signed my name too, would I be liable for those as well? What did she use the money for? Did Sally give any thought to Mary Beth when she left? Did she offer to take her? Did Mary Beth even know her mother was deserting?*

I thought about my reaction when Mary Beth told me she had gone to bed with Bill. It was her act of defiance. It was her way of breaking away because she knew exactly how her hot-tempered father would react. *Had it been right for me to withhold her last year's tuition? Should I have at least given us both the chance to work at a relationship? A grandfather? How could I be a grandfather? How could I be one of those white-haired, doting monarchs offering gum drops and chocolates to an infant grandchild? At fifty, I was too young for fallen arches and a rocking chair.*

The telephone jarred me from my thoughts. It was Mark Hammond. "Hey," he said with no cheer in his voice. "Thought I'd save you a wasted drive. They sold Taj and they've shipped him."

"To Maine?"

He hesitated, almost not wanting to say the words. "Not sure. Arthur parceled him in with a block of horses to a new buyer. It was a cash-and-carry deal and he isn't giving details. Afraid of the I.R.S. All he would say is that the new buyer lives in Maine but sells to Canadian processing plants, maybe Western Canada or Montreal."

"Montreal, I hope?"

"I'm just not sure. There are a couple of auction houses, one in Indiana. Not sure about the other one. He's a big horse. I guess they figured he'd bring more by the pound than at the racetrack. Prices are high right now."

I was stunned. Poor Taj had never had a chance. Not an even break. He raced his heart out and his reward was a crowded rail car to the killers. A voice kept repeating that Taj never had a chance. Nor could I ignore the observation that I hadn't given Mary Beth a real chance either. Was there a lesson in all this? Was a mightier power than I meting out the same kind of justice I dispensed?

"How will they get him there?"

"They'll truck 'im up to the border and stick 'im in a box car with two hundred other horses. The vet gives 'im a hurried look and they're across. After that, I'm not sure. If you drove like hell, you might catch the horse at the border. Or I guess you could fly and land in Canada but I don't even know where to tell you to go. All I do know is that the new buyer is from Maine. Whatever you do, he won't have much time once he hits that boxcar. Sometimes they pack 'em in so tight, some don't survive."

"I appreciate this, Mark. Really."

"It was the right thing to do. Good luck to you, pal. Hope you find 'im."

I called Saundra on our private line. Mornings she usually attended to household chores, shopping and the like, before her other work day began.

"Emergency!" I said.

"What's wrong?" She was used to hearing the word so she didn't react immediately.

"They've shipped Taj. Mark doesn't know where. " I answered her question before she asked. "He said maybe Montreal, maybe western Canada, maybe an auction house. Damn! I owe that horse for all the money he won, and he's entitled to his retirement. I'm not letting him go."

She went silent for a moment. "What can I do?"

"I need to contact the buyer. I'll offer whatever it takes."

I felt her shudder on the telephone. "God, I remember those horses we saw packed in a PEI stall, just waiting for a boxcar to the killers. There must have been twenty horses in a twelve-by-twelve stall. No food. No water. No room to move. Manure all over each other. Poor Taj. I could strangle that Warren for letting this happen."

"There's no time now to lament. Sit tight while I call the owner and see where he's headed."

She hung up without fanfare, and I started dialing the telephone number Mark had given me for the first owner. There is nothing like the incessant ring of an unanswered telephone. The mind conjures all kinds of fates and disasters. I found myself *willing* someone to answer. Even a janitor would suffice.

"Come on, come on," I heard myself saying. "Answer the damn phone." No answer. I slammed the phone down.

It rang almost immediately. "Hello..." thinking it was Saundra with some news.

It was the last voice in the world I wanted to hear.

"Hi, Mary Beth..." I sparked. "Can't talk right now. Problems."

"Dad, please. Tell me."

I hesitated, wondering whether or not to waste the time.

"It's one of my horses. My favorite. They claimed him some time ago. I wanted to buy him back and just found out he may be on his way to Canada, to the killers."

"Oh, Dad, I'm sorry. I'll call..." she hesitated. "Dad? How are they sending him to Canada?"

"Train, probably. I'm not sure. They could truck him to the border and then a train if it's western Canada." She read the exasperation in my voice.

"Dad, let me call the railroads. I can get information on what train would take him and where."

"I don't even know for sure where he's being taken."

Her voice was pleading. "Please let me try."

"Where are you now?"

"At work."

"I'll fax you an information sheet and a picture of him. He's a big animal. Can't miss him."

"I'll call right away. We ship salvage on some of those railroads. I may know someone I can talk to."

She gave me her fax number, and I was sending the brochure and photo even as we spoke. "Thank you, Mary Beth, thank you very much."

"It's all right, Dad. I love you. Danny loves you, too."

"Funny. I almost said the same thing."

"What?"

"That I love you. I guess I've been hard on you."

"Sometimes. But I figured out it's because you care. You just don't know how to *say* you care. All those times you yelled and screamed at me. It took me a long time to understand, but Bill says it was the only way you knew how to protect me."

"*Bill* said that?"

"Yes. He's pretty smart that way."

"Treats you well?"

"Very well, Dad. We're happy. We just wish you could be part of our lives."

I didn't answer.

"Bill says you were carrying a big load because of the divorce, and...well, Dad, maybe we can see each other soon and talk...can we?"

"Maybe it's time, Geishel."

"Oh God, Dad, oh God!"

She wailed. "You haven't called me Geishel since I was a little girl."

"It was my nickname for you. You were always waiting on me, so submissive. You'd rub my shoulders. Light my cigarettes. You were a little geisha."

She laughed.

I laughed, too.

"Dad, do you remember when the kid across the street called me fat?"

"The Germ? Yeah, I remember. I told him if he ever hurt you again, I'd shove him in a garbage can, hook him to the rear of my car and drive him around the block ten times."

"He never said another word. Dad, I've got another call. I've got to go. I hope you find your horse. Let me know if I can do anything else. I'll call again if anything turns up on my end."

"Thank you, Mary Beth."

"It's all right, Dad. Danny and I love you."

"Gotta go. But let me know if you discover anything. I'm calling the owner's farm right now." Without further delay, I hung up and started dialing the owner's second telephone number. No answer. I waited and telephoned Saundra.

"Any luck on your end?"

"I called Warren…well, he sells horses to the killers so he would know."

"Good thinking."

She interrupted. "He said he only ships from the island so he doesn't know where the States would ship from, but he thinks they would haul Taj to Bangor and then onto a train at that point. The boxcar could be stalled at the border for two or three days until the Canadian vet clears the horses for entry. After that, he doesn't know how long it would take, but, if you fly up to Montreal and talk to the buyers there, Warren said they'd work with you to rescue Taj."

"Great! Great, great, great!"

"One more thing your wonderful wife has done. There's a Newark-to-Montreal flight leaving tonight at eight. I reserved a seat, your overnight bag is packed and I reserved a car rental for you at the airport."

"You didn't miss a thing. That's my baby."

"You can buy me dinner at the Manor. I'll accept," she chided.

"Deal," I said.

"One more thing. I think Warren's pretty hurt over this thing."

"Hon, call him and thank him. Tell him as soon as this is over, he and I are going to the island and buy some horses. Tell him that."

Her voice brightened. "Right now!"

"I'm going to check with the owner again. See if I can find anything more." I hung up but I might as well have kept talking since there was no answer at the owner's. Just as I was about to try for the third time, the phone rang.

"Dad, it's Mary Beth. I've got something. I think it may be important." Her excited voice instilled hope. "There's a railway train that leaves South Portland for Montreal and western Canada. The railroad man told me that sometimes they ship horses by truck up to South Portland. There's a private meat processing place there that has a shunt for its own railroad car. He couldn't say for sure but he told me that Taj could have been sold to the private facility in South Portland or they could be shipping him to Canada. Either way they go through South Portland."

"Mary Beth, that's great. Did he have any address information?"

"No, but I checked our directories. They list a meat processing plant named Carnton's Meat Processing, 221 Saco Lane, South Portland, Maine. I haven't been able to raise them on the telephone. They're probably closed at this hour."

"Mary Beth, that's terrific. I've got to call Saundra and cancel the flight to Montreal. I'll drive up to Maine. If Taj isn't there, I'll drive up to Montreal. I'm excited, Mary Beth. Got to go. Thanks again."

I hung up and called Saundra. "Hi! Cancel the Montreal flight. I'm going to Portland, Maine."

"Huh? Portland, Maine? What's up there?" she asked, a note of suspicion in her voice.

"There's a meat processing plant privately owned. Mary Beth located it. I'll drive up there. It's only seven hours and I can make it before morning. This may be the break we were waiting for."

She didn't share my enthusiasm and I could sense the wheels turning. "Have you really given this much thought?" she asked.

"As usual, there's some objection on your part," I fired.

"I'm not objecting. But you're going to drive seven hours to a meat processing plant you could telephone from Montreal. In the meantime, Maine could be a long shot and Montreal could be the place where Taj is going. Everything seems to point to Canada, not Maine."

"There's another reason for going to Maine. The first buyer lives there. He buys horses and ships. If he decides to race Taj, he'll keep him in Maine until he breaks down. Why would he ship a horse to Montreal if he can race Taj locally and sell him later if he doesn't pan out?"

"For one thing you don't even know if this meat processing plant accepts horses. For another, the man might get higher prices in Canada. I just can't see driving all the way up there even if Mary Beth's information is true. And for a third you have State v Montero scheduled for trial day after tomorrow. You can fly and get back in time for the trial but you'll never make it if you drive."

"I can't just sit still. Taj could be on his way to the chutes right now. And you can get an adjournment on Montero. Just notify everyone, please. And no, I didn't call the plant. I just have a gut feeling Taj is there."

"But you can still travel faster by telephone than by car. Fly up to Montreal tonight. Call the processing places tomorrow and I'll keep trying the man who bought Taj. Then, if Taj is in Montreal, I can telephone and ask them to hold him and you're already there."

"Look, Mary Beth tried to help. I don't want to hurt her by ignoring her information."

She was quiet for a moment but I could hear the exasperation as she exhaled.

"I guess you have to decide what's more important, Mary Beth's feelings or Taj. And I can't make that decision for you."

"Right now they're both important. I'll stop by and pick up my bags. Cancel the Montreal flight. If there's any penalty, I'll pay it. I'll feel better if I drive. Please, Hon. I need your help."

"I'll have your things ready for you. Is there anything else you need?" Her voice sounded the surrender.

"I'll leave some notes on pending cases. But if I forget something, I'll buy it on the way up. Lean on them to adjourn Montero."

An hour later, I was driving Route 95 headed toward Maine. There was a traffic jam going through New York but by the time I cleared Hartford, the road was open. At times, the speedometer tapped one hundred and I had to slow myself down. My heartbeat kept pace with the car. It's odd how swishing past objects at a hundred miles per hour focuses attention on the roadway. Travel at a monotonous fifty miles per hour and the mind drifts: road hypnosis seeps into the brain and miles go by with no conscious recollection of location. On several occasions my mind wandered and I jarred awake wondering where I was or how I had gotten there.

I thought about Mary Beth. How we'd parted when she decided to move in with Bill. Being a strict Catholic, I reacted exactly as I thought I should. But I was regretting my decision. Had I really reacted as my feelings dictated? Or had I reacted the way I *thought* my grandfathers would have reacted? They were from the old country. In those days a daughter stained was a daughter in exile. But I had been born in America. My thoughts should not have been of the old but of the new. Teen pregnancy and common-law relationships were no longer anathema. My maternal grandfather had been a very austere man. When his third daughter took up with a married Portuguese man and became pregnant, he banished her from the house. I spent summers at Augie's house, watched my Aunt Selma sneak in the side door to visit. If I heard my grandfather's 1928 Ford putt, putt, putting up the road, I sounded the signal and my aunt hastened away.

Did it make sense? I saw Selma's astonished and alarmed face as she rushed away from the house, cowering as if driven into shame. I saw her as she clutched her child, as if the old man would beat her and snatch the child away. It never changed. Even when her boy, Sonny, was a teenager, he could not see the grandfather whose blood coursed through his veins. Like his mother, he was an outcast. Her illegitimate son saw his grandfather exactly once and that was at the funeral.

As I drove, I thought of my own actions. Had I done the very same thing? Was I treating Mary Beth as Augie treated Selma? I had been relentless as a father, but I cared about her. I played the role of mother and father. Tight curfews, private schools, weight control, strict discipline. I never met a crisis or a problem without overreacting, without shouting my disapproval. I was concerned out of love for her, but I failed to show it. The screaming and shouting had made her wince and cower. Cower such as Selma had done as she hugged the dark buildings to secret herself and her child from my grandfather's view.

I remembered once that my anger drove me to pound my closed hand on a dinner plate and it shattered, spewing splinters of glass over the table. Was this the loving father I thought myself to be? I loved my child. I thought I was doing what was right for her. Or was it right for me but not for her?

Was that the reason she needed to escape? Was she escaping the home I provided for her, or was she escaping me?

The miles clicked by. Connecticut, then Massachusetts. There was little traffic on the road. I gassed the car in New Hampshire. There was a diner just off the interstate, and I stopped for a hamburger and some coffee. A dowdy waitress scribbled my order on her pad, then called it in to the cook without looking at her notes. She clanked a cup across the counter and poured the coffee as if she could have done it with her eyes closed. When the hamburger came, it was served on toasted white bread with the crust cut off. I was too tired to argue so I munched it and only then realized how hungry I was.

Two truck drivers hunched against the counter at the far end of the restaurant. One was a burley man, black wavy hair, a neatly groomed beard. With a suit, he could have been a stock broker. He spoke with an air of knowledge and distinction. The other was younger, blond hair that was almost invisible, an ear ring in the left ear. The heavier man made eye contact and nodded. He had a horse emblem on his tee shirt, some kind of reining horse.

"You into horses?" I asked, raising my coffee as if toasting his health.

"Yeah, I got a quarter horse I ride, gruella colored." He softened to the conversation with a stranger. "You ride?"

"I race standardbreds. You travel up through Maine?" I pursued the conversation.

"I live in Maine," he retorted with that deep New England pride for which Maine is known.

"Maybe you can help me. Ever hear of Carnton's Meat Processing, near South Portland?

"I used to ship cattle, sometimes horses up to them." He wheeled his counter seat around to face me and shoved the rest of his pie aside. "Never liked shipping the horses, all crowded and shoved together like flies on a sticky board." He puffed his cigarette and let the smoke curl out of his nose.

"I'm looking for a horse I was racing. He's kind of a pet. They claimed him while I was away, and he broke down. He's been shipped north but I don't know where. Someone said Montreal has a stockyard. My daughter located Carnton in Maine and thought the horse might be going there."

"Not there, I don't think." He shook his head in thought. "No, not there."

I felt my heart leap into my mouth and my stomach twist into a knot. I put the coffee down. "Not there?"

"Carnton tapered off a while back. The old man keeps the place open and processes deer and wild game during hunting season. I don't think he handles horses or cattle anymore. The animal rights people got on him and started picketing his place. Small area like that, it doesn't take much pressure. Thing is, most of those horses were better off dead. Some lame, some sick, others too old even to stand."

"Are you sure? I mean about him being closed."

"Pretty sure. Like I said, I used to ship to him. Hasn't had a shipment there in two years, maybe more." He inhaled again and let the smoke escape through narrowed lips. "His son drowned in a boating accident on the Saco. Then the activists got a hold of the old man and he ain't been right since." He shoved his plate and the money toward the waitress and rose from counter seat.

"Any idea where they'd ship a horse from Jersey? There's a man who buys lame horses and sends them up to Maine. Sometimes he races them. Sometimes he just sells them for meat." I pressed the issue, hoping for any information I could uncover.

"That's a hard one. Sometimes they ship to Canada, or to an auction or even a private buyer. The Amish buy some for wagon horses. If a private buyer takes them, it's hard to say where the horse would go. The killer plants are keeping a low profile. Afraid of those animal nuts. Needle in a haystack. If I had to make a guess I'd station myself at the border though."

I nodded.

"What kind of horse?" he asked again.

"Standardbred," I answered, "almost seventeen hands."

"Big one." He'd lost interest in the conversation and shoved away from the counter while the droopy-eyed waitress brought his change. He ignored the money and stood up and stretched. "Got a long haul, pally." He crushed his cigarette in the ashtray and motioned to the younger man.

"Good luck," he said and barreled out the door.

I turned to the waitress. "Do you have a telephone here?"

She pointed sleepily to the other end of the diner.

I dialed home. The door shut behind the driver, and I felt a sense of desolation overtaking me. Everything seemed hopeless. After several rings, Saundra answered. It was later than I realized and her voice was sleep ridden.

"Hi," I said.

"Hi, yourself. Are you all right?"

"As soon as I wipe the egg off my face."

"Huh?"

"You were right. Wild goose chase."

"Are you up there already?"

"Naw. Got as far as New Hampshire. Ran into a truck driver who knew about the processing plant. Thinks they've been closed for about two years. That they only handle deer processing now."

"I'm sorry, Hon. I know you had your hopes set on Maine."

"I did but I should have listened."

"So what now?"

"Maybe I'll drive up to Bangor. See if I can find out anything up there. My old law school chum, Mike Murray, has a law office there. Anything new on your end?"

"I spoke to Warren this evening. He feels pretty ratty about Taj. But he did give me some ideas. He said they probably are shipping Taj to one of two places, possibly a small, local racetrack in Maine or Montreal. He mentioned Bangor as having a small racetrack. They use it mostly for qualifying horses and fairs. It's located just as you come off the exit ramp for Bangor. Warren thinks they'll race him in Maine first. I tried the Maine owner twice more. Still no answer."

"Sounds like I'm right to drive to Bangor."

"Wait!" she near screeched. "I thought you were hanging up. Sorry. I called the stockyard in Montreal. Had to use some of my high school French but as soon as the man heard me trying to speak French, he reverted to English. They're not expecting any U.S. horses for at least a week, perhaps more."

"And the bad?" my voice and my hopes dropped.

"Judge Hartman gave us two days on Montero. There was a message waiting for me at the office. No adjournments and no excuses."

"Do you have the address for the killers in Montreal?"

"Did you hear what I said? Hartman wants this case tried and off his docket."

"I guess that's the ball game." The heart went out of me. Montero would take at least a week to select a jury and try. But Hartman was a no-nonsense judge. Some judges could be pushed again and again. Others were soft but eventually took a stand. But not Hartman. He ran his courtroom by the book, and he'd jug me for contempt if I didn't show up.

"I do have a little good news."

"Don't hold me in suspense, you beautiful dame."

She laughed a sweet little laugh that resonated like glass. "Warren knew the name of the man in Maine. Said he sells horses up there all the time. If Taj can race, he'll doctor him and send him to the races. County fairs are big up there. Bangor has a state fair that lasts a week and has a lot of racing activity. There is no drug testing so they can shoot the horses up and still race them. Warren had said Taj could race if they shot him full of Novocain or something like it. "

"I love you. Do you know that? I love you." I said but the words sounded hollow and meaningless.

"I love you, too. Get some sleep then drive home tomorrow. I'll prep the file for you. And I'll keep trying the telephone."

"Deal. Wish me luck with the traffic." I was devastated by the judge's ruling. It wasn't a difficult case and there had only been one adjournment. There was no need for him to lean on me that way.

"Luck." She sighed and then continued. "Everything else is fine. Nothing catastrophic at the office. Mary Beth called. She felt really badly about the misinformation. I think she's worried you'll be mad at her." I heard her tense as she completed the sentence as if expecting the worst and, for a moment, I measured my words carefully.

"We need to talk about that, Love. I've been doing some thinking on the way up here."

"Good. It's nice to know you do…think, that is." I could almost feel the smugness. "Any conclusions?"

"Well, I just need to talk…to you…and maybe to her as well."

"She sent a picture of your grandson, Danny."

"Un huh."

"He's got your round face and your chin, brown eyes, light skin. They call him Spike because his hair sticks straight up like it's been greased." She giggled a little.

"Spike! That's a name to be reckoned with."

"Hey? I love you," she said.

"Me too."

"One more thing," she added, "didn't your friend in Bangor have an investigator working for his office?"

"He did. Yeah," I drew the words out slowly, *"he did."*

"Well?"

"Know what?"

"What?"

"I'm exhausted. I'll find a motel room and start home tomorrow. As soon as I get back, I'll call Mike Murray and talk to his investigator. Take care." I hung up. The waitress called a motel down the road and woke the owner. I had a room waiting for me when I arrived. The frown told me he didn't get many night callers. He handed me the key and mumbled something about jiggling the key. Outside the tiny office, the sea wind refreshed my stagnant mind. Even a bed smelling of cigarette smoke and mold felt good after the long day. But it was a restless sleep.

Somewhere in the distance of dream, I heard Taj nickering. He was in a long file of horses headed into the plant for processing. When I saw him, I knew he was saved, but then he disappeared in a herd of horses that surrounded him. The herd disbursed but I couldn't see Taj. I could only hear his frightened nicker. I jolted into consciousness and drifted to resume the dream. At five, I jabbed at the telephone and dialed Mary Beth. It rang with the incessant clang of a phone that does not wish to be answered. Twice, I nearly hung up. Finally, Mary Beth moaned a sleepy hello.

"Geishel?"

"Dad! Oh Dad, what's wrong?" she blurted.

"I'm sorry. I shouldn't have called so early."

"No, it's all right. I'm glad you called. What's wrong?"

"Me. Geishel. I'm what's wrong. About a lot of things."

She sprinted to awareness, alert to the conversation. "I'm sorry about a lot of things, too."

"Can we talk when I get through this business?"

"I'd like that, Dad. We always did talk things out."

"You were my little confidant. I could talk anything over with you. Then your mother intervened and things didn't go so well. I made all the wrong moves."

"I know, Dad. I made mistakes too."

"That day. The day you told me about Bill. It all exploded. When you told me you had been to bed with him, I gave you that choice to stay or go and you wanted to go."

"I was kind of dumb. I was hurt when Saundra came into your life. Jealous. So I acted like a dumb little girl."

"I was really hoping you wanted to stay, so we could buy some time to work things out."

"I knew I hurt you, Dad."

"Guess I didn't do such a hot job as a father, did I?"

"You're a great father. I know now that when you yelled at me, you were trying to protect me. I couldn't see it then. Maybe having Danny taught me something. Dad, you've got to see him." A mother's pride was in her voice. "He's so roly-poly and chubby. He looks like you."

"I think I'm ready to be a grandfather now. Maybe when I get back. But God help him if he looks like me."

She laughed and I felt purged, like someone going to Confession and feeling the weight of sin shuttled away.

"I couldn't sleep," I said. "I kept thinking about things, the absence, the loss of love and companionship."

"I've missed you, too. Holidays would go by. I'd want to call but I was afraid."

"Well, I yelled all the time. Who'd want to call someone like that?"

"Me. I wanted to call. I missed you. Sometimes I'd dream we were all together just as a family should be. It would be Christmas and we'd have the Village set up, the train running, the tree decorated. We'd be sitting down to dinner and later we'd go out and have a snowball fight."

"Yeah, and then sit by the fireplace and watched the fire crackling into hot embers," I interjected.

"And stuffing ourselves so full of dessert we couldn't move." She laughed. I'd not heard her laughter in years but she sounded like the little girl she still was...to me.

"Yeah, fun, wasn't it?"

"Well, I'll let you get back to sleep. I'm sorry I bothered...no, I'm not sorry. I'm happy I called."

"Me too, Dad. We'll talk when you get home. Find Taj first. Then he can be part of the family, too."

I slipped the phone down into its cradle and dozed a few moments more. By morning, I was awake and ready to travel. I ate a hurried breakfast at the same diner and started back. When one is in a hurry, everything seems to journey in slow motion. Cars that rip past to unknown destinations suddenly take meaning. They have drivers. They have passengers. Grubby little children stare as one pulls alongside. Does it matter where they are headed?

My thoughts turned to Taj, to horses. Was there a bond between man and horse? Did we tame this magnificent beast, or had it gracefully consented to be our slave? I shuttered at the thought of my amiable giant being shunted along with the other horses, moving toward his doom, moving out of my life. How could these animals be so trusting? How could man be so inhumane to them? I thought of the drivers who whipped the horses, not the cart. I remembered that in the South Pacific, they left wild horses in a corral on the wharf. Left them there for three or four days in the hot sun. No food, no water. It subdued them and made it easier to load them onto the freighter. Perhaps that was why nine of seventeen horses had died only days after arriving at their destination.

And yet, the horses trusted man. They bonded to him in every form of human endeavor from circus to war. They suffered whip and spur and gunshot. They suffered thirst and hunger and exhaustion. They pulled him across the mighty plains of America in its formative years. They carried the rider that alerted the colonies to the invasion of British regulars. In all life, I could not think of a single, domestic beast more affable to man and of more use. Yet, as trusting as they were, that was just how abusive some men were to them.

In my mind's eye I visualized Taj being led down the long chute. Someone puts a .22 to his head, just behind the ear and pulls the trigger. Or, they'd jolt him with a charge of electricity, stun his senses, and the great horse collapses in free fall. That great spirit is no more. That friendly nicker is no more. I saw the faces of each horse as they passed. Felt the hopelessness of searching for one horse in hundreds. My desperation increased. My anxiety hit new heights. And then I prayed.

Lord help me to find him. He's my friend. When in despair, Taj listened to me speak my heart. His presence was always comforting. All I ask is to find him so I can lead him to still waters and green pastures. I know he's only a horse but surely even they deserve your mercy.

If there was blame to be assessed it fell, not on the killers, but on those who placed their charges into harm's way. I had failed Taj just as I had failed my daughter. Why should God hear me? I hadn't been a very nice guy to the people who loved me.

I returned to New Jersey to prepare for State v Montero. Miguel Santo-Del Montero had been charged with driving under the influence and criminal manslaughter. A few well-meaning friends invited Miguel to celebrate his birthday. According to Miguel, a tall, muscular and swarthy man of forty, with raven-black hair and bottomless, brown eyes, his so-called friends spiked his teapot with bourbon while he dined on Moo Shoo Pork. The MSG acting in concert with the alcohol could have worsened his intoxication or, at least, dulled his senses even more. Miguel missed a stop sign and ploughed into the middle of a sub-compact vehicle, killing the driver and passenger. On a personal level, I felt the manufacturer of the small vehicle was more responsible for their deaths than Miguel's drinking, but the manufacturer wasn't on trial.

Jury selection took two days. I kept thinking about Taj, and all the "what ifs" flooded into my mind during the trial. The case droned on. Two days into the trial, Judge Hartman suspended the proceedings while he attended a judicial conference in Trenton. For a moment I thought I'd be able to resume my search but the judge buttoned down the loopholes by ordering both lawyers to check in with the clerk every day.

At my office I telephoned Mike Murray. From him I obtained the name of his investigator and hired him to see if he could find Taj. I forwarded photos by fax machine as well as a description of the horse. Saundra continued trying to contact the first buyer and only succeeded in raising a stable hand who could only say, "Boss no here."

Judge Hartman returned and called the prosecution and the defense into his chambers. He pressured me to enter a guilty plea and cut a deal with the State's attorney. But there was no deal to be cut. Montero's case was a win-or-lose situation. If he lost, he did time in jail and lost his driver's license. If he won, he'd face a hearing on whether or not he retained his driver's license.

We commenced the trial again. The State introduced the police, copies of their reports, photographs of the scene, results of the breathalyzer tests, video of Montero performing physical tests, the medical examiner's reports on the causes of death. They felt smug that they had a pretty tight case.

By way of defense I introduced Montero, the friends who had been with him on that evening (though none accepted responsibility for spiking the tea) and my key witness, an expert who testified that the MSG alone could have dulled Montero's senses, giving him a natural high and causing him to operate a vehicle in an erratic manner. Then I innovated a bold move and put the state trooper on the stand. I insisted he perform each and every physical test he administered to Montero. One test consisted of standing on one leg, eyes closed and touching the nose, first with the right hand and then with the left. The other was the sway test in which the defendant, Montero, had to stand with his two feet together while the Trooper observed his stability. And, of course, the walk-the-line test. There were twitters in the courtroom when I had the officer perform a breath test on me. Reading zero. No alcohol. Then, I took a bottle of bonded whiskey, poured some onto a cotton ball and put the ball in my mouth for thirty seconds. The officer performed the breath test again. Reading 3.6, off the scale. My point was that Montero could have had whiskey in his mouth without having been intoxicated.

On the eighth day the trial ended. On the eighth day Mike Murray telephoned me and told me Taj was racing at the fair the following week. And on the eighth day, Miquel Montero shook my hand and walked out of court a free man. Even the prosecutor said my closing argument was outstanding. As I faced each juror, I wasn't pleading for Montero. I was pleading for Taj. He didn't deserve to die in a slaughterhouse.

Getting a room in Bangor when the state fair was in town was just about impossible. Not only were the rooms scarce, but they tripled the price because of a special event. I found a spot on the edge of town, typical of the home-built motels, weathered and grimy with road dust, sparse furnishings, cheap locks but neat enough inside. Shower, no tub and the sink enamel worn from use and spotted with rust. Modern technology had struck my room because there was a hot plate, a coffee pot, packets of sugar and coffee, even a plastic spoon and napkin. The owner didn't know much about the racing at the fair but, by his prices, he did know the fair was in town.

I met with Mike Murray and spoke to his investigator, Carl Streevos, on the telephone. He'd lived in Jersey, decided to abandon the rat race and relocated in Bangor twenty years earlier. The man was a marvel. He furnished me with the name and address of the owner and even pinpointed when I could find him at the track. And he was worth every penny he billed me.

Mike hadn't changed much in the twenty years since we'd graduated Seton Hall Law School. His hair had thinned to the point of baldness, the sharp, bold features still chiseled out an Irish face, deep, stern brown eyes and he still dressed in brown suit, white shirt and coffee colored tie. We dined together at the Lobsterman Café, a local seafood place, long on food, drink and atmosphere.

We spoke of our law school days. Mike had married a chemical engineer and they eventually engineered seven children. Trust the Irish to follow Catholic doctrine. We laughed about his moving from Jersey to Maine but he was happy there. Back when he moved there, a lawyer either worked for the water company or he waited tables at a restaurant and hoped for an opening. Even Bangor, though, had moved into the modern age, and he was doing pretty well for himself.

Before we closed the place, the conservative Irishman leaned forward to tell me something. His eyes looked a bit grim when he did so and that instinct which tells one that all is not going well suddenly struck the pit of my stomach.

"Carl told me something he didn't tell you." The chair groaned as he leaned back and let his words sink deep. "The guy who bought your horse sold him to a local man. There's a little girl involved. Apparently she took a liking to Taj and is with him much of the time."

"Oh," was all I could manage. "Tell me about the family."

"I'm coming to that," he admonished. "Her father trains and works horses locally. Takes in a few boarders. About two years ago the little girl came down with some disease, maybe meningitis, maybe an accident. I'm not sure of the details but she hasn't been able to walk. He lets her jog your horse and she's pretty attached to it. Hubris is tough and he's pretty protective. You may not be able to buy this horse if he thinks it will hurt Samantha."

"He must be financially strapped with her kind of medical bills."

"He didn't have medical coverage so it drained all his resources. I remember the case because the papers carried the story. For a while they had an organization collecting money. Donation containers all over town. Like most of those things, it eventually petered out. A lot of nice people tried to help and they did, but like everything else, it passed."

"And you think I might have a problem buying Taj back?"

He shrugged. "I don't know. I suppose if you raise the ante high enough, he'll sell. God knows, he needs the money. But he thinks the world of that little girl. Anyway you can meet him at the backstretch tomorrow morning around seven. He'll be jogging horses then. Samantha will be with him. She always is, from what I hear."

"So why didn't Carl tell me this?"

"He didn't have the heart to disappoint you. Said you sounded like a little kid who'd lost a toy," he snickered.

We both had a rolling laugh but Carl had been right. I was lost without Taj.

We parted with a handshake, the kind that says everything to a friend that needs to be said. I returned to my motel after declining Mike's invitation to stay at his home, set my alarm and went to bed. By six I was showered and dressed. I tossed in a packet of coffee, heated the water and brewed what was a fairly decent cup that later gave me heartburn. I had time so I thought about Taj. I thought about Mary Beth as well.

The fairgrounds were active for that time of morning, especially near the racetrack. I strolled along the pathways, searching through the barns for Taj but did not find him. Unlike the patrons that started flowing in around eleven, the horsemen were up early. There was a brisk chill to the air, measured in the breath of horses wheezing and blowing into the morning mist. It took me two hours before he came onto the track. When he did, he was noticeably thinner and his head bobbed because of the lameness. He nearly stopped when he saw me but I refrained from walking over to him. The trainer walked him toward the entrance to the track.

When I first saw Samantha, her father was lifting her from wheelchair to the jogging cart. She was frail and mousy looking. Her stringy blond hair hung down around her shoulders. When she sat in her chair she was sullen and unsmiling but when lifted behind the great horse, her face brightened and she sparked to life. She grasped the reins firmly and clucked to the horse. She was talking to him, soothing him, urging him on. I watched as they became one, the towering horse and the tiny girl. *Crippled in body but with the spirit of a titan*, I thought. Taj had become her mentor and she, his willing subject. They took the first turn slowly as if she were nursing that sore leg with gentle handling. She didn't work him hard. Just breezing him. At each passing, I saw the sparkle in her eyes, the youthful power of motion, something she could not do on the ground. Behind the cart, Taj was her legs, her will, her motion. He was her pass to freedom. Behind Taj, she escaped the wheelchair that bound her and aimed, like an arrow, into the stratosphere of freedom. Something in her innocent laughter reminded me of Mary Beth.

Taj felt the freedom too. He snapped to tall attention, threw out his chest and rose to full height. His legs churned like pistons. His stride lengthened. He flattened on the turns to reduce wind resistance and hugged the rail to take advantage of the shortened distance. Another training horse attempted to overtake him, but he refused to relinquish the lead. The other horse drew abreast. Its driver screamed to gain the lead. Taj just flattened down again and increased his speed. Halfway around the other horse caved and Taj raced comfortably away.

When Samantha finished, she pulled alongside her father. I was astonished by the precision with which she executed the stop and turn. Then, Hubris lifted her from the sulky and ended her freedom by confining her to the wheelchair. Her face, though bright and pale, became solemn again and the spirit slipped out of her. I strolled over to them and smiled. The man flashed me an ugly glance.

"You did a nice job handling him," I directed my comment to the little girl. "I saw how you eased him into those turns to save that front leg. Great work." Then, I faced her father whose reproachful look unsettled me. "I'm Grant Larsen. I race in New Jersey and around the circuit. I'd like to talk to you about Taj Mahal." The girl winced as if in pain but her father's blue eyes held me fast like a cobra waiting to strike.

"Ayeah," he said, "I heard you was comin'. Hubris Haney, but don't know if I got anything to say to ya though. Maybe."

"Can I take you and the little girl out for an early lunch?"

"Samantha's her name," he volunteered. "Ayeah, she can handle a horse. Been doin' it since she was five." He smiled at the waif as if trying to reassure her.

"Like a pro," I said. I found myself staring into that tiny, innocent face, watching as she twisted the long strands in a trembling hand. She could have been Tiny Tim or Little Orphan Annie except that written on her lips was her pain, and in her face her sorrow and in her eyes the fright that I had come to take her friend away. I bent nearer to her.

"Is Taj your friend?"

She nodded shyly. I felt like an outsider, someone intruding on a special and intimate relationship between father and daughter.

"He's mine too. I made him a promise long ago that when his racing days were finished, I'd turn him loose in a green, grassy field and let him enjoy his final days. Do you think I should keep that promise?"

She shrugged, not wanting to answer an obvious ploy.

"Do they call you Sam?"

"They call me Samantha," she replied, finding the courage that was in her. She twisted her hair again with her other hand. "I don't like Sam. It sounds like a man."

"Good for you. Samantha is a lovely name." I turned my attention to Hubris. "Now, how about having lunch somewhere, Mr. Haney? On me—"

She gazed at her father. "He did really good, Hubris," she interjected. "I eased him on the turns because that left front leg is still weak. Did you see him flatten down on that last turn?"

Hubris nodded, then signaled she should not have cut me off. She obeyed and faced me again as I continued talking.

"We could talk about Taj. I could tell you some things about him you may not know. Would you like that?"

She turned to her father who grabbed the handles of her wheelchair as he spoke to me. "Ah no, we'll take you to lunch. At the farm. We can talk there. Too many busy ears at the backstretch. It's an old gossip mill." He signaled to a groom who took Taj in hand. "See he gets a bath and rub. Plenty of grain and some electrolytes. And rub that leg good. I want him fit for tonight. Two-thousand-dollar claimer."

Samantha grimaced at the word "claimer." She knew she could lose the horse if someone put in a claim slip on him. But two thousand was a lot of money in that neck of the woods.

The groom asked where he was to stall Taj, and Hubris directed him to return the horse to the farm and turn him out in the pasture by the barn. The groom nodded then walked the horse away. Taj turned his head and nickered to me. It was not a gesture wasted on Samantha.

We drove in Hubris's van. He'd jury-rigged it so Sam's wheelchair could be lifted in and out. Samantha favored a seat by the window so the cool breeze could blow the blond hair off her ashen face. From the rear seat, she could reach the rural mailbox so when Hubris pulled into the driveway, she reached out and sequestered the mail. For nine, she was very mature as she read off the letters.

"This one's from the phone company. They want their money or they'll cut off the phone." She giggled a little and went on. "Here's a letter from the feed company. I know what it says. No more credit for feed unless you pay the bill in full. Mr. Tucker always wants his money right away. When Dad goes in to see him, he accepts whatever Hubris has to give him."

The farm was neat and cared for. A wood frame house that had recently been painted white and trimmed with cocoa-colored paint so it looked like a gingerbread house. The front porch had the traditional white posts, rocking chair, hammock with a small, wicker table nearby. The dwelling was encircled by picket fencing around its perimeter, separating it from a round pen, a red barn, a small jogging track. Beyond the track, several large paddocks lush with grass from the Spring rains struck the viewer as being manicured and well trimmed. We sat on a veranda in the rear yard. I stared down at the red bricks and watched a stream of black ants flow along the cracks and disappear near the grassy edge.

Hubris pointed to a little fountain not twenty feet away.

"Ayeah, Samantha loves to watch the fish when she's not busy. She'll get lunch all by herself. Don't like me fussing with it or helping her. I put everything in the house low so she could reach it. I'll venture you've never tasted the likes of her seafood salad or hushpuppies. And she makes a passable coleslaw too."

"She's a remarkable child," I said and then asked, "Why can't she walk?" She was out of earshot so I knew the question was safe.

"Couple of tom-fool boys cut her off on her bike. She slid down an embankment with the bike wrapped around her legs. Says she heard something in her back snap. Doctors say there's a small chip laying right up against the spinal cord. It's cutting into the nerve so it pains her to try and walk."

He looked at the stream of ants, got up and walked to the implement shelf and pulled down a spray can. First he sprayed a large rectangle around the entire colony. Then he sprayed the area where the ants had been parading. I watched them scatter and wondered if they understood the necessity for their eradication. At the first spray they scurried in different directions. But they were contained within a larger square and when they reached the rim of their world, they began to die. Those that didn't die would reconnoiter and form again at some other location. They'd be there for Hubris to spray again another day. I thought about how organized the ants had been. And I thought about how strange it was to be focusing on ants when my interest was in purchasing Taj. I thought about how methodical Hubris had been in his approach to destroying them.

I didn't really have to be there. All I had to do was attend the races, drop a slip into a claiming box and the horse was mine. But like the fascination the ants held for me, I was enticed by this old monarch and his crippled daughter. And like the ants, somehow I believed he and his daughter would survive to be sprayed by misfortune another day. For ill fortune stalks us all. Perhaps it was time fortune turned a smile upon them.

"Can't they do something for her?

"A yup. They can. Only she won't let 'em. See if they move that chip just a fraction when they try to remove it, she may never walk again. Can't say I blame her."

"But it could move on its own and she'd still be paralyzed."

"Ayeah, but that's her decision, now isn't it?"

Samantha called Hubris from the door. Lunch was ready. We pushed through the screen door and assembled around the table. Samantha led us in grace and then began serving. Seafood salad, steak fries with vinegar, spinach, Italian bread spread with mayonnaise, finely chopped coleslaw. She'd made a pitcher of lemonade and another with unsweetened iced tea with lemon slices floating on top.

"Quite a meal for a young lady," I said, staring at this wisp of a thing that seemed so efficient and well organized.

"Thank you," she replied, pushing the hair back from her face as she served herself. "I'm not used to compliments except from Hubris. It's just something I do since the accident."

"You call your father by his first name?"

"We're from Maine. We don't hold on protocol. Hubris is his name. Samantha's mine. Why complicate matters?"

We ate mostly in silence, an occasional comment as it occurred to one or the other. I was fascinated with this young girl. She was so unlike Mary Beth. Her disability did not faze her at all. Yet I found myself drawn to her, chastising myself for expecting Mary Beth to be as self-reliant and independent as Samantha. Had I expected too much from my daughter? Had I treated her unfairly? I didn't ask what happened to Samantha's mother, but it was apparent she had assumed the lady-of-the-house role and fulfilled it admirably. At the end of lunch she served coffee, hot and steamngly black. Blackberry cobbler with a sprig of mint, she had made herself. Hubris helped clean up the dishes and then excused himself to see to other horses in the stables.

"You're here to take Taj, aren't you?"

"I'd like to. He and I are old friends."

"You said you'd tell me about him. Will you now?"

I hesitated, stared at her placid face, then I nodded. She pushed nearer the table and I pulled my chair around to face her.

"When I bought Taj, he was a sorry horse. Depressed, unhappy. They had him racing, but he wasn't doing well. I don't know why but I just fell in love with the big guy. Do you know what he would do to me?"

"Un uh, I don't." Her grey eyes widened as she awaited the answer.

"When I walked into his stall, he raised his head and put his muzzle right on top of my head. Lightly though, I almost didn't feel it there. It was his way of telling me I was very short but it was all right with him."

She laughed and her face crinkled into a soul-warming smile. I'd not seen her laugh. The happiness seemed to well right up out of her and burst into the atmosphere. "He's very gentle for a big horse."

"He is that. And I fed him carrots and praised him. He thrives on praise."

"Yeah! When I drive him he is ever so careful around the turns. I have to urge him on. And when I visit his stall he never makes a move. The other horses are frightened of my wheelchair, but not Taj. I love him so..." And she caught herself in mid-sentence and dropped her eyes away from mine. "I mean I've become very attached to him since he's been here."

"That's easy with him. He's a really fine horse."

"Hubris says I shouldn't get too attached to him. Someone will probably claim him. He's racing in a two-thousand-dollar claimer tonight. Won his last two races so he has to go up in company. That's what Hubris does. Buys a horse cheap and gets him racing well. Then, he puts him in a claimer and makes a profit on him. Sometimes it works." She laughed then like a child laughs. "Sometimes it doesn't. But they like big horses up here. Hubris got him cheap because they found some damage to his leg. He has some remedies he tried on Taj and he's trained well. If they claim him, Hubris will put the money away for my operation."

There was no point in feigning surprise with a mature nine year old. She had that indelible mark of someone who's been through the mill and would see through any sham. "And you don't want to go through the operation." There was definition in my voice as I leaned back in my chair.

"I don't want Hubris to spend more money on doctors. The pain is not so bad. And I'm happy here. I don't even have to go to school because they have a retired nun come three times a week. And the first doctor told me that if the bone chip moved even a smallest bit while they were operating, it might sever part of the central nerve and cripple me forever. Then, I'd have no hope at all. "

"Suppose the chip moves on its own, without the operation?"

She shrugged noncommittally.

"Well, suppose someone else paid the bills? Someone like Taj if he wins races?"

"Ha!" she shook her head in disbelief. "Racing in a cheap claimer? Do you know what they pay up here? Three hundred fifty dollars. Hardly enough for feed." She leaned back in her chair. Her questioning eyes fastened on me and there was a brightness I had not seen in them except when she was driving Taj.

"Well if he did well, couldn't you race him somewhere else?"

She shrugged and twirled her hair again but I saw she was relaxed. *At least she was comfortable with me*, I thought.

"You're going to claim Taj, aren't you?"

"Actually I'd like to buy him. That doesn't necessarily mean you'll lose your friend."

Her cheeks quivered a little at the thought of losing him. She did not resist but she also did not relent. She turned her face away when she saw me staring.

"It's all right. Hubris told me this might happened. I guess he saw how I attached to Taj when he first came here."

"You haven't had him very long."

She sighed. "I know. But does it really take such a long time to love something?"

"Sometimes, it does." I whispered, almost to myself.

"Do you have children?"

"Mary Beth. She's my daughter. Must be twenty-six now."

"Do you see her very much?"

"I haven't seen her in four or five years." My thoughts drifted from Taj to Mary Beth, to her child. "We used to be very close. Not so close now."

"Did she do something terribly evil?" Her face contorted at the word evil.

"No. Not really. She was just unlucky."

Samantha was not about to abandon the topic. "Hubris and I are very close. He's takes very good care of me since Mom died."

"I'm sorry," I said, "about your mother."

"It's all right. She's been dead a long time. As long as I can remember, it was just Hubris and me. I don't know what he'd do without me."

"You help him a lot. But wouldn't it be better if you could walk? Wouldn't that help him a whole lot more?"

"Perhaps." And she persisted, "Why don't you see more of your daughter?"

"Pride, I guess. She did something that hurt...hurt very deeply. I didn't have the courage to say what I really felt."

"Oh," she uttered, watching a sage-colored cat slink along the window sill. "Was it such a hurt you can't forgive her?"

"I can't even forgive myself...not ever."

She looked puzzled. "What did you do?"

"A lot of things I'm not very proud of."

"Is that why you want Taj so badly?"

"Partly. I made a promise but I have something to set right." I hesitated because she penetrated my heart with her gaze.

"Can you keep a secret? It's a secret I am not very proud of."

"I can." She began twisting the long tresses of her hair.

"I owned a Doberman named Poco." I didn't know why I was confiding in a nine-year-old child. I was comfortable talking to her. She understood. Her eyes searched my face with wisdom far beyond her years. Perhaps her pain had made her more mature. Pain can do that to a person. Suddenly I wanted to confide in her, wanted her to know my shameful sin.

"My first wife and I were battling a lot. Mary Beth was just a kid and heard it all. The more she heard, the more I stayed away. I didn't want her involved."

I glanced at her again but she was intent on my confession.

"I came home from a weekend away and my wife started provoking me with everything the dog had done wrong. She had diarrhea and the floor was a mess. My wife had left it there for me to clean. In anger, I struck the dog with a small bat and hit it in the head."

I halted and watched her reaction. Halted because I was choked up. Halted because tears flowed down the channels of my nose. Halted because I could still see the twisted, anguished face of that dog and in her eyes was all the love and loyalty she had always borne me.

"Two weeks later Poco had a stroke. A month later she was dead. I blamed myself for what happened. I murdered her as surely as if I shot her with a gun. Murdered her because I was divorcing my wife and finding a new life and Poco didn't fit. Now, I have to help animals. I have to atone for my sin."

"Atone. The nun says that means to make up for." Her eyes were frightfully narrowed and watered. "You hurt your friend and you feel guilty?"

"Very. I have to atone, to make it right. I cannot tell you how much anguish I feel over that shameful incident. I can't forgive myself."

"You didn't want to kill her." The words were sympathetic and soothing.

"I didn't mean to hit her head. My wife knew how to drive me into a rage, but I didn't mean to hit her in the head. I just didn't know what to do. My marriage was breaking up. There was another woman in my life. I wasn't living at home. I was building a law practice and raising a kid because my wife wouldn't do it. I just had no place for Poco. I didn't think of giving her up for adoption. I don't know what I was thinking. " I emitted a long breath and with it, the tension I'd felt confiding in this little mother confessor. When I looked my hands were shaking.

She nodded and we lapped into a pensive silence.

"Do you feel guilty about your daughter too?"

I didn't have an answer. Hubris let the door slam behind him.

Saved by the bell! I thought.

"That tarnation stallion is chewing hell out of my stalls." He stopped momentarily and surmised that a deep conversation had been going on between Samantha and myself. He sat at the table and poured himself another coffee. "I imagine you'll put a claim in on Taj tonight."

"If I don't, what guarantee do I have someone else won't?"

"None. There's a lot of Easterners coming up through Maine for the summer. Big money. They'd claim him just for the sake of having something to race. Ayeah, some trainers will dope him up so he doesn't feel any pain and then race him until he collapses."

I stared at Samantha as I spoke. Her face reflected the nonchalance of one who has no control over her destiny. Still studying her, I spoke to Hubris. "Of course someone else could put in a claim. They'd have to draw to see who gets him. I don't know if I want to take that kind of risk."

Hubris gazed at me with questions in his eyes, but Samantha was smiling as if she already knew where I was going.

"What he means, Hubris, is that he is willing to buy Taj rather than risk losing him in the race tonight. He made a promise to Taj and he has something to account for."

"You *are* a bright girl. That's exactly what I had in mind."

Hubris snapped alert. He had a hundred questions and wondered what Samantha and I had talked about for so long a time. He wondered but he didn't ask.

"And what did you have in mind?"

"Well, I'll make you an offer for Taj. Couple of conditions."

Samantha's face went sullen as she heard her friend being bargained for. Hubris glanced at her. "It's something we may have to do, Samantha."

"I know. I know." Something glistened in her eye, escaped and flowed down her cheek. "That darn old operation."

Hubris turned his attention to me. "And?"

"I'll offer ten thousand for Taj. I can have the money wired up in a day or two, and you'll prepare a bill of sale."

"Ten thousand? The tarnation, you say. Are you Santa Claus or somethin'? Ayeah, even if they claimed him you could buy him back for two or three thousand."

"Perhaps, but you haven't heard all the conditions."

"Thought so." His eyes narrowed into that all-knowing look that said "I've been here before."

"I will buy Taj for ten thousand. You will scratch him from tonight's race. Next condition. I will leave Taj in your stable. Not to be raced. Just to be cared for. I will board him here and pay for his feed and care, vet bills, farrier ...all of it."

Samantha nearly leapt out of her chair. "Stay? Here? Taj? And I could still jog him?"

"Yes, you could still jog him. But hold on Samantha, there's another condition."

Her mouth dropped a little. "I know what it is."

"Shoot," I said.

"You'll leave Taj here if I go for the operation."

Hubris's face glowered with shock.

"Samantha, I have some very good friends in New York. They can find just the right doctor. I'm sure I can work out a payment plan for the hospital and the doctors. So here is my condition. You let me set up an examination with one of my medical friends. If he says he can perform the operation safely, that you'll walk again, Taj stays here until you are on your feet and ready to help Hubris. I'll even stable some horses up here to race. When you're ready, Samantha, and only when you are ready, you bring Taj back home, back to me, so I can fulfill my promise to him. I just can't not keep my promise to him."

"I understand. It's not right to make a promise and not keep it. I know that."

Hubris was stunned, not only by the offer but by the bond which had formed so quickly between me and Samantha.

"Why you doing this, Mister?" he asked, collapsing into a kitchen chair.

"Samantha reminds me of my daughter, Mary Beth. Things didn't go so well for the two of us. Sitting here, talking to Samantha, kind of reminded me I wasn't as good a father as I thought myself. I have some broken fences to mend. "

"Ayeah," he replied, "I've broken a fence or two in my time."

"You know, I hadn't seen or heard from her in years. Yet, when Mary Beth knew I was searching for Taj she pitched in to help me find him. They grow up in your home and you never really know them. Don't know why. All I've ever shown her was anger."

"Maybe she loves you because you're her father," Samantha commented.

"Not for what she can get from me?" I asked, watching the cat strike the glass with its paw.

"She does get something from you. She gets the same love from you that you give to her. Taj loves me because I love him. I think he loves you for the same reason."

"He does?" I was flattered by the revelation.

"He told me that. He said you cried once when he got hurt."

"Taj told you that?" I rose and started to pace. "He told you I cried."

She nodded assent.

I looked at Hubris, and with my eyes, asked if I could take Samantha with me. He didn't understand. I lifted her out of the wheelchair and watched him almost keel over with shock.

"Let's go see Taj and see what he thinks." She lifted that sweet face and gazed at me. I saw the angel in her, innocent and loving and I knew Taj would be in good hands. At that moment, I knew Samantha would walk again and I knew Taj would come home.

"I have a little grandson," I said as I carried her down to the stable.

"What's he like?"

"I don't know. I've never seen him. My daughter was afraid to tell me she was dating. We argued and she left home. I have an old ghost to confront. We both do, Samantha. You owe it to Hubris, to yourself and to Taj. I owe it to Mary Beth and Danny. Little girl, there's so much life out there, and you have a chance to see it from outside a wheelchair. And Taj can't get home until you bring him. You have to walk him right up to me and hand me the lead line. I'll miss him until then, but I know you'll care for him."

We stood outside the stall and the great horse turned and nodded. I think he was agreeing to the bargain. Then I opened the stall door and carried Samantha inside. Gently I swung her onto the great horse's back and supported her limp legs as she settled into the saddle of his back. She snuggled into a comfortable position and glanced down at me. There was radiance in her small face, a glow of infinite happiness.

"Can you imagine," I said, "what it would be like to ride him? To gallop him along the edge of the woods or along a deserted beach? It's such a feeling of power when one bonds with a horse, more than any other animal. A dog will love you and it will be loyal. But when a horse bonds there is a meeting of souls, Samantha, that borders on the infinite. Sometimes I think that God must ride horses because they are so very special."

She nodded at almost every word, still stroking the great horse with her tiny hand.

"I've never been on him before," she sniggered. "He feels much taller than he looks, like I'm on top of a building." She leaned forward and rubbed his wither. "All right, Taj. For you, for Hubris, I'll do it. But I need to talk to the doctor myself. I want to hear him say that I will walk again."

Then she turned to me and smiled. "You need to mend your own fences. You need to put your grandson on Taj."

I slipped her off Taj's back and carried her back to the house. She settled in the wheelchair and laughed. "I won't be needing you much longer."

With Samantha and Hubris wide-eyed, I wrote out the check for ten thousand and another for one thousand.

"The additional is for feed and board. Have the vet send the bills, if any, to me directly and I'll pay them from my business account."

Suddenly I realized that Hubris had his hand on my shoulder and was squeezing gently. "Ayeah, you really are Santa Claus."

With that, I shook his hand and left. But the miles were angry because I could not get home fast enough to try the new Grant on my wife and family. A kinder, sympathetic Grant. A devoted horse and a little crippled child showed me the way or perhaps it was the light of God that illuminated the path. I did not know. I would never know. All I knew was that I liked the Grant who had given a little girl a chance. I liked the Grant who was ready to be a grandfather. I liked the Grant, who, like Scrooge, transformed every day into Christmas.

Conclusion

A YEAR LATER, I TELEPHONED SAUNDRA AT MY OFFICE. The Court Clerk obliged by letting me use the judge's phone. It was the end of a three-day trial, and, after living with the parties and the facts for nearly two years, I was elated to be liberated.

"How about dinner?" I asked.

"You need to be at Winter Hills first. And soon because it's important."

"What's wrong now?"

"Nothing!" she giggled. "It's a fun surprise. Mary Beth and Danny are there waiting to show you something."

"Something to show me? And you're not going to tell me?"

"Nope. But I'm on my way right now. Please say you'll come."

"Not even a hint."

"Nope."

"I always said you were evil to the core."

She laughed. And it was good to hear her laugh. So much of my anger had hurt her over the years.

"I'll do it but only because it will make you happy."

"It will. I'll meet you there. And then you can buy us all dinner. You made enough on the trial."

"Done." And I set the phone down gently.

Winter Hills Farms. I was proud of the name because I had selected it. I was proud of the racing stable, too, because we had some fine horses. Usually, I tried to visit every other week because it was a sixty-mile drive from my office. I turned my car in the direction of Winter Hills, wondering why in God's name Saundra wanted me there. Obviously it was because of Mary Beth and Danny. But why Winter Hills? And what was the surprise in seeing Mary Beth when we'd begun bonding almost a year earlier? I alighted from my Lincoln and aimed toward the barn. And then I noticed two men, a child and a horse coming toward me. My eyes settled on Warren, Hubris and Samantha. The girl was leading Taj Mahal and she strode directly to me, not a hitch in her step. She did not hand me the lead. Instead she shoved out her hand and shook my own.

"I can walk. I can even run. I've trained Taj Mahal to saddle and he's got a good gait. I think his canter is the best one. The leg is as healed as it's going to be and as long as you don't push him too hard, he'll carry you for twenty miles."

In her eyes, I detected a bit of sorrow but also a bit of hope. She had grown, filled out. Her face was brighter, touched by optimism. Her smile almost translucent.

"Hubris bought me my very own horse. Her name is Puppet's Pride. She's a Standardbred out of Puppet but I use her only for trail. In the spring we'll breed her and race the foal."

"That's great, Samantha." I let the lead drop and stretched my arms out for a hug. She leaped into the embrace, then pulled away and did a little dance.

Hubris stood by her. He squeezed her shoulder and said, "Mr. Larsen kept track of your progress every week after your operation."

"I'm not surprised," she laughed. "He wanted his horse back."

"And how," Warren added. We all bowed with laughter. And I found an inner peace that I had helped this little girl. It did not lessen the pain I felt over Poco, but it vindicated me as if I had made amends to Mary Beth and Danny. As I turned, Mary Beth and Saundra were behind me. They were smiling too. A little wallowing ball of mirth and joy waddled toward me. His eyes were shining and his round face was undeniably from the Larsen strain. My ancestors would have been proud of him. I lifted him and pressed him to me. He felt warm and comforting and he lay securely in my fold.

Warren and I renewed old ties and ultimately we purchase ten race horses at various sales. I am proud to say he has done very well in training all of them. Just reinforces what a little faith can do. I took everyone out for a glorious dinner and the night's conversation was brimming with hope for the future and the excitement of living. Several times Samantha came over to squeeze my hand and tell me about her Puppet's Pride. In a year's time she had matured into a young adolescent. It was good to see her smiling.

The party glimmered like a glowing spark long after the participants had disbanded. It was not sugarplums that danced in our dreams but the glory of the Winner's Circle. And like the Roman adage repeated behind the chariot of conquering generals, the Roman saying: *All glory is fleeting.*

I visited Taj again a week later with my grandson. I brought the great horse to his field, the field where he spends his days with his friend, Dusty. He still nickers when I bring his carrots. He still raises his head and places it lightly on my own to greet me. There are days when I visit him alone because old friends should have time alone. And there are days when I visit him, holding my Danny's fragile hand and hoisting him on the back of that huge animal. Taj turns to look at the fidgeting tyke balanced astride his broad back, and in his eyes, I see the wonder of that young life.

THE HORSE WITH THE GOLDEN MANE

What he saw in those eyes spoke to him of abuse and pain, of a misery so deep and a disillusionment so penetrating that he could scarcely believe what he was seeing. Those eyes, so proud, so bright and kind, so puzzled that men had hurt him, spoke to Pierce Bernard as if the man *heard* the words rather than *felt* them. Pierce was stirred to compassion, for compassion was the innermost self of the man.

He raised a hand to stroke the nose of that magnificent beast, but the animal shied away. He lowered his hand and gazed at the flaming horse, the horse with the mane of gold that sparkled with sunlight like fire raging through a withered prairie. An athletic horse, trim and fit, endowed with conditioned chest and leg muscles. Red Leader stared at Pierce, his eyes softening momentarily. The man meant him no harm; he sensed that. But he was far from docile. He strung himself to full height, snorted and blew like a steam engine, then reared and defied Pierce to come into his paddock. But Pierce merely stared back at him, searching for something in the animal's soul. When he found it, he unlatched the gate and stepped in.

Red tossed his head in annoyance and galloped to the far end of the enclosure. It was not a large square, barely one-quarter acre, with a small round training pen in the rear. Pierce watched as the animal flung his heels toward him, then pitched and weaved his head as he paced near the round pen. It was a sign of defiance. Still, Pierce did nothing. He knew the horse needed patience. He knew the horse could be intimidating. Something in the animal's eyes read like a storybook and spoke to Pierce of the animal's past. Something in the animal's manner told Pierce the animal needed a friend.

The man stepped forward. The horse stopped and regarded him. It was not so much a challenge as studying the landscape in the way plains animals are apt to gaze at some distant figure. At times it appeared the horse was staring beyond Pierce, but the man had his attention.

Pierce inched forward, closing the gap slightly. The sun glistened on the magnificent red coat, and then the red horse drew himself up, full, and charged. As he closed, it was apparent he could easily trample Pierce. The man accepted the challenge and stood his ground. He anchored his feet and faced Red as he bore down. As the horse veered away from him, Pierce circled and came up behind Red, raised his hand to drive the animal forward. The red horse stopped. He was puzzled. His dance of fury and his charge had failed to unsettle the man. He snorted and blew again until spittle foamed in his nostrils.

But the horse stood as Pierce strode to him. The man had noted something in the horse's turn. He crouched when the horse settled and approached him quietly. When Red calmed, Pierce gently lifted the left front leg, carefully plied the bone. He massaged the white band that separated the pastern from the hoof. When he felt something, he let the leg down but kept his hand on the bony portion.

Fracture, he thought. *Not a bad one and probably half-healed.* "You've got spirit," Pierce said, half to himself. "Big fella, too. Probably sixteen hands." His fingers moved like a surgeon's around the bony mass. "I'll wager you've got heart too." He said this aloud, catching the horse's attention again.

"That he does," the man behind him said. "Lots of heart."

"Hi, Doc," Pierce replied, not turning to look at the vet. "I came to pick up a few wormers, just thought I'd see what you have here." Then he stood up, a little stiff from having crouched and shook the vet's hand. Stiffness seemed to be a way of life lately and it hurt when the vet grasped his hand in greeting. Pierce stood alongside the vet so he could speak without taking his eyes off the horse. He was slightly taller than Donnie, his brown hair tinged with less gray than a fifty-five-year old man would show, a deep tan weathering his linear face. The horse ambled off to the far end of the paddock allowing Pierce to face the vet. "Something special about this horse, something tame but untamed. Never know what he'll do next."

Donnie himself was muscular and short, perhaps thirty-five, soft black hair pressed back around a flat forehead and a boyish face that accented the his English stock and cheeks that seemed to outline the determination that burned within him. And there was compassion and kindness in ashen eyes that focused on the red horse. It was not uncommon in this redneck area to find people with pale grey eyes, descended from the English who had settled the area. And, like his ancestors, Donnie had a square build as if he had been a boxer or wrestler, but he had been neither. His whole life had been spent caring for horses. He knew them. He loved them. Although he had practiced for many years, he never lost his tender bedside manner. His hands caressed rather than handled a horse. Force or impatience was never part of his itinerary. He never hastened to finish no matter how busy he was. And he worked long hours and late into the evening. He could perform any surgical procedure his equipment would permit, but he never conquered the flustering pain of putting an animal to sleep.

"You've lost weight," Pierce said, for indeed the vet had a trim, well-toned torso. Slight-shouldered but strong arms and hands that went about their work with self-assured skill. "We need to get out for dinner again."

"Don't get much chance to eat the way I'm running these days," Donnie replied. "I've got one barn with fifty-two, all thoroughbreds and all flighty." Then he faced Pierce full and smirked, "You've taken a shine to Red Leader, have you?"

"Red Leader," Pierce repeated. "Red Leader. Sounds like a litany, doesn't it? Flows right off the tongue." He brushed back the lock of hair that flopped over his right eye. "Something about him. Something special."

"Pretty good race horse," Donnie offered. "Was anyway." Then, scrambling in his bag for the wormers, he asked: "How many?"

Pierce took his eyes off the horse. "Give me a dozen. Maya likes to have extra."

The vet's eyes tilted slightly downward. "Surely not. I thought..." he stammered to a stop. "Your wife," he mumbled. "She sure takes care of her horses."

"She's been away so much you thought she left me, huh? Everyone does. She's coming back. Just got a big book order so she flew off to New York to close the deal." His eyes narrowed as he studied the vet's face. "I know what they're saying. They think I'm going crazy. Treat me like Maya never existed. They'll see. She'll be back...just wait."

The vet looked uncomfortable, as if he'd touched a nerve and wanted to swallow his tongue. "Surely not, Pierce. I don't think you're crazy. I just plainly forgot how much she's into her book. How's it going?"

"Great. Just great. She was on her way home a month ago when her agent told her he'd lined up a contract with the California Library Association. Big order. Maybe two, three thousand books. She closed that and her agent sent her off to New York. Another big deal. What a woman."

"She's quite a woman to put up with the likes of you. Haven't seen her in quite a while." He averted the man's gaze, staring at the flaming, chestnut horse that had approached them as if wishing to hear the conversation.

Pierce's lip quivered a bit as he stared at the horse. "Maya is a bug for horse care. Wants them wormed six times a year. Has to have twice the season's hay we need. I don't know how many times we've argued about that." He leaned closer to the vet and whispered, "I know what people are thinking, Doc. She's not coming back. Not ever." He straightened up and raised his voice. "Well, they're wrong. All those people who said she wasn't coming back were wrong. She was...back. Just two months ago she flew into Lexington Airport. We spent time together at the Radisson. You know that fancy place near the center of town? Had a wonderful dinner, romantic evening."

The vet raised his hand to calm Pierce. "It's okay, Pierce. Even if people gossip, well surely you know country people. But I believe you. And I know that hotel. First class." He nodded then placed his hand lightly on the man's shoulder. "Let me tell you about Red Leader," he said softly, mouthing the words carefully as if to sooth the agitated man. "Maya will love him."

Pierce brightened when Donnie said this. "Sorry, Doc. Just burns me up. They stare at me like I'm a freak. Why don't they just mind their own business?" The red horse had moved closer again. Pierce inadvertently placed his right hand on the horse's withers. The animal did not move as though gauging the measure of the man who stroked him so gently. "So tell me about this horse." His faced relaxed.

"Standardbred. Raced in New Jersey and piled up a bunch of wins. Earned over one-hundred thousand dollars. Took a wrong step and incurred a tiny, ribbon-fracture in the left front pastern. The owner was told to rest the horse for a year. Instead he moved him to another training barn and never told the new trainer the animal was hurt. Insisted the trainer put him right into another race without even jogging him. Well, he broke down. Not before he won the purse money though. They didn't think they were going to get him to the barn, let alone anywhere else."

The vet reached into his pocket and pulled out a treat. The horse nickered and moved to receive it, then nudged him for another. The vet obliged, then handed Pierce the wormers.

"How'd you wind up with him in Kentucky?"

"He landed with a vet I clerked with in Alabama. The owners didn't want to pay any board bills and told the vet to put Red down. My friend took him for the amount of his bill and called me to see if I wanted a nice trail horse. I didn't need one, but when I heard the bad deal Red got waiiiillllllll..."

"You figured you'd find a soft-hearted guy like me who'd take him off your hands. So far, you've stuck me with two dogs, two house cats, three barn cats, a broken-down mare, and a frustrated old parrot who hung upside down all day until he fell over dead. Do I look that much like a bleeding heart?"

Donnie laughed, something he managed almost without seeming to, as though the laughter was there, but his thoughts elsewhere. "I surely didn't have anything in mind. The horse is a nice horse, but he can be a handful. They always had problems getting his harness on. He'd refuse to warm up before the race. Once, he bolted right up into the stands and scattered patrons all over the place. He's got a kind eye, but he can fool a man, too. Still, he needs a friend and until...until Maya gets back, maybe you need a friend too." The vet stared into the vast space beyond the paddock, lush with green, full grass and still wet with dew. "I just wish you wouldn't take this book business so seriously."

The horse nodded his head as if in agreement.

"I've got a friend. How about a vet who baby-sits horses? Or cries when he has to put an animal down?"

"You're an easy guy to like, Pierce. Love animals. Care well for them. And you and Maya surely had a special..." he stopped.

"Special relationship? We still do Donnie. So she went away for a time. It's something she wanted to do. She'll be back."

"She's been on the road for a long time," the vet added, then moved nearer to Red Leader and bent to check the injured leg.

Pierce's face tightened and he quavered as he spoke. "No, now that's not true, Donnie. She'll be home any day." His face softened then as he glanced back at the horse. "Sure is a looker. The horse, I mean."

"Smart too. He learns fast. Well, why don't you take him on trial? He'll make a nice trail horse if you can settle him, and I don't know anybody down here handles a horse the way you do."

"Well, Maya will probably kill me taking on another horse. She won't let me near a horse sale."

The vet looked away, down toward the white, linear barns of his property. The buildings were stark white with freshly painted weathervanes, unpainted cedar doors, nests where mud wasps were building.

Pierce looked the horse over again. "Anything else wrong with him?"

"Not a thing. Rest him. Massage that ankle. Put him on some kind of joint supplement like GlucoFlex or Corta Flex. That fracture has healed so he can be ridden. Lightly, at first. He's got all his shots and I've got a Coggins in my office. You don't need a health certificate unless you're transporting out of state." He paused then, "I wouldn't send him back to the races."

"I'm done with that," Pierce injected. "Not after what they did to Diamond's Pride."

The two men walked back toward the gate, each staring at the ground while conversing. They had been friends almost from the start, eight years earlier. And they shared a mutual love of animals. That passion for horses bonded them as friends and they had shared many a dinner together. When Donnie divorced his wife, Pierce guided the equine vet with legal advice. In that manner, country people are beholden and they never forget a friend. Because he was a friend, he avoided the sore topic of Maya. It wasn't a pleasant secret to hold, nor did he wish to hurt his friend.

"What exactly did happen to the filly?" the vet asked, putting the last of the wormers into Pierce's hands and shaking off the money he offered.

"I hired a trainer–driver in Ohio. Gave him orders that no one was to train or jog that horse except him. I got a call from him telling me that horse had to be put down, that he had an accident with Pride, and she couldn't get up. When I asked for more details, he gave me a blow-by-blow account. Mind you, he put the horse down without even asking me. Said the track vet made the decision, not him."

They reached the gate and both men stopped, still staring at the ground, the comforting, golden May sun engulfing them. Donnie noted a watering beginning in Pierce's eyes.

"We can talk about something else," the vet said.

Pierce then jerked his head back to get the hair out of his eyes.

"My trainer wasn't jogging him after all. He sent a young kid out there to condition her, a beginner. Another driver cut too close to Pride's sulky. In a panic, she reared. When she came down, her leg went through the wheel spokes of the other cart and snapped the cannon bone. He lied to me, the skunk." Pierce pounded his fist into his hand as the picture of that accident streamed through his thoughts. "Well, I called him back and asked him how many horses he was training for me and he answered thirteen. 'Wrong,' I said, 'you're not training any.' And I pulled every damn horse out of his stable. It bankrupted him, but he deserved no better. We were his biggest client."

The vet shook his head sympathetically. "Sometimes we just have to let go, pal. Some things got to be faced and accepted. Then we move on." He greeted Pierce's eyes with a direct gaze. "We have to forget, move ahead." Pierce felt the vet wasn't talking about Puppet, but about something else. Perhaps Maya. He fidgeted uncomfortably.

Pierce jabbed a toothpick into his mouth and began chomping it anxiously. "I guess, Doc." Then he turned to the horse. "Now what about this beautiful red horse here? How much do you want for him?"

Donnie smirked. His face was always placid and serene but concentrated. "Pierce, you're just the right man for this horse. He needs a friend, not a trainer or driver, just a friend. I know you'll take care of him."

"And Maya," Pierce interposed, "she's going to love Red, too. Handsome horse. Beautiful golden mane."

"Sure," the vet said sadly. "Maya for sure."

The older man's face brightened like a child who has discovered an Easter egg. "Send him over tomorrow. You going to be around?"

Donnie shook his head. "I'll have my assistant drop him off. I'll fetch the Coggins papers now and send you the title when I get to it."

They shook hands again. The vet held Pierce's hand longer than usual. "Pierce..." he hesitated. The older man focused on him. "You've got to let go..." the vet said, his eyes skittering side-ways, "I mean, things like Diamond's Pride, you've got to let go...of things like that." He almost spelled out the words, but when Pierce's eyes hardened, he let the hand drop and nodded. "Thank you for taking Red. I think the two of you need each other."

The men parted company and Pierce drove off. Donnie stood staring at the vehicle as it motored down the tree-lined thoroughfare leading to Highway 910. Donnie was not wondering about the horse, but about the man. Pierce, too, was wondering. He was wondering about the horse. He was wondering what Maya would say when she saw Red. Would she be so angry she would not see the horse's beauty? Or would she fall in love with him as she had with Challenge? He didn't know. He'd call Maya tonight and tell her the news. He didn't like to bother her when she was marketing her book. Yes, he'd call that evening.

Then second-guessing himself: *No, I'll call after the horse is here. She won't make me take it back... I don't think she will, anyway.* He smiled then and his eyes sparkled with happiness.

RED CLATTERED OFF THE CRIMSON TRAILER, anxious to be free. He was lathered and sweaty from the hot, airless ride—a horse with a new home and a new friend. The man had not really known what he would do with Red, but he admired the animal's courage and spirit. And Donnie was right. With Maya away, he needed a friend. The man knew he was searching for some missing piece to his tattered life. Perhaps the horse could help him find it.

In time, he would learn that Red was exceptional; that the chestnut gelding learned routines quickly and was alternately sweet and defiant, depending on his mood. Pierce would learn the horse had great sensitivity and that he would respond to kindness. Red was a horse aware of his sur-roundings, noting every change in his environment. But that day he charged out of the trailer and jerked the lead so hard that he lifted Pierce off his feet and dragged him a foot or two. Pierce felt like a sled being tugged along the road, but there was no snow and the gravel hurt his bottom. The horse jerked again and Pierce released the lead. Red snorted and rolled his head.

The mutinous horse trotted down the road, but his path was limited. The private road on which Pierce lived was lined with fencing on both sides. In the distance, Red saw the large A-frame home that dominated the hill. On both sides of the house, the land sloped down into the road. Across the road, there was ample pasture, separated into two paddocks. Red searched for open space, but there was only the road ahead or behind. He glanced up at the treetops and saw he was enclosed by ridges and hills.

Even if Red had turned in the other direction instead of toward the house, he could only have gone as far as the creek. Southern Moor was bounded on all sides by streams and beyond those by the barbed wire of neighboring farms. The road divided the property and the fence separated the fields.

The angry gelding slowed and stopped. He blew and did a war dance, but he was confused by the unfamiliar terrain. Pierce heard him snorting as he tried to rise. He had been dazed by the sudden jolt. He shook himself off and arose so he could take the measure of the horse that defiantly trotted toward him. He was a magnificent animal, light red chestnut, golden mane, smooth, athletic body, and slender, handsome face. And in that face Pierce saw something besides defiance. Something in Red's eyes did not speak of hate but of fear.

Yes, there was insolence, but there was something else, almost pleading to be understood. As Pierce arose and approached him, Red eyed him warily. A beating surely was to come. There had been so many before by other men. Why should this man be different? He drew himself up, full, his ears forward, waiting for the blows. But Pierce merely stood. Then, imitating another horse, he darted around and toward the horse's hind. The lead stretched to its fullest.

"Hyahhhh!" he shouted, forcing the horse away from him. The horse responded, stepping a few feet, then turning again to face him, surprise crossing his narrow face. Pierce moved behind him again. The horse countered by following with his head, preventing Pierce from "nipping" his hind. The man strode directly toward Red, never hesitating, never slowing. The horse lifted his head and gazed down at the approaching man. Red retreated. He stepped back and eyed Pierce again. The man moved at him again.

"Back!" he commanded, stepping right into the horse.

Red backed, a step, then another, then another until Pierce halted.

He watched as Pierce backed away, motioning the horse forward with his hand. Then the man reached into his pocket and withdrew a treat. Red regarded it suspiciously but stretched his neck forward to accept the apple-flavored wedge. Pierce snapped off the lead. He did this with respect and dignity accorded royalty for Red was royalty. He carried himself like a king and he commanded respect.

"It's all right, red horse," he cooed. "My fault. Anything else you want to try?"

But Red did nothing. Only a glimmer of relaxation surfaced as he understood that Pierce held no whip, had not raised his hand, had, indeed, made no motion to harm him. He was so used to men striking him with hands or whips or buckets that the softness of the man's approach frightened him more than the abuse he had known. He worked his mouth nervously, his attention focused as Pierce reached to stroke the soft, flaxen mane. The red horse shied a bit. Pierce slowed the motion and continued speaking, moving nearer each time, then gently touching the horse's nose, he found a sweet spot in the center of his forehead. The man rubbed his finger in a circular motion, almost caressing the white snip. For a moment, Red forgot, dropped his head and let Pierce rub. Just for a moment, he felt kindness, love.

"No whips here, Red. If you can't respond because of love, well, it isn't worth a thing if you respond because of fear. That's what I tell Maya. Do it out of love or don't do it at all."

And that was a promise easier in the speaking than in the keeping, for Red would be a vexing horse, requiring patience and a firm presence. One day he would be completely docile; the next, defiant and angry. But he understood. Smart enough to read the man's thoughts, his movements. Even when he pretended not to be looking, he was watching. Pierce snapped the lead on again and clucked.

"Now come and let me walk you around your new home. Get you used to things. This is a nice, little two-acre parcel. Produces good grass and clover; clear, cool stream running through it. You'll have a quiet paddock all to yourself. Good way for us to make friends. "

Pierce led him around the perimeter. Red followed reluctantly, looking warily from side-to-side, but complying when asked for a turn or his attention. The man checked his leg, the one with the fracture, gliding his fingers over the trouble-site like a skilled surgeon. A large bone mass had formed where the fracture was healing. Otherwise, the horse was sound. His chestnut coat glimmered in the noon light. They toured the entire paddock, a rectangular field with run-in shed at the rear and round pen toward the center. After a time, Pierce set him free.

Red galloped the field and charged the fence, wheeling away just inches before he reached it. He snorted, blew, pitched his head defiantly. It was a battle cry, a war dance, a dance that challenged the authority of any man to tame him. And when he had done and shuttered to a pensive stop, he stood quietly surveying the green fields beyond and the hills surrounding him. He saw the high ridges behind the fields, ripe with walnut and cedar, yellow poplar, white oak, and he contemplated the hills that swooped down into the shallow creek. It seemed he stared forever into that space. Perhaps, he heard the voices of those long dead who still dwelled in the shadow of the forests. Perhaps, he heard Audra Clements's husband crying out from those hills as his tractor tipped and crushed him. Perhaps, he heard the deer that traipsed through the runs and grazed in the fields. Pierce didn't know. He only knew that when he approached the fence, Red breathed anger from his nostrils and dashed away. He was daring Pierce to catch him. But Pierce did not. He did not even try. The horse was bluffing. Despite all Red's antics, Pierce understood and would not play Red's game.

"Go on, stretch your legs. Get it out of your system. But for a horse with a broken leg, you run pretty well."

He challenged Pierce with a flinty look, then continued racing along the fence, searching for a low spot he could jump. Finding none, he continued galloping around the paddock. And the admiring man thought it was good to see him run. In the end, though, Red limped to a stop. He still suffered soreness from the fracture and needed time and care.

Assured he was not totally lame but only aching, Pierce left him to his freedom. Red paced along the fence line for some time but settled toward evening as though the coming of twilight made him less restive. When checked again at dark, he was grazing quietly in the far corner. Silhouetted against the dark hills, even ungroomed, he was even more magnificent.

Something stirred inside of Pierce, something he had not felt in a very long time.

"Ah, love, let us be true to one another," he recited, recalling the words of Dover Beach. Then he walked the long road back to the house, to wait for Maya's call and, for the first time that day, he wondered if the call would ever come.

THE MAN WAS LONELY AND HE LONGED FOR MAYA. He wished she could see this magnificent beast. He wanted her to share with him all the joys and power he felt when he saw the animal galloping, his muscles rippling and taut with power. When they first moved to Kentucky, he and Maya had been together all the time. He never minded that Maya was taller than him. He never minded that she spent hours reading or writing her "book." It was the book, she said, that would make her worthy of him. She very much wanted to be worthy of Pierce. And she told him that. Told him he was so much more worthwhile, so much more sophisticated. Pierce was a man of wealth, a man of respect, and Maya just an insecure girl with a dream.

In time, much time, he discovered that her family emigrated from Mexico when she was a young child. Even in a small village there can be political enemies. Her father had the misfortune of angering someone in political power. They left Mexico in haste, with not much more than the clothing on their backs. In her early days she traveled from state to state, wherever there was work. By the time she was ten, she was a seasoned field hand, but fate smiled kindly on her because of her literary ability. Educators remarked at her talent and pushed her into advanced classes. By the time she completed grade school, she had procured several grants that enabled her to attend a private high school and to board without cost to her family. Shortly after, the family returned to the Yucatan Peninsula, to the place of their birth. The government had changed and they felt it was safe to return. Safe, until her mother died of an undefined cause. Safe, until her depressed and lonely father stepped in front of a fast-moving truck and ended his life.

Maya was in school. She heard from a relative what had happened. She never saw her parents again, but their memory plagued her with doubt. Perhaps if she had been with them, nothing would have happened. She did not return to Mexico. There was nothing to return to. So she stayed in the United States, found work, and avoided involvement with anyone.

Pierce often thought of her early days and how providence had brought them together. Returning from court, he had seen her wandering about the street, looking up at the towering structures around them. Her face was soft and bright, linear and lightly tanned, marked by the high cheekbones of her lineage, a tiny nose, almost too tiny for someone of Hispanic descent. He found himself staring into luminous brown eyes dancing with youth and vibrancy. Her hair glistened like black gold, and hung down to the small of her back and swayed as she moved and it was steely-black and soft. He recalled asking her, in Spanish, if he could be of assistance. She replied laughingly, in English. Pierce detected a slight humor on her lips at his Spanish.

"You asked me if I wanted yesterday," she tittered.

"Oh God, I've always had trouble with the word for 'help,' and I was just asking if you needed assistance. Are you sure? I thought I said *ayuda*."

"You said *ayer*."

"I am sorry."

"Why did you speak Spanish?"

"I wanted to impress you. Your facial features look Spanish. That's what I get for being smug."

"I think it's funny."

"I guess it is at that."

"No harm done."

She was slender, sensuously curvaceous, shaped like a dancer, but not petite. He watched as the silky, red floral-print skirt, ballooned with the light breeze, showing shapely legs that slid down to a well-proportioned calves and delicate ankles. She had milk-colored skin, smooth like the creamy texture of lotion. Maya was seventeen years his junior, but she seemed secure with an older man. And Pierce loved her high-pitched laughter, so child-like, yet so mature.

"Anyway… Really, can I help?"

"I'm looking for a lawyer," she replied, tilting her head as if a child peering at her mentor. They were standing in front of a towering building that housed two-hundred lawyers and he found himself hoping that "he" was the lawyer she wanted to see.

He stared at her momentarily. *Nothing pretentious about her. She's real. No lipstick, no eyeshadow, nothing false. A natural beauty.*

"Does your lawyer have a name?" he smiled back.

"Pierce Bernard," she answered.

"Oh God, not him. I can't believe you want him," he chortled.

Her face worried into a frown. "Is something wrong? He was recommended by the Lawyer's Referral Program."

He shook his head vigorously, chuckling to himself.

"A terrible man. Terrible. "He caught her staring at him as if his private joke were provoking suspicion about his motives. Then he felt sorry about his little prank and answered. "No, there's nothing wrong with me. At least, I don't think there is." And he thrust out his hand to shake her own. "Pierce Bernard."

She jolted him with her touch. There was energy there, a shock of innerself they both felt. She was warm, pulsating. He lingered, holding the hand's fragile warmth within his light grasp. She, too, found herself staring, sensing the energy between them. Before her she saw a man of forty or so, more a boy than a man, for he had a wave of brown hair flecked with dabs of grey that flopped in front of his right eye. She laughed as he blew from the side of his mouth, trying to will it back into place. It flopped again and she laughed harder, a relaxed laughter, placing a hand over her mouth so as not to be rude.

"You're like a little boy whose hair won't stay back."

"I don't like hair spray and water only holds it for so long."

"Try a little baby oil. Just a touch."

"I'll remember that." And then he realized they were both staring at each other and something was happening between them.

He wore a dark, grey suit with a burgundy shirt that appeared custom-made, a sheer white tie with an onyx scrimshaw tie clasp. She liked his appearance, elegant yet casual. So casual that he wore black loafers and not the formal shoes of a trial attorney.

"Maya del Rey," she introduced, staring back into his own lively, brown eyes.

"Maya. What a lovely name. No nicknames for you. Are you Mayan?"

"Yes, I am Mayan and part Spanish. My family came from a small village near Chichen Itza', only don't try to find it. It's not even on a map."

"I've been to the ruins. Fascinating."

She tilted her head and shot him a coquettish glance. "Oh, we moved here when I was very young. They didn't even have ruins when I was there. I haven't been back...ever."

"Are your mother and father still living here?"

"They went back a number of years ago. Both dead."

"I'm sorry."

She nodded and Pierce continued the conversation.

"Why don't we go up to my office? The car fumes will kill you down here and besides, it's quieter there." He turned and led the way. She followed, swaying rhythmically as she kept pace with his aggressive stride. He felt a surge of pride as she walked alongside, as if she were his and they belonged together. They remained silent until they were in his office. His secretary nodded as they came in, read off several messages, and returned to her typing.

Maya was astonished at an office that reflected the man. No marble flooring. No cold, mahogany desk. His personal office was more a living room than an office. Deep green carpeting complemented with chartreuse, velvet drapes, a brocade sofa situated in front of a simple, dark-stained desk, pictures of a dog, a black leather chair behind the desk, multi-lined telephone, brass nameplate, business cards prominently displayed, the usual writing implements. There were no law books or degrees on the wall, so Maya concluded that his library was in another room. And she saw no evidence of another lawyer in the office.

"I am surprised about your office," she said, noting a photo of the sunset at the Aruba Yacht Club on the shelves behind him. Another shelf held a photo of a Jamaican waterfall and on a far wall, a bullfight scene on a black, velvet background.

"I keep it casual. It relaxes the client before they get my bill."

"Should I be concerned? About your bill, I mean." Her eyes twinkled but showed no alarm. She was comfortable with this man.

He shook his head, then, still staring at her, went on. "I'm staring. I'm sorry."

She nodded assent and met his gaze.

"From the moment, I saw you I felt we had known each other, somewhere, some other time." He chose his words skillfully and with precision. He wanted nothing out-of-sync with the moment. "The Sicilians say that one has been struck by a thunderbolt. It means he is overwhelmed because a woman has captured his heart." He stopped talking and she studied his face as one who searches for a sign.

"Are you Italian?" she asked, settling back in her chair. He heard the air whoosh out of the cushion as she did so. It was as if the same air whooshed from his heart. If she was upset by his statement, her face showed neither alarm nor concern. Pierce released a sigh of relief.

"Not exactly," he smiled, and the lock of hair slipped down over his eye again. He brushed it back with his hand this time.

"My original ancestry was French. The name was Benoit. The family relocated to Sicily. When my ancestors went through Italian Immigration, the Immigration officers couldn't say the name so they wrote Bernardi. When the family moved into the United States, the immigration people at Ellis Island shortened it to Bernard. The old man wanted to be a citizen so he kept the name that way. I'm really American but my roots are in Sicily."

"Well," her voice dropped as she produced some papers from a folder. "I won't hold it against you, if you'll review this book contract."

"I never do this," he blurted. "I mean, say these kinds of things. I feel stupid. Absolutely stupid. I just felt perhaps we had known each other somewhere else or were meant to. Does that make any sense?"

"In another lifetime, perhaps," her voice fluttered, half giggle, half assent. She cocked her head, peered at him with sultry, inviting eyes. "We are reincarnated lovers," she mocked, almost whispering.

He hesitated then, fearing he had pushed too far. A radiant beauty emanated from the woman, a power to love with great depth, to journey with a man to earth's end. "I'll review the contract." He took the papers and began studying them carefully.

It was only a simple contract. Maya held a part-time job as an editorial re-writer in a large metropolitan newspaper. She did some reporting, but her dream was to be a reporter and to work on foreign assignments. Pierce grimaced when she said this. He wanted to be near to her, but her notion of traveling isolated and saddened him. He concealed his disappointment by continuing on with the contract and reading the various terms. It was only a tentative offer for her to write a book. Nothing was certain but she wanted a professional to prepare her contract.

"Will you represent me, please?" Her tone was helpless, not as confident as it had been, and he realized then that she had been frightened by the prospect of meeting a lawyer. He also understood she trusted him and his heart soared because there was a chance he might actually see her again.

"I wouldn't consider anything else." He realized then that they were still gazing into each other's eyes—he, wondering whether they had both encountered fate, and she, wondering if she dared trust her instincts. "I wonder..." he hesitated. "Oh hell, let's make a deal. I'll review the contract. No charge to prepare a new one." He leaned forward so he was as near as the desk permitted. "Please have dinner with me. There's a lovely place called Lascos, wonderful Italian food. Small, very quiet. If I don't entertain and delight you," he said, shoving back from the desk and throwing his arms up as if to simulate flight, "you never have to see me again. Well, only until I have to review the contract with you." He laughed, a hearty laugh filled with boyish tones.

Something about him must have intrigued her. She laughed and told him she felt very confident he was a gentleman. No, she offered, she wasn't attached. Yes, she would have dinner with him, but no, she would not accept free services unless she paid for dinner.

HE TOOK HER TO LASCOS, HIS FAVORITE ITALIAN restaurant. Lascos with its dark, insidious hallway leading to the larger restaurant in back. Lascos with its aroma of tomato and pizza. Lascos with its wonderful light pastas and nutritious soups. Lascos that had seen the cream of Newark's politicians and the hierarchy of the Mafia chieftains. But it wasn't the food or the history that intrigued him. Lascos was a relic, a remnant of the past tucked away in a deteriorating section of the city, boarded up buildings alongside spoke of an aging quarter that had long since seen its day. Yet, for all the degeneration, Lascos had maintained its Roman ambiance. Once inside, the dark hallway lit with amber light showed an old linoleum floor. Booths lined the sides of the hallway with a single, yellow lamp at each one emitting only a limited sphere of light. The tables were of heavy oak, stained dark to match the interior décor and the seat backs were high enough to blot out the voices of neighboring patrons. Outside the perimeter of the table lamp was a shadowy darkness that seemed quaint and inviting. The booths were another world, distant from the restaurant and private. One could spend hours and never know there was anyone else in the bistro.

Pierce savored the little place because it was the last of its kind. The newer generation of Italian restaurants were stacked with fawning, servile waiters, impressing people with their snappy gestures and suave speech. In particular, he hated the Bon Apetite that waiters in other restaurants seemed obligated to say. Not so at Lascos. The waiters engaged in small talk that was meaningful and sincere. And they did not serve a course and greet you with the Bon Apetite. They pointed out the delicacy before the patron and explained the care with which it had been prepared. Not many people ate there any more. The waiters were all Italians, imbued with charm and old-world grace. They spoke with an accent, remnants of a day when Europeans funneled into the United States, with the hope of every new immigrant. And when they found America the land of opportunity for a selected few, they settled into the oblivion of time that ushers them into old age.

Most of them enjoyed waiting on people. It was not a job but an art, a talent. For these waiters, timing was a talent, a skill to be acquired and retained. Dining was not merely a conduit to eating food. It was a time of bonding and love. And so, they had plied their trade on a young America, hoping the *barbaro* would appreciate their uniquely delivered services. But the barbarians of America did not understand the nature of a meal, and they rushed through it like so many ants gathering particles for their colony and now, the same waiters who had once had so much hope, sat lazily at the bar in the far back room and stirred to action only when people such as Pierce appeared, because he alone understood the true nature of dining.

A short, thin, clean-shaven server with a black jacket, wrinkled white shirt and a wilted bow-tie motioned Pierce into one of the booths and set down the settings and menus. Then, with a snap of the wrist he unfurled a napkin and laid it, first in Maya's lap and then in Pierce's.

"Bon Giorno," he smiled, revealing a gold-filled incisor. "Nice to see you again Counselor." He was a fragile man, almost emaciated for one who worked in a restaurant, and his skin had yellowed with age as had the thinning hair that barely covered his scalp. His hands were knotted and tainted with liver spots except where the fingers were stained with nicotine.

"Nice to be here again, Giancarlo. Been a while."

He shrugged, motioning his head toward the outside door. "Not many come anymore. In a little bit no one will come and then, I go back to Sicilia."

"You go back to Alia, eh?"

"I go back to Messina. Alia is your town." He jerked his hand up as if hitching a ride and then lifted his order pad. "Can I get you something to drink?"

"A nice wine, perhaps," Pierce suggested, looking at Maya.

"I like red wine, but anything you order is fine."

Pierce looked again at the waiter. "Montepulcciano. The oldest year you have."

Giancarlo smirked. "We don't have Montepulcciano for five years now. You know this. I get you Chianti."

"Chianti is like water. Something else."

"Barbera. We have a nice Barbera. I drink myself." He made a kissing sound with his lips and strolled away. In the background a 1940s radio bleated out *Come Back to Sorrento,* and it reminded Pierce of his grandmother's early days, listening to Italian soap operas on a staticky radio.

"Alia. What did he mean by that?" Maya asked when the waiter was out of earshot.

"It's a hill town in Sicily. About sixty kilometers from Palermo. My maternal grandparents were married there and then immigrated to the U.S. The story is my French ancestors got on the wrong side of a political argument and had to leave in haste. They took to the hills and ended up in Alia. I never did figure out which side of the family I belonged to."

"So you're Italian,"

"Never tell a Sicilian he is Italian. They aren't even remotely related."

"Oh, it's like that, is it?"

"It's like that. And please, don't ask me if my relatives were in the Mafia. Most Sicilians are hard-working people. But the country was taken over by so many nations they have their own, strange culture, and it differs even within the country itself. My grandfather was shoemaker. That's what he did in New Orleans. My father helped him and turned his entire paycheck over to his father until he married at twenty-nine. By then they'd moved to Newark, New Jersey."

"What did they do then?"

"Well, that's the skeleton in the family closet."

"Oh," she smiled. "Am I in some kind of danger?"

"You've been watching too many movies." He stared straight into her eyes. Bottomless, brown, provocative eyes. He then studied the shape of a face that curved down into a determined chin. She laughed and he felt as if he had heard her laugh before...many times before. Like music, it soothed and comforted him although his hands shook when he moved the ashtray out of his way.

Giancarlo brought the wine and pulled the cork.

"Barbera D'asti," he said, "nice."

Pierce took the cork and sniffed it.

"Passable," he quipped, motioning the waiter to let the wine air.

Then the man left again, giving them time to talk. When sufficient time had passed, he returned to pour the wine, tilting the glass and letting the dark, burgundy liquid ease into the container. He held the glass into the dim light to show the color, swirled the glass to release the bouquet and nodded triumphantly as if he had scored a point.

Pierce smiled, nodded asset, then sampled the wine. "Nice," he said. "For once you haven't disappointed me."

"When I fail you, eh? When?"

"I have to think."

"When you discover, you let me know, eh. I take you order now?"

"I'll have the baked rigatoni," Maya answered.

He wrote, then peered over the pad at Pierce.

"I'll have the spaghetti Bolognese with meatballs."

Giancarlo shook his head. "Ma no. You have the veal parmigiano."

"Now you are ordering for me?" Pierce teased.

"The meatballs are not fresh."

"Then I'll have just the spaghetti."

"Ma no. The veal is tender and sweet. We made the sauce this morning. I tell you the veal is better."

"You recommend it?"

"Si. I recommend it."

"Okay. You did well with the wine. Bon. Molto bene."

"For sure, Giancarlo tells you the truth."

He spun on his heels and stepped away quickly.

"You tease him incurably," Maya said.

"We go back a long way."

"How long?"

"He loves it. I met Giancarlo when I was in college. He had just started working here and I used to come when finances permitted it. First time I met him he asked me what I wanted to be and I told him I wanted to be a lawyer. So he told me that when I opened my practice, he wanted to be my first case."

"Was he?"

"He came in wanting to become an American citizen. I filed the paper and acted as one of his witnesses. We've been bantering with each other ever since. But if I came in with a patron, he treated me as a special personage so I'd make a good impression on my client. Changing my order was his way of telling me the food wasn't fresh. He takes pride in his service, but the clock is ticking on this place and frankly, I dread the day when the doors close."

They lapsed into silence and then spoke of other things. Time was non-existent in Lascos. The city had fallen down around it and only Lascos had survived. It survived as if time had frozen its old-world ambiance. Outside the city was in decay, but inside, the walls of Lascos were murals of Italy though difficult to see in the darkness. One entered into the darkness, passed three booths and saw the main dining room with a bar to the right. Pierce had always sat in the center booth because there would be no intrusions except for an occasional visit from Giancarlo.

The food was still good, a blend of Sicilian and Southern Italian cuisine. Maya enjoyed the bread, the aroma wafting up to delight her senses.

"How'd you ever find this place?" she asked, nibbling gingerly on her food.

"Old man Lasco was a friend of my grandfather. It was his favorite restaurant. I think the owner was Sicilian and came to my grandfather for help when he immigrated here. I always thought my grandfather held a financial interest in the place, but no one ever confirmed or denied that. When I was sixteen, my father and my grandfather celebrated my birthday here. I had my first glass of wine. It knocked me on my can, but I couldn't let them know that. I've just always come here. It's quiet and very private. The waiters seem to time their presence so they never intrude."

"And you bring your lady conquests here to impress them," she laughed, her cheeks crinkling.

"As a matter of fact, you're the first woman I've ever shared this place with. Somehow I've always felt it had to be that special someone."

"I'm flattered."

"You probably don't believe a word I said, do you?"

She thought for a moment, then stared into his eyes. "I think I do."

"Funny thing is I didn't even have to think about it. I just knew this was the right place."

"You've had other women in your life though."

"Not many. Worked through college and law school. Then into practice.

And trial work keeps me pretty busy. I do a lot of my own typing on trials, contracts, that kind of thing. I get a better feel for a case if I do the work personally. My secretary does the routine stuff. Forms, real estate. Besides, I'm not exactly the Errol Flynn type. Bulky and short; big nose, deep eyes, fat face."

"But no, you treat yourself too poorly. Your nose has character. And it's just right for your face." She peered at him for a long time, emitting light sounds from time to time. "And your face is round, not fat. You have kind eyes, and an innocent smile like a little boy and, for a lawyer, you're...well..."

"Go ahead, for a lawyer what?"

"Very sincere. You exude confidence and a sense that you care."

"Well, I'm the one who's flattered now. An attractive woman like yourself must have a lot of interested men."

"A friend. A very long time ago. He was too possessive."

"Was he Spanish?"

"Of course. He needed a wife who was pregnant in the summer and barefoot in the winter. I couldn't be that person."

"Did you love him? I mean, like a first love?"

She blanched at the question. "Could we speak of something else, please?" The finality in her voice told him he'd resurrected a tender topic and he moved away from it with sudden skill.

"So what do you want for yourself?"

"I enjoy writing, reporting."

"Is that what you do?"

"No. Well, yes and no. I'm a technical writer for an electronic company. I write the descriptions of products they want to sell. But it's not very challenging. My part-time reporting job is my real love."

"So you want to be a reporter."

"Not just a reporter. An investigative reporter. Crime, that kind of thing."

"Wow! You shoot high."

"I don't fool myself. I'll probably always be a technical writer. The money isn't bad. It's just not very exciting."

He caught himself staring at her again. On his lips words were forming, dispersing into the air, then lighting on her willing ears.

"Western wind, when will thou blow/The small rain down can rain? / Christ, if my love were in my arms/ And I in my bed again."

"What was that?" she asked with deep admiration in her eyes.

"A poem called *'Western Wind'.* I don't know who wrote it."

"You like poetry?"

"I find interest in many things. Music, literature, law, people."

"What kind of music?"

"Classical. Country, blues, jazz, slow jazz."

"Do you dance?"

"Not very well. What about you?"

"I read a lot. And I like Latin music, the rumba, tango. Piaff. I love Edith Piaff."

Pierce beamed. "Okay, twenty questions. Favorite actor?"

"Jimmy Stewart."

"Favorite movie?"

"Philadelphia Story."

"Favorite female actress?"

"Katherine Hepburn."

"Favorite book?"

"Gone With the Wind."

Laughing, "Wait a second. How about you?"

"All right, go!"

"Favorite actor?"

"Spencer Tracy."

"Favorite book?"

"The Four Feathers."

"Movie?"

"Inherit the Wind."

"Female actress?"

"Katherine Hepburn."

"Why *Inherit the Wind?*"

"I always loved that passage in the Bible. He that troubeleth his own house, shall inherit the wind. And the fool shall be servant to the wise."

"That's so profound. You really are a challenging man."

The hours raced by. Giancarlo's look went from business to weariness to annoyance as they focused on each other. Pierce paid the bill and looked at his watch.

"God, eleven o'clock. Where'd the time go?"

They both arose. "Let's go back to my office."

Her eyes rose a bit at the words.

"You kept your end of the bargain. We'll finish that contract." His voice dropped a little. "Then, Maya del Reyes, I'd really like to see you again."

She hesitated a moment.

"Wait," he said, "the Art Center is having Bach's Brandenburg Concerto. Do you like classical?"

"I like all kinds of music."

"Please say you'll come."

HE RECALLED HER ANSWER AS HE PREPARED FOR ANOTHER DAY with his animals. It brought a smile to his face as he did. *She is so beautiful,* he thought. He stepped out onto the porch and surveyed the green fields before him. He savored a deep breath and let the air seep slowly from his lungs as if sampling a fragrant wine; it was the fragrant wine of morning honeysuckle when the aroma was strongest. He was in communion with the universe, the land. He relished the sounds of the canary-like cardinals singing to their mates. The rippling hush of the forest creeks soothed and calmed him. The wind whooshed through the treetops with its awesome power. Each day he rambled out the front door and faced the rectangular paddocks before him. Dusty and Power Blaster were in the front field; Lonesome Dart and Diablo in another field to the right; Uno and Willie in the paddock next to Red. He was happy. Maya would call soon. He'd know when she was coming home. With that, he started down the steep drive and the road to the barn.

All the horses waited at the gate for their morning feeding. Everything was at peace. The air was sharp and clean and crisp; the wind from the west, bending the tall cedar branches eastward and into the sun. Pierce inhaled the fragile fragrance of damp morning grass. He felt good to be alive, but sad to be alone so much of the time. More time to spend with Red. More time to spend missing Maya.

He sauntered down the road to the converted tobacco barn they inherited when they purchased the Randolph farm. The old tobacco farmers had faced it where the west winds would sweep into the building and dry the hanging leaves. Weathered and silver-gray, tilted precariously left, boards termite-eaten or broken, it had seemed hardly worth salvaging. Pierce could afford to have workmen repair or demolish it. His investment strategies and law practice rewarded him with ample funds. But he was a self-made man and Southern Moor Farm was his dream of freedom. He wanted that freedom, that freedom to spend with Maya, his animals, his land. He recognized the seventeen-year difference in their ages between them and wanted every minute he could spend with his lovely wife. The barn was part of that freedom. It was their project.

He and Maya removed the broken boards and replaced the termite-damaged supports. Board by board, they hammered home the loose nails. Like surgeons, they pried away the damaged metal roofing and installed lemon-yellow aluminum sheets and chuckled when they realized that only the birds would see the colored roof. When it was done they hooked a chain to the front bumper of the pick-up and the other end to the roof-top. This was the way farmers pulled their buildings upright. Slowly, Maya eased the truck backward, letting the chain tighten.

While the truck held the building in place, the two of them worked diligently as they nailed into place the cross-supports that would give it structure. Maya returned to the truck. The moment was theirs.

Slowly, she eased the truck forward, letting the chain go slack. Pierce sucked in his breath. Would the barn stand or fall?

It stood. Proud and staunch like a resurrected titan.

Maya leapt out of the truck and into Pierce's arms. They hugged and kissed with the joy of their accomplishment.

"It's done," Pierce cried, kissing her cheeks, face and forehead. "We can move the horses in this afternoon."

She squeezed him tightly, then bounded away and jigged like a pogo stick until the wind went out of her. All this he recalled as he walked to the barn. It was yesterday's memory.

Yes, he missed her. *Why'd she need to write anyway? They had been happy at Southern Moor. Wasn't that enough?*

Her absence drove him mad. He almost returned to the house to call her, but he knew she'd not be in her hotel room. Pierce wasn't even sure he knew where she was staying. He'd submerge his loneliness in working with Red. He knew the horse but a short time, yet he knew the animal. Although Red was gelded, the animal saw himself as a stallion. Pierce knew about animals. He was comfortable with them, as comfortable as with people. It was a natural instinct as if he had been raised with wolves and knew the things an animal instinctively knows. And he knew Red was a proud and determined horse. His task would not be an easy one; to befriend an animal that man had abused, to earn his trust. And yet, once he succeeded with Red, Maya would return. He knew that too. It was his dream. She would end her tours and return home because he had succeeded and was worth something again. Her writing dreams merged into his own dreams of a life together, the life they once had. So he focused on Red. Red, his savior. His companion. He needed him as surely as he needed Maya. The endless hours of desperation would unfold into hours spent without sadness, without loneliness because he had a challenge. And Red was certainly a challenge, a stubborn, unrelenting gelding.

On the racetrack, he had fought fierce battles on the pace. He never raced without heart or the will to win. On the back-stretch, though, he resisted. He bolted, reared, struck like a stallion and he suffered for it. So he raced. And before each race, the rebellion rose up within him. He struggled to be autonomous and because he did, he suffered the whip and the fist. These things Red told Pierce in the only way an animal can. Bring a rake near him and the horse cringed and tensed. Raise a hand and the animal jerked away. Fold a towel near him and he tried to break free. He spooked at the slightest sound or movement. Fear welled in his eyes and spilled over into his actions. So told the tale that Red had been punished for his spirit as if spirit were an evil thing to be assailed and obliterated. But Pierce loved that feral spirit for he, too, held an untamed and wild strength. And he, too, was no longer confident or sure.

Pierce fed the other horses then stopped by the small paddock. Red approached the feed bucket, halted, stared at the man. The sunlight streamed from behind him and steam wisped up from the dew-soaked ground.Pierce studied the horse then slowly shook his head.

"I'll never understand the mentality of a man who would order you euthanized," he groaned. "Why?"

The horse merely puzzled at his words. Pierce saw the horse's mouth working and knew he was considering approaching nearer. He lowered his voice still and watched the horse's ears spike straight up. Red was paying attention.

"If I knew who that man was…" he fumed, "I'd stuff him in a garbage can and roll him off a cliff. What a damn beautiful animal." He muttered this, his jaw working side-to-side.

Red took a step nearer. He knew the other horses had been fed. He wanted his grain, his carrots and his hay. But he was shy of his new surroundings. He had trusted the vet who fed him treats, but only for the treats. He didn't trust anyone else.

The other horses were already munching their forage, orchard grass laced with red clover. Pierce only permitted them two days grazing per week. Maya didn't want them foundering because of lush grasses and legumes. The remaining time they spent in paddocks with little or no grass. But Red resisted coming near the man voluntarily. He wanted his food but nothing more.

"If you want your grain, you'll have to trust me," Pierce cooed. "I'll stand right by your bucket while you feed. No work today. I want you calm and getting just a bit bored."

The chestnut gelding stared at him, snorted, turned and walked away, looked back over his shoulder, stopped and turned again. Pierce could almost read his thoughts. He followed the horse into the center of the paddock, waited for the animal to halt. Then he made a wide circle, cutting Red off from the back of the paddock. With that, the horse turned and headed for his grain. Pierce followed slowly, waiting for the animal to become engrossed in his grain. He stood watching Red eat. The horse was a nervous horse, not vicious, just flighty. He'd probably always be spooky, but in time, he'd come to trust Pierce and learn from him. If Pierce knew one thing about the animal, it was that Red was an intelligent creature. He learned quickly.

When the horse was done, he moved away from the feed bin. Pierce covered the ground between them, holding out a carrot. Red advanced, stood before the man. Pierce studied him, then offered the carrot. The horse stretched his neck to take it. The man took a slow half-step backward. Red stood for a moment, considering a step forward. Then he took it, moving near enough to reach for the carrot.

"Good boy," Pierce whispered. "No one here will ever harm you, Red."

Yes, he thought, *Maya will love this horse. He'll make a fine mount.*

Perhaps she would call tonight. He could tell her then of his limited success with Red. Perhaps not. She didn't always call when on assignment or working. *He'd have to understand that. Have to understand she was just being Maya and had to* have *her space. Yes, if he loved her, he'd have to understand that.* Things would be different when she came home. He'd be different. More understanding.

He caught the red horse staring at him.

"You know my thoughts, don't you big fella?"

But the horse just stared as if reading into the man, as if quizzical about thoughts the horse did not comprehend.

WHO IS HE? WHAT DOES HE WANT? He stands there a long time looking at me, just talking. I don't want to be his friend. He's smaller than most men and he speaks quietly. I don't understand the words, but I sense what he means. Still, I don't trust anyone. I trusted them when I was a colt. Then, I was sold to other men who tied me to a post and whipped me until I bled. They said it would take the starch out of me. So my head was tied. I could not move and they beat me. I hadn't done anything. I was just frightened of all the new things I saw. I still hear the whir of the lash cracking me. No, I'll not trust him. I'll not approach my food as long as he is there.

He has that strange fur on his face though. I've seen it on other men. Does it mean something? He just watches me, talks. Something about him makes me want to look at him from time to time. I toss my head and race around the paddock. It doesn't seem to bother him. He just smiles and watches. He probably admires how handsome I look. Somehow, it's almost as if he knows what I am thinking. But how could he? He's just a man-animal and they are not very bright. And he's very small. Hardly comes up to my muzzle.

He could have struck me when I pulled him off his feet. But he didn't. How strange. Is he a herd leader? Or will I be dominant? And he has strange thoughts. He thinks of someone else, not just me. He speaks of a Maya but I do not know what a Maya is. I think it may be a person, but I am not sure. I know he misses this Maya very much.

What others did to me was wrong, he says. I do not understand the concept of right and wrong, but I know he feels badly about something. The herd boss, Power Blaster, spoke to me across the paddock fence yesterday. He told me that once when he was racing for this man, the man saw a bruise on his flank, touched it ever so lightly with his hand and water began flowing from the man's eyes. Blaster did not understand this, but he knew the man felt badly about his wound. He turned his head and signaled that it didn't hurt. He said he came to love this man because he was so kind and always came with apples and carrots. He does that with me, too, drops carrots in the feed bucket. I won't eat when he is there, but when he comes again, the carrots are gone.

What kind of man is this? He feels sadness when an animal is hurt? All I have ever known is men who punished me when I needed understanding. I was afraid and they terrified me with beatings. They whipped my head, flanks and hind. It didn't matter. Pretty soon, I flinched no matter what they tried doing. Then they brought me where there were crowds of people, strange noises and other excited horses. I had to race against them, work hard to gain the finish line before the others. When I didn't, the men struck me with water buckets and towels. I didn't mind competing. I liked beating other horses. It was like being at play when I was a colt. But I don't trust people. They hurt you and they make you work hard. They make you race even when you are in pain.

It is quiet here. There are two fields right across from my paddock. A horse named Challenge is buried in one field. I am alone in this paddock, but I can see all the horses. Right next to my paddock, separated by electric fencing, they keep Willie and Uno. It's called the diet pen. I don't know why. Willie is wretched to Uno. He gives him no peace. He eats all the hay until he is filled and then runs Uno off. Willie is large-boned and bulky, a bay horse with a huge head and a hay belly. He has a haughty attitude, but the other horses tell me he is nothing special. The man has to separate them when he feeds. They tell me a lady lived here once, but she has not been here for a long time. The man tells them she will return soon. He knows they miss her. I think he misses her too. But the animals that live here are his friends. I suppose that is enough for him.

He is different though. He does not tack the horses for racing. When he leads me into the barn, all he does is groom and curry me, spray me with something that keeps the flies away. It smells awful. I crinkle my nose and pull my lips back to show my teeth. The little man laughs. He thinks my displeasure is humorous. I'll repay him when he worms me by spitting wormer on him. Well, it's apple-flavored so he won't mind.

He feeds me treats, cleans my hooves and checks my shoes. I do not understand what he wants of me. Why is he so kind without asking for anything? The man's hands are gentle. His eyes sparkle when he touches me. He says "the hands hold the power of love." I do not understand the concept of love, but I understand tenderness and a kind touch. Horses do not love, they obey.

The woman he speaks of does not visit us. I would like to see her some day. The man says I will. He says she will come home and they'll ride again. Perhaps that is Maya. Why is she never here? Why doesn't the man have a herd of his own?

Sometimes, he takes other horses into the barn and puts them in cross-ties. Mostly, the horses just graze and relax though. Diablo and Uno are trail horses. Lonesome Dart is the youngest and is not very bright. I'll be dominant over him. He does nothing more than tease his mother and Power Blaster and nudge the other horses when they are turned out together. Power Blaster doesn't let him get away with raiding his feed bucket and Dusty nips and kicks him, but the others are more tolerant as if they understand he is immature. But I think he is retarded.

The man does other work, too. He rides Uno. That's his horse. Often he rides Diablo but Diablo belongs to the woman. He doesn't ride Willie very much. Willie is an arrogant horse with an attitude worst than mine. He boasts that he's bucked the old man off seven or eight times. He doesn't like amateur riders so whenever the man wants him to do something he doesn't want to do, he bucks him off. And the man doesn't whip him either. Strange.

I'm not sure about Willie. He is dominant over Uno and mistreats him with kicks and bites. Willie would eat all the food on the farm if given the chance. I don't think he and I will get along and I don't think I'll be dominant over him, so I hope the man doesn't put me in the same field with him.

The man is back now. He's watching me eat my carrots, keeping his distance. Each time he comes a bit closer. I don't understand why he watches. What's he trying to see? Always he says: "Hello Red. How's my big, red horse?"

I'm not his horse. I'm not anyone's horse. So what is he talking about? I won't eat while he is around. But he does no harm. Never raises his hands around me. Let him stand and watch if he wants to. I'm not afraid of him. I don't care how nice he is. I don't trust him. I'll stamp and gallop around the paddock, show him my strength. He'll not come near me 'cause I'll just move off and away. No! People hurt horses. They are not to be trusted. But I may sneak in for a nibble of grain or carrot. Then, I'll race away again.

BUT AS HORSES ARE APT TO DO, RED DID NOT IGNORE his carrots, nor did he avoid the man. He approached his feed bucket, looking at the man that stood before him. The gelding tensed and raised his head, ears forward. But Pierce stepped back and more to the side. The horse focused on him, took a step forward.

"That's right. Now another step please."

With that, Pierce backed up and the horse followed. Pierce drew nearer. He blew gently into the horse's nostrils and rubbed his bearded face against the horse's nose. Red reveled in the moment. The man showed kindness, patience, things he was unused to. Pierce stepped into the horse's withers. He stroked the animal's neck, sweeping his hand occasionally to the ears. He scratched the inside of the ear, then the back, massaged the poll and Red's neck. The animal stood, not fully understanding a kind touch, yet not wanting to move away from it. Red snorted gently, nickered to the other horses. They nickered back and Pierce felt the horse settle.

He spent two hours with Red, asking nothing more than to approach the horse and be accepted. When he'd done, he brought Red two carrots and stood while the horse munched them. It was a quiet day. A day that would be repeated. Pierce worked with the horse. He spoke to Red that he awaited Maya's call—which never seemed to come. Yes, the man spoke of his wife. He spoke of her with disappointment in his voice. He rejoiced when Red did well and celebrated his achievement even if he suffered the loneliness of dragging hours. But he wished Maya would come home so he could brag of his accomplishments with the horse.

Somehow Pierce fixed on the animal, felt that working with the Red would while away the time until his Maya returned. There was a common bond there, the abused animal that had been driven off by men...the man who restricted his wife's freedom and had driven her away. The two seemed intertwined, as if they were both in need of a friend. If Red could resolve the issue of trust, Pierce would resolve the problem of his loneliness.

They had been such lovers, the man and the woman. How had such lovers come to a parting? They had seldom argued. They seemed never to have grown old in their adoration for each other. They enjoyed the horses, even spoke of adopting animals. They rode the trails together. It was from his love of animals that Red Leader had come to live on their farm. But he had come there long after Maya was gone. So Pierce had much time to think. Think about the million errors one makes in life. Errors that cost him in terms of love and companionship and tenderness. He'd known little enough from his father and less from his mother. Maya had been the only love he had ever known. And he would do anything for her.

Always, always, though, Pierce noted the sadness when Maya watched the television news or read the headlines. The subject usually came up at breakfast while he read his newspaper. Or pretended to. More often than not, he simply watched as she busied herself in the kitchen. Then, she'd slide into conversation as she prepared their food.

"It must be nice to have a by-line," she'd comment. "Nice to see one's name in print. I guess one could do the same by writing a book, but it's really not the same. Writing a book is for money. But writing a newspaper column is to inform the public, to expose wrongdoing, to make bad things right. Don't you think?" She tilted her head and gave him a naïve glance that resembled innocent questioning of a smug, little child.

"Today's hero is tomorrow's has-been," he would say. "If you write a book, it's read again and again and you can do it again. People would want you to write other books. If you write an exposé, tomorrow it's uprooted by another story. And the journalist is forgotten."

Maya put her head down. The lower lip jutted out in disappointment. "Perhaps if I just had a part-time job somewhere. Someplace where I could write small items. Perhaps that would suffice."

She stared at him again, *willing* him to concede.

"Maya, I do not control you. As a grown woman you're free to do as you choose."

"But I don't want to upset you, honey-bins."

He hated when she called him that. The term was derisive, baby-ish. It was as if she were his mother, not his wife.

"Perhaps you're bored with the farm, with retirement, with...with me."

Shock spread over her face. "I love it here. I love you. I love the animals. I just want to do something more." She wiped her eye with a white knuckle, then brushed back the hair that flopped before her eye. "I just thought perhaps a small job would break the monotony. I always loved editing and re-writing. I just want to be Maya."

"There's a lot of work on a farm. Perhaps we should think about selling, moving to the city again. Or maybe traveling. A cruise," he replied, setting down the newspaper and shoving away from the table.

Then, she arose with him, stepped toward him and kissed him lightly on the lips. "I don't want to move." She knew he wasn't serious, but it was a game they played when the topic of working arose. "Tell you what. I'll make you poached eggs and toast for breakfast."

He loved her poached eggs. And it was his favorite breakfast. Soft, yellow yokes, salted heavily and ready for dipping his toast. They were always perfectly done, not because she used a timer, but because she watched how the water boiled and removed them at just the right moment. She loved watching him sop his buttered toast into the soft yoke, watched him blot up every bit of yellow on his plate.

Pierce did not eat his eggs so much as he relished them, savored them, foregoing even his morning coffee until he had savored the last bite. Then, and only then, did she raise topics that might cause him consternation. He was always in a fair mood when he'd had poached eggs. Maya knew how to time her requests and she knew how to play Pierce. He was easily manipulated if one knew what keys to press.

"Let's take care of the horses," she smiled.

He nodded, pushing his chair away from the table. "I'll think about it. The job, I mean."

He didn't though. Think about it. It was not a subject he wanted to hear, nor think about. Maya was his companion, his partner. They shared everything together. He did not want to be apart from her. Not for a minute more than he had to. While she was there...there on the farm, he felt secure, safe. When she was away, there was a desperate emptiness. His past was speckled with punishments in a dark broom closet, alone, in darkness, for some minor infraction. Maya was his light and, when she was absent, the clocks figuratively stood still and time was his mortal enemy. When she returned, he did not greet her with a smile, but with a scowl. He was troubled that she had been away and he could not admit that he missed her. He shook off the thoughts of Maya. He needed to focus on Red. What to do next? What lesson to teach? He needed to get inside the horse's head, to know the key to gaining his trust and confidence. The animal was flighty, high-strung. Everything spooked the animal. Wind gusting through the shrubs caused the animal to stare as if some invisible predator was about to attack. A rock might lie in his paddock for days only to have the animal discover it and startle. Like steel, Red coiled into a mass of tension when the unknown assailed him. It would not be an easy task, taming a flighty horse. Especially not one that had been abused.

After Pierce left the paddock, Red sauntered to the fence line and communicated with Diablo. The animal had belonged to Maya and he loved her. Because Diablo had known the woman, Red's curiosity grew. It was not long before Diablo told the chestnut gelding about the man and the woman who had lived there.

THEY CALL HIM PIERCE. THAT'S IIIS NAME. Mine is Diablo and I am part Spanish like Maya. I am one of the trail horses here, and I was here before Maya went away. I was her trail horse and her friend. But they kept me in Challenge's paddock so she would have company. Although I was her horse, Maya loved Challenge. I think she saw in the old, arthritic mare, the desperation of an abused woman. If Pierce loved his horse Uno, Maya loved Challenge. Like Maya, she was an aggrieved woman. To Maya, Challenge was as much a prisoner as she felt herself to be.

The mare was twenty-six when she came to the farm, fifteen hands, crippled and twisted in her hind, hooves off-set at odd angles so that she dragged her rear feet rather than lifting them. Yet, Challenge carried herself with aristocracy and dignity. She knew who she was. She knew Maya loved her. The woman, who felt comfortable when alone, strangely felt human compassion from a horse. It was as though Challenge understood her sadness and bonded with her.

Maya loved Pierce as well. He was impulsive, reckless, fun-loving. He quoted poetry and introduced her to classical music and delicious red wine. He entertained her with stories and held her when she wearied and nodded off to sleep. He held the power to make her love him all over again simply by gazing into her eyes. It was a magic time.

But there was, too, a time without magic, for Maya had not been married to Pierce very long when she discovered that the exterior was not the inside of the man. Internally, the man was beset with insecurities. He needed appreciation, attention, and encouragement. He held himself in poor esteem.

Maya was secure. Secure in her own world. She loved Pierce and she loved the farm. She also loved to write and be recognized. When the worlds collided, as they did invariably from Pierce's insecurity, Maya suffered quietly, never saying a word to hurt her husband.

Each day she awoke, yearning for the day to be different. Each day she paced down to the barn, fed the animals, checked them over and turned out the hay. Each day she hiked the field to Challenge and led her back to the barn to medicate her. And each day, she greeted Pierce with the hope that light would bring new growth and understanding in him.

It was not that he was cruel or selfish. He was frightened. He needed constant reassurance she would not leave him. They often spoke of it because she understood and loved him. And once, when he became despondent, he swallowed a large amount of sleeping pills and nearly died. After that, she lived in the fear of one who holds the life of another in her hands. She dared not speak of leaving to find work. She would do that when the time was right.

So the woman focused on Challenge because Challenge was her lifeline. The animal accepted that role. She required special shoeing, bran mash for feed, liniment for her legs, bute for her pain. She accepted the woman's love and companionship. In a sense Maya used Challenge to enjoy her private moments, moments when she could be by herself and away from Pierce. Not because she did not love him, but because she was a private person who could not live outside herself.

In time she had to have Challenge shod lying on her side because she could not support her weight with one foot upraised. It became more diffi- cult to feed her because her teeth wore into sharp points that stabbed sores into her mouth. Maya spent more and more time with the old mare. She drifted further and further away from her dream to be a reporter. She drift- ed further and further away from Pierce. She just wanted to be Maya and, no matter what the cost, she would have her way.

It would have remained so except that Pierce awoke one morning and saw no sight of Challenge. Then he saw her, lying motionless in mid-field. Her head was up, but she was not moving. He called to Maya, alarmed at the prospect of losing the old mare, for Pierce recognized the danger in that ani- mal's death. He was thinking that Challenge was done for. He was thinking that he and Maya were done for, too. Everything seemed to be falling apart.

When Challenge could not rise up from the ground, Pierce whipped her with a towel trying to get her on her feet. I nickered to her that it was time to walk to her favorite spot in the shade of the old sycamore at the far end of the paddock but she was silent. I didn't understand why she would not go.

I didn't understand why Pierce whipped her either, but it wasn't the way men beat a horse when they are angry. I think he was trying to help. Something in his voice was desperate and pleading, but Challenge could not stand. When she did, she started circling. She nearly fell on the man, but he vaulted out of the way, and she went down again. Another man came. It was the man who often gave us shots. He studied Challenge for a time and helped Pierce get her on her feet again. But again she circled and fell. Then the man stuck something into her. I thought it would help as injections sometimes helped me. But it did not. Instead, I heard her moan, watched her relax. She peed all over herself and then she didn't move any- more. I raced around the paddock and galloped straight at Pierce and Maya but stopped short of them. I didn't want to hurt anyone, only to show my frustration because I was much attached to Challenge.

There was water flowing from Pierce's eyes. And Maya refused to come near me, just stood there staring at Challenge. I never saw that before. They pushed Challenge into a hole and covered her with dirt. I stood and watched. So did the man. Maya came up to him and rubbed his withers. I saw the man put his arms around her. They held together for a very long time. Then, he turned again and rubbed my head. And more water flowed from his eyes.

I nuzzled him from behind and he touched me with his hands, soothed my withers and moved along side me. He blew gently into my nostril and hugged me with an arm over my neck. And he was so upset, he clung to me. I could easily have heaved my head and unsettled him, but somehow I felt the need to be near him. I don't know why I don't know what Maya felt. She was very rigid and very still. She was thinking about a lot of things and somehow I had the feeling I might never see her again. Horses know about that kind of thing.

I think sometimes Pierce knows what I am thinking before I do. And that is strange for humans are not horses so how do they know this? Yet, he knew I had feelings for Challenge just as I know he has feelings for the woman. But Challenge has been gone a long time now.

I think the man will need us. The woman had been very sad. She wanted to do something very badly and it meant she had to go away. Pierce did not like to hear her words. To the horses they both spoke softly and with kindness. But they did not have kind words for each other. They did not even look at each other.

The woman shouted that the man kept her like an animal, caged and with no freedom. I do not understand that. Maya came and went around the farm as she pleased. She saddled and rode me alone on the trail. She took care of Challenge until she died. Then she told the man she did not even have her friend to take care of. I thought I was her friend. Perhaps she had forgotten because she was angry. The woman did not know it, but I still see Challenge. She is out there in that copse of woods. She does not like the anger between the man and the woman. She would like to kick the man for being so stupid. She would kick the woman, too, for being so selfish. Surely she must understand the man's need to have someone?

Yes, I think he will need us. The woman spoke of leaving to follow her *dream. The man said he would not let her go. Maya went anyway. I was hurt she did not care about me enough to stay. The words just grew more angry and hostile every day. Some days they did not even speak. They used to ride together. They were in love. Sometimes they would stop and peer into each other's eyes. They spoke soft words and touched lightly. Sometimes Maya leaned in the saddle so she could reach to kiss him. She touched me on the flank so I'd move closer to the other horse. They spent hours riding on the trail. There was happiness in her eyes and contentment on the man's face. It was not as it is with horses... they loved only each other. Did the man do something to hurt my rider? I don't know. I only know that one day she drove off in her car and never returned. The man says she will come back. I do not think so. I think all he has now is the farm and all of us. Even the dogs, Tribute and Saber, ran off when the woman didn't come home. I think they went to find her.*

EACH DAY HE TRAINED RED AND WHEN HE FINISHED, Pierce traipsed across the luxuriant field of orchard grass to a copse of trees not far from the creek's end. It was the place where Challenge was buried. It brought him closer to Maya because Challenge was Maya's friend. From there he smelled the scintillating waters of Woods Creek, listened to it as it murmured its somnambulant song. A chittering squirrel seemed to welcome him there and the place was tranquil and distant.

His thoughts drifted to his wife and her love of animals. Maya did not see Challenge as an abandoned and crippled old mare, but as an ailing monarch that had ruled a herd and had come to outlive her usefulness. The old horse was rescued from certain death when Maya found her wandering along a deserted road, not a house in view. She pleaded with Pierce to take on the aged horse, nurse it back to health, let it live out its days in the quiet of their verdant fields. Because he loved her, he agreed. Took on the damaged old filly, so crippled her hind swung around to meet her ribs, so crippled she dragged a left rear leg that was twisted and misshapen. Perhaps he saw in that horse the same aristocracy and dignity he saw in Maya. Perhaps it was the way her eyes pleaded with Pierce, begging him to take the weathered, old horse.

Maya loved Pierce. He was full of mischief, romance and vitality. He rattled off poetry, quoted the great novels, lavished classical music and brought her gifts as elegant as diamonds and as simple as a single wild, lavender flower. From the day he met her, he pursued her with all the charm at his command. They loved. And loved again. They spent weekends in old seaports. Found obscure restaurants that served up sumptuous seafood. Walked along wind-driven sandy beaches and scurried from the water's edge when the waves rushed in. They strolled hand-in-hand as he regaled her with stories that made her laugh. He mesmerized her with the depth of his talents. She wished she could do as much for him, but she regarded herself as lowly and merely a shadow in his wake.

She loved his recklessness, his fearless approach to life. If he rode a horse and was thrown, the injury never prevented him from re-mounting. Nor was he ever at a loss for something to do, some new adventure, some new romance. He loved her. He possessed her. And in that possession lay the seed of their discontent. For Maya loved him, but she desired a life of her own. The lure of journalism still beckoned to her like an unfulfilled dream. She was not content to remain on the farm, not content to whittle away her days. The very traits she admired in Pierce drove her to be like him, to be worthy of him.

If there was any sore point in their marriage, it was her desire to accept a foreign assignment, to write, to live history. There was so much difference in their ages and Pierce had achieved so much. But Maya suffered because she was young and the young often suffer because they have achieved nothing and do not know where they are going. Such is life. We learn where we are going only when we are too old to get there. We learn what we have only when we lose it. Maya had been so young when she married Pierce. She had only just begun life. The throb of accomplishment was just a flutter then. Maya did not want fame or fortune or riches or even acclaim. She only wished to do that for which she had been created. She had no children because she was barren. Yet, she searched for another purpose, another direction. She was determined. Pierce was unrelenting. Because she was unhappy, she focused on Challenge. The animal needed her. She needed the animal. It was her escape from the only unhappiness she knew. Her heart was divided. She loved Pierce, but before Pierce, had been her dream of journalism. Each day she awoke, yearning for the day to be different. Each day she paced down to the feed barn, fed the animals and groomed the sorriest. Each day she negotiated the washboard field to Challenge. She led her back to the barn, showing infinite patience. She groomed and medicated the old mare. Spoke to her and loved her. And each day she saw Pierce, hoping that the light would bring new understanding in him, that he would be again the charming sorcerer he once had been and he would comprehend her desire to meet her own needs.

The old mare required almost constant attention. She was not just a horse. She was Maya's companion, her mentor. She stood stoically as Maya groomed her matted mane. She puffed like royalty when Maya spit-shined her with conditioner. Challenge had never enjoyed such personal attention, so in a sense, Maya was her first friend. She grew feeble from the constant drain of malnutrition. Her bones disintegrated. She developed goiter. How she came to be wandering along an old road they would never know. She was as much a captive to men as Maya was to her ambition. But, while Maya trusted Pierce, the old mare did not. She sniffed every treat he offered, was uneasy when he stroked her. The mare accepted food from him and then sauntered away. It was as if she understood his possessiveness was the cause of Maya's unhappiness.

What once had been a loving bond between two people eroded until it was a silent war. She and Pierce seldom touched. They seldom made love and, when they did, it was perfunctory and dull. The dogs sat between them on the couch so they lost the closeness they once had shared there. They slept together, but often withdrew to opposite bedsides, as if the cold war permeated the bedroom as well. Though they ate meals together and occasionally celebrated a special occasion, the conversation was polite and sparse.

On both their mind was the oft-asked question: Why do we stay together?

Maya answered that she hoped tomorrow would be better and that Pierce would become the man he once was. But each time they discussed her leaving, Pierce's possessiveness surfaced. It was not as if he resented her leaving. Rather, it was that he feared that she would never return.

"Silly," she would say. "I love you. Why wouldn't I return?"

"I just have a feeling," he answered. "It took me so long to find you. Why do you have to go?" Then he would note the sadness in her eyes and he hated himself all the more for denying her that final happiness.

"But Pier," she whined, "I need something more than just a farm. I don't feel useful here. I want you to be proud of me. To say that I am your wife and you are proud of what I have done."

He smiled, trying to avoid the topic. "I like you just the way you are. Hey! I know. We need to take a trip. Perhaps Europe, maybe Italy. Rome, Venice, Florence. We need a break."

She pouted and turned to hide her tears. "It's not the same. I love traveling with you, but it would just not be the same." He felt remorse, guilt. He loved her and wanted her to himself, but she had a right to her own life, her own interests.

"Even one or two days a week would be better than nothing," she offered, wiping her eyes with her knuckles.

"I guess I'm not enough anymore."

"Pier, it has nothing to do with you. I want to be able to contribute to our marriage, to come back with new things to say, just as you take pleasure when a horse you are training, does what you ask of it. I've never made a secret of wanting to be an investigative reporter, now have I?"

"No, you haven't. But I'd miss your company."

"I'd miss you too." And then, seeing the hurt in his eyes, "Pier, it's probably a foolish notion on my part. Let's just drop it. We'll just keep working with the animals."

"I've been thinking, Maya, why don't we start an animal rescue farm? We could get tax status, expand the kennels, add some more paddock space. Provide a real home for some badly treated animals."

She sighed deeply and her eyes flashed disappointment as she nodded assent.

"We'll see," he sighed, the ache in his heart already beginning.

He spoke to an editor friend at a local newspaper. He found her a part-time position on the staff. She wrote articles, did re-write again. She even reported on minor accidents or local crime. It only served to deepen Maya's discontent. The more she retreated, the more Pierce withdrew, spending longer and longer hours in the field. He plunged into his work and ignored the world around him. Maya was part of that world. She watched him take risks. Nursed him when he suffered injuries. More than once he ventured onto the hillsides with his tractor only to collide with trees and drop down the slopes. It was a death-wish in a desperate man.

They were both headstrong and determined, yet Maya would not hurt him. She often kept things hidden for months, exploding only when her rage overcame her. Maya harbored slights in silence, overlooking Pierce's stubborn refusal to talk. Pierce, however, overlooked nothing. He frequently sulked for days before blurting out a problem.

When an animal was in jeopardy, they called a truce. They thrust their differences aside to nurse the animal. The old bond resurfaced. They were one again. Once done, though, they regressed into their cold war. Animals were their common ground, but only until the danger was past. Then Pierce walked around with his head down and his face sullen, and Maya went about her business as if there was no one else on the farm.

When Challenge had first been brought to the farm, she was placed in a paddock alone. She did not walk off the trailer so much as she fell off, nearly toppling Pierce as he skittered out of the old mare's way. The horse was arthritic, bent with age and ill use and unable to move easily. She needed pasture and time to heal because she was old. Old from lack of care, from lack of love. She could have used a guardian, such as Red, but he was not to come until much later. Thus, she remained alone for a time and, when Maya was sure Diablo would not harm her, she settled him in Challenge's field to encourage her to move. When Challenge died, Maya's outlet died with her. There was nothing more for the woman. Her desire to be useful was fueled more and more by the passage of time. It was a life-clock clicking away the days, months and years of being a childless woman. Finally, she could contain it no longer. It burst like an overwhelmed dam spewing water and debris into the downstream channel. She would simply tell Pierce she wanted real work as a reporter. If he loved her, he would understand and support her. Not an easy task.

"Pier," she cooed, cozying up to him so he felt the full warmth of her body. "I need to tell you something." She stared into his eyes, waiting for him to say something, but he remained still.

"Aren't you going to ask me what?"

He still said nothing.

"It's not all that bad."

He shook his head, staring into the space beyond her.

"Go on," was all he said.

"I've taken a position with a larger newspaper. It's the *Progressive*. Dan Merin needed a road reporter and saw some samples of my reporting. If it weren't for you getting me a position on the smaller paper, I would never have gotten the chance. Thank you, thank you, thank you."

Pierce still said nothing.

"He started me right away. Tomorrow, in fact."

"How many days will you work?"

She hesitated, looking at him with innocent, dim eyes. "I set my own schedule. Work as much or as little as I need if I'm on a story."

"I see."

"No, you don't. You never see. It always has to be Pierce's way."

"Is that the way you feel?"

"Pier, it's an exciting assignment. I'm really flattered. I mean, he called me and asked me to work for him. Don't you see how important that is to me?"

He nodded but turned away, the hurt seeping into his eyes and a cold fear striking him within.

"I just wanted to thank you. I thought you'd be proud of me."

"I am proud of you…as my wife. I don't need anything else."

"But this is different. They're making and selling drugs in the county. Young kids are being hooked and enlisted into the sales ranks. Some of them aren't even nine years old and they're hooked. Pierce, someone has to do something about it."

Drug runners were using the county as a distribution point. Her editor wanted them tracked down, wanted to scoop the police who he felt were doing nothing. Each night, she returned, exhausted but bubbling with excitement. It was an excitement Pierce hated. He withdrew from her, refused to talk about her work. More and more, Maya turned to that work to hide from the guilt she felt. Just as Maya had turned to Challenge, Pierce turned to farm work and the horses. He hid his heartache in his friendship with them. He hid from his own feelings that he was a failure. He needed to succeed at something again.

After Maya was gone, he somehow conjectured that his success with the horse would presage Maya's return. He fixated on his potential success. She'd love him again and abandon her thoughts of journalistic glory. And he repeated the lie, over and over to himself, that his Maya would return and love him once more. Because he could not bear the truth, he lied—to himself—to his senses—and then, the lie became the reality and the reality became the truth, to him, and then, for Pierce Bernard, there was no lie, but only the truth he saw.

HE COMES EACH DAY TO CHALLENGE'S GRAVE. Then he walks me along the road where the grass is lush, wet and fresh. He speaks to me in human tones and, though I do not understand the words, I no longer resent his attention. In the morning he brings my grain, laced with carrots or slices of apples. I keep wondering when he will ask me to race. But he doesn't seem to want anything. I am still cautious with him. He seems to understand that. Yet, I find myself heeding his call because he never fails to bring something good to eat or to stroke me with gentle hands. Uno nickers to him in the morning and I have taken to calling the man too. When he is late or too slow, I display indignation by rearing and bucking around the paddock. I've even crushed the feed bucket once or twice to teach him timeliness, but, when it became too narrow to reach in and eat, I stopped.

He grooms me every day, sprays me with foul-smelling liquid and places a fly mask over my face. It took a long time for me to understand it keeps the flies away. He thought it was cute when he forgot to put my fly mask on and I picked it up in my teeth and flung it around. Then I raised my head so he couldn't put it on. My former trainer would have cracked me with a whip, but he only laughed and begged me to lower my head so he could fit me. And he told me that God punishes horses that take advantage of short men. He does not command or order. He just asks and waits patiently until I comply. This is a very strange human. But I am beginning to like him.

He is not lean like a race horse, but a little plump and, when he walks, his feet toe out. I've known race horses whose feet paddle out like that. They always shoe them differently so they don't clip themselves. But this man wears soft shoes and they make no sound as he walks. Nor does he walk very fast. When I get ahead of him, he slows me down and tells me that he has only two legs and cannot keep pace. Sometimes I jar him with my muzzle to push him faster but he pushes back.

I am frightened of many things here. Wind blowing the weeds terrifies me. Loud noises remind me of the race track. When the man raises a hand to pet me I often shy, thinking he will strike me. My last groom whacked me with a feed bucket because I would not calm down. But this man is never anything but quiet and placid, soothing me with words and singing little ditties that make no sense at all. He takes me to the things that frighten me, makes me stare at them and grow accustomed to them and then the fear is not so great. When I do well he praises me. It makes me feel good to please him. I have never done that before.

Each day the man comes and rubs my injured leg. He paints an awful smelling liquid on it and it stings for a while and he massages until the ache is gone. I don't know why he does this. No one else ever cared if I was hurting. But every day, several times, he massages my leg and every day it seems to get better. Sometimes after he has gone away I gallop around the paddock. It's good to know I am getting better. But one day he will send me back to the races and I will not stay here. At least, this is what I think.

He will want me to do something because the other horses all have something they do. The man comes and takes Uno. We call to each other, *but they disappear into the barn. When they emerge, Uno has something on his back and the man stands on a box and lifts himself up. Then my friend carries the man down the road and they disappear into the woods.*

Often I wonder where they go, the man and Uno. My friend, Diablo, says they go out on the trail and sometimes it's a scary place, but sometimes it's quiet and there are good things to eat along the path. I don't know what a trail is. Perhaps one day I'll find one. But I like Diablo. He's the herd boss in his paddock. He says he is a Kentucky Mountain horse and that he has Paso blood. Sometimes I catch him staring off to where Challenge is and I know he is thinking of her. I think he loved her, but he never says.

But the man is coming down the road now, and he usually brings me something to eat. So now I must be still and not let him know what I am thinking. Horses are supposed to be dumb and it would not be good if he thought I was smart enough to know when carrots are coming.

Yes, the more I am around this man the more I like him. He is different. Not a herd boss, but different. I think I will be nicer to him, perhaps, even join his herd. Diablo said I should, but since he is in another paddock, he can't hurt me if I don't. Still, there is something sad about the man. I feel sorry for him. Yes, I think I'll pay more attention to him. Let him feel as if he is training me. For a man, there is hope for him. I'll let him feel he is training me when, in fact, it's just the other way around.

EACH DAY, RED GOT STRONGER. THE FRACTURE HEALED and bulged where calcium deposited. It is the healing power of the body, the infinite living body that repairs itself and protects itself from further harm. And so the man came each day, groomed the red horse, massaged the sore bone and spoke to the horse of the pain in his heart. So finite is the human mind that it requires someone in whom to confide. That is what the man does. He confides in Red. And it makes Red feel proud to know he is trusted by the man, so he listens when the man speaks.

"She called last night, Red. God, I miss her. Did I tell you she took a local assignment? She's reporting on drug use in the county. Dangerous.

Wish she wasn't undercover. Heard the phone and jumped out of bed. At least I think I heard it ring. When I picked it up, there was no one on the line. Those sleeping pills knock hell out of a man and sometimes I think things happen and find I was only dreaming. Losing my grip on reality." He hesitated, stared the horse in the eyes. "I tell everyone she is on a book-signing tour. They don't need to know she's out of the country."

He moved the horse into the center of the barn and clipped the cross-ties to the halter.

"Funny how dream and reality begin to blend when you get older. I told her I loved her and wanted her to be happy. I'm not sure if she could hear me, but at least I said the words. There is always static on the line and I never know where she is. "

The horse snorted and nosed Pierce for carrots. The man always brought carrots, stuffing them into his pockets as if he could bribe the horse into good behavior. From one pocket, he produced a large carrot and from another, he produced a bottle of Old Overholt. He offered the carrot to the horse. Then he upended the bottle and swigged a healthy jolt. The fire burned his throat as it coursed down to his stomach.

"God that burns, but it does warm a man's soul."

Red nosed him for another carrot, but the man grasped a curry and began stroking the horse's mane. He loved the golden fire in that mane. Loved the horse. Each day, he'd grown more attached to the animal. Each day, the animal bonded more and more with him. And Pierce held to the animal like a life-line for indeed the horse was thus. The man needed the animal as much as the horse needed him. Pierce had nothing else to cling to. Red had nowhere else to go. And Maya was not there.

He continued speaking as he groomed the horse.

"I miss her, damn it. Shouldn't rein a woman tighter than a horse. What difference if she had a job? What difference if she wanted to be somebody? Now I look back at all the times she guided me through tough times and wonder what the hell I was thinking." He'd taken to the country and his speech eroded into country slang. He did not always understand the locals, but he no longer spoke with the refinement of an attorney.

The big horse nodded as if agreeing with Pierce's lamentations. Pierce continued talking to himself as well as the horse.

"I should have been more understanding. Yes sir, when she comes back it will be different. I'll be a new man." He quaffed another nip from the bottle and stared out into the roadway. Then he returned to the grooming. He slid a brush down under the horse's neck and stroked gently, moving the crusted dust with strong, circular sweeps. The dust erupted like a cloud of fog. The wind kicked up and blew the dust back at Pierce, causing him to sneeze. Still, he continued the grooming, finishing one phase, then imbibing another drink. By the time he'd completed the grooming, he was unsteady and stumbling.

The barn was quiet then. Lined with weathered, oaken stalls, concrete flooring, overhead lights, the smell of disinfectant and fly spray. It was a horse barn that also reeked of dead tobacco and manure, an earthly, robust aroma, that bit into the nostrils but was not at all unpleasant.

Red relaxed and lifted his feet mechanically as Pierce ran his hand down a leg. He burrowed through the dirt packed within the hoof, scraped along the sides until the hoof was clean. In this fashion, he cleared all four feet while sipping as many drinks as he had cleaned feet. Still, each time the man spoke, the horse found the words soothing and sweet. His ears jutted forward, focused on the man's conversation.

"I think she's coming home soon, Red. Believe me, you'll like her. Maya's a wonderful girl. Warm, loving. Boy, can she make love. Never had a woman so sensuous." The voices that stirred him were long silent. The burning fire extinguished. He tipped the bottle twice and noted the bottom coming up. "Need a little more sauce. Seems I need more and more to do the same job. Forget. That's what it does. Helps me forget. Forget what we had."

He tossed the bottle into the waste, reached into his hip pocket for another. Red eyed him curiously. It wasn't often Pierce drank. When he did, he got sloppy with the horse. On several occasions, Red shied and stepped on the drunken man. The horse always regretted that. The man did not seem to notice.

"Maya," he slurred, "were you mine? Or did you belong to culture, to the world? I thought it was just you and me." He garbled the word *just* as if his tongue stuck on the 'j'. "Sometimes I think you weren't real at all, just an image, something I imagined. I'd feel you lying next to me and, when I reached, you weren't there. Like a phantom, sometimes visible, sometimes not." He wiped his mouth with his arm and leaned against the horse.

"No, she wasn't real. Just my imagination. She never was. A product of my loneliness and now, she's gone and the loneliness is still there. Am I going mad? Are my senses betraying me? She was real! I'm not going mad."

He thought of the times she slipped in and out of bed before he ever knew she was gone. She was quiet, so quiet, it was as if she did not really exist. He *thought* that sometimes, thought that she did not really exist. How could she disappear even in the house? He'd hear a sound in the living room and hunt her there only to find an empty room. Moments later, she appeared in the doorway as if she had always been there. Yes, he thought, she had an ethereal quality about her, as if she hailed from another time and place and not his dimension at all. It was then that he recalled her words "in another lifetime, perhaps."

Yes, perhaps it had been another lifetime. How else could she be so wraithlike? She glided around the house rather than walked. And he was unable to detect her presence. Yet, when she was near, she was truly with him. Her entire spirit consumed him, and her warmth set blazes in his heart that made the ache all the more terrible when she was absent. Was he going mad? Had the shock of her leaving set his mind adrift? He could no longer separate reality from illusion.

The horse nuzzled the man for a treat. Pierce produced a chunk of carrot and twirled it in his fingers.

"Know how we got married?" he asked, swaying as he spoke.

"Romance, horse. Romance. We flew to Tahiti. Three days later, we married. I carried her over the threshold. Damn near fell on my face," he laughed. "Right after the ceremony, we honeymooned on the island of Moorea. Beachfront bungalow. I can still hear the waves sloshing under the rafters. And when it rained, it beat against the thatch roof. We made love to the music of that rain. She always dabbed herself with jasmine just before bed and the scent of it raged in my brain loosing all the fires of love. Her body shook with passion, heaved with fervor; her moans drove me into a blind craze, two bodies united in one sensuality, one fragment of the infinite. Afterward, we lay against each other, her cologne still drifting up from her warm body. We listened to the slowing rain drops suspended on the roof's edge, then spiraling into space. And it was safe and secure there, isolated as if the bungalow was our very own island. Cowering in the face of Moa Roa, the Great Mountain beyond. And Maya and I honeymooned right across from it." He realized then he was drunk and babbling, but it didn't matter. He was adrift in his recollections.

He staggered into the tack room. Red grew impatient when the man did not come out. He emerged, red-faced and smelling of grain. Pierce placed a saddle pad on the horse's back and worked a bit into his mouth. For a drunken man he was amazingly gentle as he did so. Then he walked him out to the field and let him graze while he held the lead. Periodically he voiced commands: walk...whoa...back. Then realizing the liquor was overtaking him, he brought the horse back into the barn, removed the bridle and held onto him for balance.

"I'm too drunk to do this today. I'll just take a pill and sleep it off. A little sleeping pill. They hide the reality of life."

As an afterthought, he added: "We went to Sunday Mass. Right there on Moorea. The Mass was in French. And they don't sing gospel songs like 'Go Tell It On the Mountain' or 'Holy, Holy, Holy'. They chant island melody and sway to the music. Hypnotic. It stirs a man as if God himself was conducting the music. We fell in love with the island and the kindness of its people. We swayed along as they sang. Two days later they were filming the Bob Hope Christmas show. I stumbled out from behind a tree and they filmed my great debut." His eyes sparkled as he related this tale...this tale that was spoken to a horse. And the horse understood the man's pain and the man's loneliness, but all he could do was listen.

"We ate tuna burgers at a small shack just down the road from our posh hotel. And pizza with chunks of tuna. The waitresses brought us fruit from their gardens and every day they put hydrangea and bougainvillea bouquets on our pillows. We rode horses along the beachfront. At night, I took that delicate woman into my arms and loved her as I had never loved before. Nobody makes love like my Maya." He swigged again, let the sharp sting settle in his gullet, then drank again.

"I loved her and yet I made her life miserable because she had a dream and only one thing stood in the way of it...my jealousy. What the hell was I thinking of horse?"

He was still hanging on the horse. Supporting himself with an arm slung around its neck. He was sloppy in the way he untacked Red. He took him out of the barn and into the field. The long grass bowed with the west wind and the smell of ripening manure floated on the air. Then he loosed his grip on the horse and lurched toward the gate. The big red horse swung round to watch him go. The man may have had a twinkle in his eyes once, but now all the horse saw was sadness. A shock of static-laden hair had flopped down over the man's eye as if it were an insignia to identify him. No matter how many times he shoved it aside, it always worked its way down again. But now, it flopped in front of his eyes as he stumbled to the ground.

"She never did look back when she left," he muttered. He recalled the early years when he discovered he had colon cancer. He was doubled up on the floor, blood seeping through his underwear. Maya was standing over him, crying: "Pier, baby, what's the matter?" He stared up at her with blank eyes. He did not understand what had happened. He had been suffering pain for a very long time. He'd noted the symptoms of a severe problem, but he ignored them. Now, he was crumpled like a withered leaf and the pain paralyzed him.

Maya called the ambulance. Waited with him at the hospital as they tested. The scope results came back showing a blockage in the intestine. They told her to go home. They would take care of him. But she would not. No, Maya would not move. She would not eat. She would not drink. Patiently she curled up in a chair in the waiting room, watching as the timeless hours passed, slowly passed, ponderously passed, passed in infinitesimal increments. She scrutinized the minute hand to confirm its movement forward. She stared at the floors, at the ceilings, at the blank, dismal hospital corridors. She jumped at every new sound and every new face that appeared. The same magazines passed lifelessly through her hands, unread, a hopeless blur. Maya closed her eyes. Tried to doze. But she kept blaming herself for not having seen any symptoms.

Why had she not noticed his lack of appetite? Why had she not observed the shorter and shorter hours he was working? Why had his frequent naps not raised an alarm? He had not made love to her in months. And when she discovered blood on the sheets, why did she not question his explanation about a bloody nose?

Then look again at the clock. God! Had only four minutes passed since she last looked. The operation continued for six hours. No word came of it. Then a nurse was leading her to recovery and there she saw a man, not her husband, for he was chalk-like and drained of all life. She visited every day, talked to him, held his hand. When he became despondent, she spoke of future plans, of travel, of riding new trails. Always she brightened his day. She researched his colon cancer, showed him the odds of his survival. She fought with doctors when they objected to his early return home.

"Keep him here, with no hope, no sign when he can return to the things he loves, and he will die. He must come home." She was vehement in her discussion. Pierce had to come home. She told Pierce this. She called him in the mornings, just as she was leaving the farm. She called when she arrived home and updated him on all the animals. She brought cards and flowers to his room. And she was there when the doctors conceded defeat to Maya and released him from the hospital.

They had sewed him up with fishing line, the wound was so deep. And it was so deep, it became infected and turned an ugly white like festering vermin. But Maya did not see the wound, or the blood or the white infection. She saw her Pierce, her husband. She could not think of leaving for a writing career. She removed the dressing with care and stared down into that great slash that gnarled and twisted his once smooth abdomen. Skillfully she swabbed out the wound, barely touching, barely causing him pain. At times, the stench nearly overcame her, but she bore down, she attended her Pierce. He was not going back into the hospital. So she cleaned the wound with warm, milky water and disinfected it with anti-bacterial powder. She packed the gauze deep into the wound so the medicine took effect in the deepest recess of his incision.

Only when she left did she retch and nearly vomit. Only when the task was done did she allow herself to feel as a woman. Only when the dressing and the care were completed, did she dare to hope that Pierce might live. Only then did she try to force food into her mouth. And when two hours had passed, and she saw that Pierce was awake again, only then did she quietly slip back to the upstairs bedroom, to begin the process of cleaning and binding the wound again. In all that time she lost seventeen pounds and slimmed to a silhouette of herself.

The thought faded again and he was back again with Red. Absentmindedly he had taken the horse back into the building. He bedded the horse in his stall and made the latch secure, still muttering to himself as he did so. Red did not understand why he had been bedded down so soon. "I am losing it, fella. Something's not right."

He staggered out of the barn. The red horse peered after him as he wobbled away. Red did not see him again that day. But there were other days. They were not always the same. There were times the horse felt sorrow for the man. He was always alone. Always unkempt and uncared for. No one ever groomed him and the horse wondered who brought the man his hay and water because there was never anyone else around. He did not ask though, did not dare to think because the man seemed to know what he was thinking. It discomforted him to have someone know him so well. The man knew when he was right and when he was off. But he, too, knew when the man was right and when he was off.

There were other times when the man was somber and serious. He worked the chestnut gelding, trained him to accept the bridle, the saddle pad and saddle. He worked him in a round pen, teaching him to walk, to trot, to canter on command. At each session the horse stopped and walked toward the man, touched him with his nose. He trusted Pierce. Even a whip in the man's hands did not frighten the animal anymore. He knew the man would not touch him with it.

And as the man worked the horse, he hummed a senseless little ditty. It calmed the horse. It calmed the man. The man wished his Maya could see his success, and how patient he had become. Pierce missed her. Yet, he wondered if anything would be different if she returned. He spoke to the horse as well. He told the animal he missed Maya. Wanted her back. He tried telephoning, but always, he could not find an address or telephone number. He was sure she had given him a schedule of her travels, but he could no longer find it.

"I just want to sleep the time away until she returns," he whispered to the horse. The horse nodded.

"Thing is I can't sleep. Not without the pills. Sometimes I doze and think I feel her next to me. Then I wake up and she slips away."

The big red horse said nothing and moved mechanically around the pen. He pitched his head in anger, wheeling in balance with the man's body language. Then, breathless, he stopped on command, faced the man and walked to him. His head was down, his mouth working. Somewhere in the process, Pierce had become dominant. The horse wanted him for a herd-mate. As the man headed toward the gate, the horse followed submissively keeping pace with Pierce until he reached the gate and left the horse loose in his own paddock. But this was only on the sober days. On days when Pierce drank, the sessions were short and meaningless.

I HAVE BECOME THE MAN'S FRIEND AND YET, I know little of him. I only know that he is kind and gentle and that there is softness in him when he needs to be soft and firmness when he needs to be firm. He is dominant, and yet he is not dominant. And he speaks to me of something that troubles him, a woman he calls Maya. I do not understand human love or emotions. Horses react to those things which frighten us. We have base feelings and so we respond to our environment and whatever threatens us. We procreate, but we do not understand the emotion that drives us. I cannot say why the woman would cry. I cannot comprehend why the man would care about her. There must be something between them, but I am not a human so the feeling has no meaning for me.

The little man confides in me when he grooms me though. He speaks of the woman often and sometimes there is love in his voice and sometimes anger. I do not think he likes her editor very much. The man says the edi-

tor took the woman away and left him alone. That is when I hear the anger in the man's voice and then, I think, they will not be herd-mates again. But other times, he speaks of the romance they felt when they first met. He tells me they traveled to many places. They danced away the nights and sat listening to the ocean's lapping waters. With the morning sunlight, they rode horses on the beaches and into the mountains and they felt and thought as one. And then the anger returns and the man cannot understand why the woman had to go away. I think he is very sensitive, this man. I think he should rein her more tightly and drive the editor off the way a stallion drives off a younger colt. Perhaps even trample him if he will not leave them alone. When I listen to him, I do not think the misery is caused so much by what the editor does, but by what the woman permits him to do. But I am only a horse. I do not know human emotions. I am only troubled because my friend is so sad.

Yet, I think he is happy when he is working with me. He teaches me to back up, to side-step, to move forward. He teaches me to move in tight circles. I walk over obstacles and in and out of mazes he constructs on the ground. I know the routines so well that I begin them before he even enters the round pen. He says I am a very smart horse. But I already know that so why does he repeat it?

He also slips a cloth pad my back and tightens a leather thing around me. It is the same thing he uses on Uno when they go off together. Sometimes he places a block next to me, steps onto it and leans across my back. He is so short he cannot mount Uno without a block and Uno is much smaller than me. One day, I think he will gain the courage to sit on me. I will surprise him, then, for he is my friend and I will not buck him off. I am not like Willie. It is a true sign of trust when a horse permits a man to mount. Always, we fear the predator that strikes from above. If I allow him on my back, then I trust him as I trust no other man.

But he is a strange man, a patient man. Last night he staggered into my stall and lay in the straw next to my feed bin. He was drinking from some kind of bottle and it smelled of grain. I have scented it before. The more the man drank, the more he sang and mumbled. He was talking about *the woman again, said her boss had her by the ear, and there was nothing in the world more important to Maya than her work. He sounded very sad when he said this and I felt sorry for him. I wondered why anyone would hurt such a kind man.*

I did not move much when he came into my stall. I was afraid I might hurt him so I stood quietly and listened to him mumble. It grew dark, and the man seemed to sleep for a time. Then he awoke and cried and, for the first time, I felt the soul of a human deeply troubled. I wished I were human so I could talk to the woman, make her see that she was hurting my friend, make her understand that perhaps no one was more important to her than my friend. But I am not human and I cannot speak. I can only feel my friend's misery, and I can only hope the woman does not hurt him again.

Dawn lightened the sky. It was morning and the morning light peered into my stall and brightened the night away. He awakened and seemed happier. Perhaps the liquid he drank has some kind of happiness in it. It made him sleep and that is good. But it made him say strange things in a strange voice, and I am not certain that is so good. He says the woman will come home soon, but he wonders if she will stay. Perhaps her editor is higher in the pecking order than the man or even the woman and, therefore, they must obey him. Horses do not have divided hearts. They obey the herd leader. They follow his lead. They have only one loyalty and as long as they keep their place, they are left alone. But this is not true of humans. Humans can love one person and be loyal to another, and they can hurt the person they love because they are loyal to another. I do not blame the man for feeling as he does. I would not want a divided leader. And I would not want my mare running off with someone lower in the pecking order either. So I understand why he is angry and hurt.

There is a horse van coming up the road. The other horses tell me that Willie has been sold. Most of them are happy to see Willie go. Uno has been treated the worst by him, being run off, nipped, kicked and tormented. Willie drives him from the feed buckets, the hay bin, even the water trough. There is an unwritten law among horses that even the least of the herd is entitled to water. Not Willie though. He just drives Uno off for any reason. He is a selfish horse. So no one is sad to see him go.

Willie ambles into the trailer as if he is king. He is putting on airs because he is humiliated to have been sold. I think he bucked the man off once too often. My friend can tolerate many things, but disloyalty is not one of them. I think that is why he let the woman go. She did not know how to be loyal, so the man let her leave. I wonder why they do not see things as I see them. They are herd-mates and belong together. No one should keep them apart. Humans are strange and they have strange ways. I am told he is older than she is and will not live long. I sense that. Does the woman sense that too? Does she not care? Or does she simply not see it at all?

The trailer drives off and Willie is gone. But there are more surprises. The man comes with a saddle pad and a saddle. He grooms me first, then walks me around the pen, backs me, moves me sideward, right, then left, then back, then forward. He positions me in the center of the ring and places the pad on my back. When I do not move, he rewards me with a carrot and slips the saddle on my back. I remain still. I am not frightened because I know he will not harm me, but I am excited to know what it will feel like to have something heavy on my back. I am calm with him.

The saddle is on and it does not feel uncomfortable. He tightens something around my waist and then slips the bridle into my mouth. When I accept this, he rewards me with another piece of carrot. He tightens the band again but only slightly, and he does not yank or pull. I wonder if he will take me on the trail.

When I am "tacked up," as he says, he leads me around the pen and then lets me loose to graze on the clover growing near the edge of the pen. He does not mow here so the clover is always full and long. Yes, I am nervous about what will happen, but I do not wish to harm the man.

The man brings the mounting block near me. I am not sure of this and so I step away. He smiles and leads me around in a circle until I am standing next to it again. Then he climbs the block and leans across my back. He has done this in the past so it is easy for me to relax. The next time he moves the block, I am calm and I do not move. He praises me and rubs my withers. I am proud to have pleased him.

He places his foot in the stirrup and stands straight up. I am confused because I don't know what he wants, but then he dismounts and stands on the block again. We repeat this lesson several times until I become bored and walk off to a corner of the round pen. He does not pursue me. I graze for a time. He is patient about this. On my own, I return. I sense that is why he is staring at me. Because he is pleased, he praises me and strokes my neck. He mounts again this time swinging his leg over me and into the saddle. I feel his weight settle lightly on my back and I start to move off. He tightens the reins lightly and tells me to whoa. I stop and stand still again. Then he taps me with his feet and tells me to walk. He guides me right, then left, then around. I know this direction from my racing days. He backs me up, then around and asks me to move faster. I do not feel as if there is a man on my back. It feels as if we are flowing into one another, that we are not separate beings at all. The wind rushes by me. He and I are one. The man lavishes me with praise. The lesson goes on. I find myself enjoying the time. When the lesson is complete, the man rewards me with carrots and a rub down. He is pleased with me. I am proud that I have pleased him. I am happy, too, because I made the man smile.

He turns me out in the large pasture and I gallop to meet my friends there. He vanishes into the landscape as my friends are at the far end of the field. Before long, I am pasturing with them and I soon forget about the man.

AT NIGHT, PIERCE, BATHED IN SWEAT, TOSSED PILLOWS into different positions, trying to be comfortable, trying to sleep. It was a nightly ritual. He willed himself not to take more pills, but always relented when sleep would not come. He swallowed the pills he had stockpiled and lay on his back, staring at the ceiling. The shadows from his lamp danced and flickered across the white plains of his ceiling until a drowsy unawareness overtook him. He slipped away from the world. Somewhere in the distance, he thought he heard the telephone. He staggered out of the bed, knocking over his lamp as he did so, and falling to his knees. By the time he recovered, the phone was silent except for the eerie dial tone he heard as he lifted the receiver. Was it her? Or was it a dream? Only moments ago he was cuddled up next to her. Was that a fantasy as well?

He heard her voice, the voice that rang like fine glass when struck. The lilting chant of the islands came back to him. But he was not certain whether it was reality or dream. Beyond the dial tone he thought he heard a voice, but could not be certain. He strained to hear and then realized, he was dozing off from the pills.

"Maya?"

Did she reply? Did he hear her whisper, "Pierce?"

"Maya, I'm sorry. I was wrong. Please come home." He hesitated. "I'll…I'll let you go when you have to."

Silence. She said nothing. Was it because she was still hurt and angry over their parting? He could not determine this. The dial tone interfered with her voice and he could hear nothing definite. It was all conjecture. Perhaps it was all fantasy. He wanted to hear her. Wanted to touch her. But she said nothing.

"I know you're hurt. Angry too. I deserve it. I just didn't want to lose you. Not ever."

A sound started, then static. "Damn, Maya, you're fading. The phone is going again. We never get a good connection. Can you hear me? Maya? Maya?"

The static increased. He strained to hear a voice, anything. Nothing came except the static, then the dial tone again. This time the tone was incessant and determined.

"Maya…oh God, Maya. I've lost you again." The phone clicked into silence as he cradled it on its rest. He lurched toward the bed, but did not lie down. Instead, Pierce sat patiently waiting for the phone to ring again. There is nothing so hopeless or forlorn as a phone that will not ring, nor any wait as long as the empty silence that accompanies disappointment. There is no hope as vast as the hope of reincarnated love. Still, he waited. Maya might call again. An hour passed. The Ambien had taken hold. It dulled his misery.

He took another sleeping pill and swigged again the whiskey. Although he lumbered in a stupor, he found himself talking to himself.

"Maya, where did we go wrong? We owned the world. Travel. Fine cuisine. Good friends. Money. Love. We blew it. I blew it."

He sagged onto the bed, half on-half off. The past loomed again. It was the month after their honeymoon. Pierce persuaded Maya to work at his law office. She did secretarial work and soon proved to be very capable at organizing and preparing files for trial. Through her efforts he established an even larger clientele among the Hispanics. She also matriculated at a local college specializing in journalism. Pierce molded her work schedule to suit her schooling, but inwardly he frowned at the thought of her working anywhere else. He wanted all her time. He needed the security.

Despite his skill at trial, he suffered the indignity of a sordid past. At five, his mother shoved his hand into a stove burner because she thought he had opened her purse. The hospital authorities took a dim view of her discipline and reported the matter to the county prosecutor. Removed from his home, he was reared by grandparents who openly warred with each other. When he was twelve, his grandfather put him to work at his egg factory. He went from school to work to home. He worked without pay until he was seventeen. With no prospects of love in sight, he deserted his grandparents and obtained a job on the Port Authority docks.

The union mobsters adopted Pierce because they liked his eloquent style. Steeped in English literature, he entertained them by quoting *Dover Beach* or Shakespearean sonnets. He wrote letters for them and, later, wrote short story assignments for their high school kids. The same mobsters who employed him also enrolled him in university, paying his tuition. When his college average was just below the acceptance level for law school, they persuaded the dean to admit him on probation. He graduated in the top half of his class, passed the bar exam immediately. With the aid of the union bosses, he soon opened his own office and repaid his union friends by representing them and their families.

But his success as a lawyer never overshadowed the rejection he sustained at the hands of a cold and unfeeling mother. Maya was the only one who had ever loved him. Now, she was gone and he was alone. He roused himself to awareness. The room around him was still. The air reeked of the cologne he sprayed on the pillows, the fragrant White Jasmine that Maya had always used. In his thoughts he could sense Maya slipping into bed, wiggling next to him. He slipped his arm around her as he always had and kissed her lightly. He inhaled the sweet smell of her hair. He slipped in and out of this reverie, and when he returned to consciousness, he waited…waited for the phone to ring.

The phone did not ring. Its failure to ring lulled him into a troubled sleep. In that sleep, he reached out and touched Maya, the Maya who once was there but was now…God knew where. He always loved to reach out and touch her. He recalled that because he lived more in dream than in reality. Other times, he had stared at her while she slept, savoring her smooth complexion, the full lips slightly apart as she slept. He gazed at her breasts, round and lush like soft mountain tops, and listened to the sweep of her nightgown as she walked.

But the thoughts were not always happy ones for then they were standing at the front door. She was holding her briefcase and he was pleading with her not to go. Her appointment was a late one with the local prosecutor. Perhaps he should accompany her. No, she didn't want him involved. This was a delicate matter. Dangerous people were involved. It would be her last assignment on the series. After that, she'd return to obscurity.

"I'm so sorry, Pier. I'd love to have you with me, but they told me to come alone."

She clung to him tightly, surprising him with the show of affection. "I'm frightened, Pier. Sorry I got involved."

He stood there, wordless and stunned by her admission. "I'm sure it will be all right but if you want, I'll call and tell them you can't." He glanced at her hopefully, knowing she would not accept his offer.

She moved away from him and shook her head. "No, I need to go, to finish this assignment. I *have* to do it."

In everyone's life, there is always something they *have* to do…something so vital that the destiny of it cannot be put off. It pounds at the door like an unpaid prostitute. Maya could no more resist the call than Pierce could resist loving her.

"I'll call on my way back," she said and, when she left, her spirits seemed high.

True to her promise, she did call. It was not a good connection. She sounded happy, but a little frightened. The officials would protect her once she testified. The danger was such that she and Pierce might even have to move. What had started as a minor investigation of local marijuana growers augmented into out-of-state drug connections directly linked to the Columbian cartels. Once Maya's cover was vitiated, they'd have to find a new life. She was reporting on dangerous men and dangerous men kill.

Pierce shuttered at the immensity of Maya's embroilment in a federal investigation. She had wanted a job as a reporter and her assignment had placed her and Pierce in harm's way. Until the trial, she wouldn't have to report to work. They'd be together again.

He brightened when he heard this and it infused him with hope…hope he had not held for a very long time. Of course, once the trial was over and they could resume a normal life—no matter where it was—she'd return to his arms and he'd apologize for his possessiveness. *Everything would be fine.*

Still, he wished for old his mob connections. They'd know how to protect Maya. He didn't trust government. They sapped what they wanted and abandoned people once the use was over. The Mafia had helped the government in their battle for Sicily only to have their native sons deported when the war was over. Double-crossed by the men they trusted. No, government couldn't be trusted, and his friends were long gone and dead. Those still alive were either in jail or had no real power on the streets. The federal government had seen to that too.

But he was drifting again and unsure as to whether he was awake or sleeping. It often happened that way. He'd slip into thought and forget where reality began and ended. He'd think of things and wonder if they had really happened or if he had merely dreamt them. And thus, he questioned himself as he thought of

Maya—his Maya. *Did she return that night? Of course she did. Then her editor sent her off again. She didn't resign her position. She had done a good job and, like a fever, the praise twisted her ego into an ugly thing. She wanted to come home. She would come home. But when? Why didn't she call more often?*

But there were no real answers, not even within that soul of soul that knows the answers. And his thoughts were waking thoughts of his lost Maya and the loneliness he felt.

HE AWOKE, GROGGY FROM THE COMBINATION OF WHISKEY and sleeping pills. Pierce hated that feeling and he hated his weakness. He needed to be a man again, to have courage, drive, determination. His shoulders were stiff. His legs ached. What had he done to cause all this pain? Perhaps he had fallen. He didn't know.

He made himself some spearmint tea, trying to settle his stomach. He made two slices of toast, shoved them aside and took aspirin instead. It only mildly relieved his aches, but he knew the morning activity would loosen the stiffness.

Today would be different. He'd work Red and perhaps even ride him. The horse had the makings of a good trail horse, but he was herd-bound and did not wish to leave the other horses. Pierce had worked with him twice daily, sacking him out with saddle pads and saddle. He had led him out of the paddock and to the trail heads, taught him to cross the little creek and start up the trail. The horse seemed to have faith in him. Pierce needed that trust. He wanted to ride this horse and boast of his accomplishment when Maya called again. Once she saw him involved with Red, she'd understand he could tolerate other interests in her own life. This was more than horse training to Pierce. His hopes of proving to Maya that he could give her some space were linked to this horse. The more he clung to Red, the less he'd cling to Maya, and in some convoluted way, hold her even closer.

Red saw him coming and nickered softly. Pierce swung over the fence and into the paddock. The horse approached him and accepted the carrot he offered and munched it slowly then nosed him for another.

"Not yet, big fella. Today you have to earn it," he laughed. He couldn't remember when he'd last laughed and it lightened his spirits. He spent a half-hour grooming the horse, shined his feet with mineral oil and brushed the golden mane until it radiated. The hair was thin like silk and the man coursed the curry through it again and again. It reminded him of the supple texture of Maya's hair.

Pierce brought the saddle into the paddock. He let the horse smell the pad and then slipped it on his back. Next, the saddle, lifted near the withers because Red had a high neck. It settled easily on the horse and the animal tolerated the weight without incident. Pierce cinched it easily, not wishing to pinch the animal. The horse swelled his stomach. Pierce notched the loose girth and fastened the breast collar instead. When the horse relaxed, he cinched two more notches and then left it again. He slid the bit into the animal's mouth, made certain it fitted correctly, then clipped the headstall and the curb chain. He paused for a moment, letting the horse accept the tack, and seeing that Red remained calm, he snugged the saddle.

It was a clear morning, a sunlit morning. The azure sky was littered with large wisps of clouds that lay like strands of white fluff hovering overhead. There was little wind to spook a horse and Pierce felt confident he could move ahead in the training sequence. He wanted a second trail horse, and Red's coming had been providential, giving the man some purpose while his wife was gone. If he succeeded in gaining the trust of an untrusting horse, he conjectured that he could once again gain the love and trust of Maya.

He squared the horse so that it stood evenly on all four legs, then swung easily up into the saddle from the mounting block. He eased down lightly. *No sense spooking the horse or making it uneasy*, he thought. He took up the reins and clucked to the horse. When Red did not move, he touched him with his boots. Red started forward.

"Good boy," he whispered, so softly the horse's ears cocked back.

He worked the horse around the outside of the round pen. Red hesitated halfway around and Pierce spun him into a tight circle, knowing the horse would prefer forward movement rather than circular. Red was a hyper horse and Pierce used the horse's natural anxiety to push him ahead.

Around the pen they went, then turn and back again. He backed the horse a few steps, worked him into a walk, clucked for a trot and received it. The horse was working well. He worked him into the larger paddock. It was all going so easily. He had laid a proper foundation and his efforts brought success. Did he dare try the trail, though? *Why not*, he answered himself.

He moved the horse to the storage shed, beyond which lay the sloping trails. Cross the creek and the trail forked into two paths. Red halted at the creek, but Pierce urged him on and nearly fell when the horse scooted across the glistening water. He started up the trail. That trail led to several others, but heading straight would take them up to the old hay barn where a year's forage lay cut into square bales awaiting use. It was not a long trail, just long enough to test Red's attitude on the open trail.

The horse was alert and tight. He blew and snorted and took each step with painful deliberation. At a moment's beckon the horse might easily explode into a bucking fit, a spin and then a rush back to the barn. Pierce halted him and let him stand. When the horse fidgeted, the man turned him and pushed him on. Although nervous, Red continued along the path, hesitating only when he heard his paddock mates calling to him. The man urged him forward.

"Easy now, Red. Doing fine. Just up to the old barn and then we turn and come home. I'll work you again in the square paddock and then we'll try the trail head again."

The trail they took was an old logging road that once had been part of the county road. The Randolph family, from whom he purchased the property, told him the road was no longer used by the county and had overgrown with brush and thorns. Heavy rains had worn a deep gorge into the roadway, but Pierce spanned it with a bridge. The horse saw the bridge and stopped. Pierce turned him and let him walk a few steps. Then he halted the horse, turned him again and brought him up to the wooden viaduct. Red put his head down to inspect the bridge. He lay a single foot on it and turned, then backed away. Pierce was patient...oh so patient. The man was learning about patience. The horse was learning trust. Red placed his left foot on the bridge, then the right. He tried turning away, but Pierce headed him straight. With a small rush, the horse gaited across the bridge to the other side. Pierce praised him and patted the horse's withers.

They moved forward about twenty feet. He turned the horse and brought him to the bridge again. Red hesitated again, but when urged, crossed the narrow passage and halted on the other side. Pierce was satisfied with his progress. He brought Red down the slope and crossed the creek again. Then he started the horse up the county road to the larger creek that bordered the property. He stopped along the way to let the animal graze on the grass that lined the road. When done, he brought him to the trail head again, urged him across the creek and onto the trail.

Red was still high-strung, but he followed direction. He sauntered up the slope, his ears forward, his eyes checking both sides of the trail. They rode to the bridge and crossed it. Pierce pushed him on. Periodically the horse stopped and stared into the woods. The man knew the animal heard something, but he didn't know what. Perhaps a rabbit or a deer.

They arrived at the upper barn. Red had relaxed. His ears were back, listening to Pierce's commands. They stopped by the old weathered building. Pierce was unaware anything lurked there. He had once been summoned by workers threatening to quit because there was a rabid fox living under the barn floorboards. Pierce found the animal wallowing toward him and shot it. The Commonwealth confirmed that it had rabies. Other than an occasional snake, he had never seen anything else that would alarm the horse.

He worked Red by the old barn, bringing him up to the entrance and encouraging him forward. He got halfway through the barn and turned Red and brought him out again. Outside, the grass was luxuriant. Pierce stopped the horse and loosened the reins. His reward to Red was to let him graze on the verdant forage. And while he did so, he thought of Maya and hoped she would telephone again.

Red stopped and lowered his head to graze. Pierce permitted this as a reward to the animal. Suddenly, Red bolted. His hind plummeted down while his legs dug hard into the soil. The force of his startle caught Pierce unaware. The force propelled Pierce backward and out of the saddle. He slammed into the ground. It jarred him, and, although he took the blow on his right shoulder, he crashed hard.

Pierce just lay there, the wind shocked out of him. For a moment, he could not rise. He didn't exactly know what prevented him, but he could not rise. He saw the frightened horse run off about a hundred feet and stop. The animal turned as if understanding he had left his rider behind. Then, comprehending that he had no rider on his back, Red gaited back up the slope to where Pierce lay, dropped his head and nosed the fallen man. Pierce saw worry in the animal's eyes. He knew Red expected a flailing for his transgression. But Pierce wouldn't harm the horse even if he could have.

The man's right side was useless. His arm hung down like the pendulum of a great clock that has been silenced. As men know things, Pierce knew that if he didn't ride Red immediately, he would not be able to control him again. He labored to breathe. His right shoulder stung when he tried lifting his arm. He grasped the stirrup and pulled himself up with his left arm, using the slope of the land to propel himself into the saddle.

Red stood frozen. The horse heard the man groan, felt him sway in the saddle. He was only able to prod Red with the left leg. Slowly he walked the horse over the trail from whence they had come. The horse obeyed. Still spooky from the squirrels that had spooked him, Red obeyed every command. It was a short ride of agony back to the barn and even greater agony removing the tack.

The torture of removing Red's saddle convinced Pierce that his injuries were more than a routine spill. But he persuaded himself that he would be all right and he continued removing Red's tack. Once done, he turned Red out into his paddock and limped home. He could hardly mount the stairs. On each step he stopped to breathe. He did not climb the second flight to the bedroom, but settled in the downstairs guestroom.

He attempted lying down, but had to prop himself up with pillows. Once down, he might not get up again. What he needed, he told himself, was sleep. He swigged some whiskey from the bottle and found some painkillers. He was so damaged, the remedy worked faster than usual. When he awoke two hours later, his entire body ached, and he was hardly able to rise. There was blood in his mouth and he coughed on arising, still breathless from the effort. He could not draw a deep breath. He lost consciousness again and lost touch with reality. In that lost reality, Maya was near and caring for him.

When reality returned, Pierce awoke and smelled the odor of sickness and death. Starched linen sheets in their dull grey over-washed condition curled around his waist and caught underneath him. He was aware of the plastic tube protruding from his nose because it made his throat dry and scratchy. It was not so much the setting, but the hospital smells of medication and wrappings and the awesome hush that descended on the place after dark. He did not know how he got there.

He looked around the room. He was alone. Oddly enough everything was in sharp focus, the single chair to his left, the rolling table on which sat the plastic water pitcher, plastic cup, and assorted plastic bowls. Even the small, sealed window that emitted only partial rays of light were within his vision. Overhead were dismal lights and a worn television set. A chunky, blond nurse of thirty or so charged into the room with a small paper cup containing pills. The woman was neat and manicured. Her hair was pushed back and made her face seem larger than it was. She poured his water and handed him the cup.

"You are one lucky guy," she smiled, taking his pulse after he had accepted the pills and the water. He stared at her. She was not comely, but she radiated some inner attraction. *Even angels don't always have to be pretty,* he thought, handing her the water and the empty pill container.

"The medication will help you to relax. Dr. Hassid will be here soon."

"Dr. Hassid?"

"Pulmonary specialist. He's going to re-inflate your lung. You did know it was collapsed?" she asked, writing his pulse and blood pressure on the chart.

"No, I didn't." He wheezed the answer more than spoke it.

"Hurt isn't the word for it. Mangled is probably a better word. The doctor will discuss your injuries, but when they found you they airlifted you here. Broken hip, clavicle, two right-side ribs and a pneumothorax. Quite an assortment of injuries. I'm not supposed to tell you anything but I'm sure you already know what's wrong with you." She wore a clean, stiff uniform that crinkled when she moved. *Too much starch,* he thought. But he detected, over the smell of plastic and chemicals, a light fragrance, perhaps a scented soap.

"I guess I was hurt," he quipped, glancing to see if she caught the humor.

She shook her head, checked the tube and the intravenous needle in his left hand. She was walking out when the doctor veered around the partially closed door and greeted him. Dr. Hassid was typically Middle Eastern, complete with swarthy skin, mustache, a slight accent and a feint aroma of spices about him.

"How are you feeling?" he asked, not taking his eyes off the chart. Pierce didn't bother to answer. He'd been through this before on other horse accidents and knew that a doctor asking a rhetorical question only meant he needed time to review the chart. Hassid replaced the chart and moved bedside.

"The x-rays show a good deal of blood in the right lung. Have you been coughing much?"

"When I bend..." he coughed. "How did I get here?"

"A woman called 911."

"A woman? Maya, it has to be Maya," his face brightened.

"Your wife?"

For the first time, Pierce felt his pain and looked away from the doctor's gaze. *"No, it couldn't have been Maya,"* he thought.

"Have you been in touch with her?"

"Not really. She wrote a pretty successful book. Traveling. She tries to call, but the connections are always poor." He hesitated to catch his breath. "No, it couldn't have been her. She'd be here by now." His face saddened as he spoke.

The nurse brought in a tray full of instruments, but Pierce couldn't see what they were. Doctor Hassid spoke to the nurse and she left to obtain something else. The doctor continued about the procedure. "What I am going to do is to dull the insertion site with a local anesthetic. You won't feel any pain when the plastic tube goes in. For a while you'll see fluid and blood draining into this plastic bag. That's normal so don't be frightened."

"It's okay, Doc, I don't much care."

"That's the sedative. But once the fluid is drained, I'll inflate the lung. We'll do a few x-rays today and tomorrow. I have to use a local anesthetic. Morphine could cause pneumonia and we can't afford that. We must make sure the lung stays inflated. I'll let you know when you can go home."

"There's no one there."

"Social Services can help you. You can make a private arrangement with them to provide any services you need."

"Who's taking care of my animals?"

"A veterinarian friend of yours. He said not to worry. He'd stop in later to see you."

"Donnie? Donnie is doing all that?"

But the medication seized him and he crept into a dull sleep, and when he awoke, the room was empty again. The bag was half full of blood. He stared at the wall, darkened with the age of an old building. He remembered the ruins he'd seen with Maya. She had wanted to visit her home in Mexico, to see the ruins at Chichen Itza. He drifted to sleep again amid his thoughts of her.

He remembered, then. They flew to Cancun and hired a driver to take them to Valladolid, a quaint little town of a few hundred people, most of them living in the outskirts. He recalled the town square with its local merchants displaying their goods. Shriveled and brown old ladies and men, younger than their looks portrayed, displaying wares woven or carved by their own hands. In the central plaza, he photographed the church of San Sebastian, its gray, twin spires poking up into the pale, smoke-colored clouds behind it. Took a photo of Maya with the same background.

For a rural town, the plaza was embellished with dazzling, white wrought iron chairs, statues, and vivid flowers of red, green, yellow and lavender. Pierce could never recall the names of the flowers, yet Maya knew them all. In the center was the main fountain shaped like a soup tureen with the figure of a young girl, her jug spouting water into the base of the structure. A walkway curled around the park, decorated with small trees and hedges and more colorful flowers. It was a place at peace, filled with exciting sights, populated with varied people, history and culture. The fresh aroma of flowers and shrubs blended with the feint fragrance of Maya's perfume. Pierce enjoyed it. He longed to see the place, to sample its food, to bargain in his poor Spanish with the merchants—most of whom spoke more Mayan than Spanish.

He and Maya sought out families that might be related to her. One by one they visited while she spoke in her native tongue, asking if there were any relatives of the del Rey family still living there. She pouted when no one could recall such a family. "Quien sabe. It was such a long time ago," the natives said.

They whiled away the hours, walking with hands clasped together, lost in the reverie of love. Although they had been married for several years, they still gazed into each other's eyes with the deep attraction that melded them. They had first become friends, then lovers, then husband and wife. They renewed that love every time they stared at each other, for there were times when life separated them and drew their attentions elsewhere. And there were times when a single gaze could blot out the world, and they alone existed.

Maya wanted to see the plaza again and thus, they went, still gleeful and free as little children who have been released to play. They abandoned their pursuit of relatives or family history and returned to the square. They sought out a petite and wizened old woman, decayed teeth showing through parched lips and the brightness in her eyes long dulled by life and poverty, because she sold shawls and such. They bargained for a scarlet scarf far below its true value, and when the old woman conceded defeat at twenty pesos, Pierce handed her one hundred and whispered: "Por los ninos."

She had no children of course, for all her children were grown and gone to Mexico City or Cancun to find work, but they laughed at the humor and parted with smiles. The memory came back to him then that a tall boy next to the old woman shouted "Ola" when he saw what Pierce had done. The black-haired boy smiled and chided them. "The old woman is a witch. Tell her to read your fortune. Go on, tell her."

"Es verdad?" Maya asked, "This is true?"

The old woman nodded, then seized her hand and pulled it forward. She peered into the palm, then put it down. "I will not read the future" she said in Spanish. "Mucho dolor."

Maya asked her what she saw that was so painful, but the old woman returned to her stitching and refused to speak.

"Then read mine," Pierce offered, shoving his hand before the woman. But after looking at the palm, she only shook her head and pushed his hand away. Pierce offered her more money, but she only nodded and sank into a stoical silence.

She said something to the boy and he made the Sign of the Cross. "Por Dios," he uttered.

"Maya, what did she say to the boy?"

"She told him the fates were intertwined and she would not curse us by revealing what she had seen."

"Rubbish," he said. "These fortunetellers are a dramatic lot."

But Maya said nothing and only stared at the woman.

By and by, they passed a young boy holding a small caiman, its mouth taped shut and a sign wired to it reading ten dollars U.S. Pierce and Maya shuddered when they saw it but turned away without saying anything. What could they say? They were in a foreign country with different laws and customs. Life was hard there. Pierce offered to buy the caiman and have the boy set it free, but Maya refused, saying that the boy would only capture it again and sell it to someone else. Then, turning to the boy, she spoke so rapidly in Spanish that Pierce couldn't understand her. Seeing the puzzlement on Pierce's face, she switched to English.

"Why do you torment that animal?"

"I don't torment him." The boy turned sullen.

"Would you like to have your own mouth taped shut?"

"He bites. Look, here, see…" He pointed to several bite marks on his arm.

"My husband will give you fifty pesos if you release it."

The boy nodded in agreement.

"But..." and she set her face in his, " you will release it so we can see the animal is free and escapes. Then, and only then, will you receive the fifty pesos."

The boy shrugged. "It's of no matter to me. I can catch another tomorrow."

"Yes, but we will not be here to buy it. Besides, tourists cannot take such things back to their countries. It is illegal now."

The boy said nothing more, but turned, motioned them to follow, and led them through a narrow street not far from the center of town. There, a steam coursed through a small canal. The boy untapped the caiman's mouth, and heaved it into the water. It splashed into the stream, stalled for a moment, then swam quickly away. Pierce handed him the fifty pesos and they walked back toward the center. The boy walked away counting his money.

The streets were confining but clean. They studied the aged buildings along the way, wrought-iron balconies and grates upon the windows. It was nearing siesta and already shutters were being closed and laundry taken in after it had dried in the warm, morning sun. A hairless, calico cat rushed from the bushes to capture Pierces' shoelace, stopped when it saw him looking and scrambled back to its hiding place. It was a pleasant day, as he recalled, the sun warming but not uncomfortable. It bothered him, though, that the old woman would not read their futures. Maya laughed. "Pier, do you really believe in that stuff? She was just trying to raise the price."

He grew somber. "I just don't believe in tempting the fates."

They kept walking, into the sun, into the oblivion of love, into the shadow of an uncertain future.

Yes, he remembered Valladolid. They had left the town and returned to Cancun where they were staying. They dined at a waterfront Italian restaurant. Maya told the waiter they were celebrating their anniversary and he seated them on the outside veranda overlooking the water. They watched the golden sunlight transform into a ruby sunset, then darken and give way as a gigantic moon crowned with luminous stars spun magic into the sea wind. He reached across the table and took her hand. The fortuneteller was soon forgotten. Later, after they had finished cordials, he thought himself silly to have taken the episode seriously. He didn't really believe the fortuneteller was trying to raise the price. Just trying to frighten them. They'd already made their purchase and she had refused the silver coins he tried to bribe her with. No, he felt she had some other motive, but decided she couldn't really read palms and the other vendor was merely trying to stop them from leaving so he could show his wares. Satisfied with his rationalization, he turned his attention to Maya again.

"I love you," he whispered.

She nodded, sipping the cordial. "Pierce, I've been thinking. I'll write an article about Valladolid. It'll make a wonderful human interest story. Should I do it?"

He pulled his hand away and looked outward toward the sunset. Maya always chose the wrong time to bring up unpleasant matters, and she had spoiled the evening by talking about her career.

"If it's what you want." She read the disappointment in his face, but her own enthusiasm overshadowed his feelings.

"I know you get upset when you think of me taking a job, but why does it bother you?" she countered.

"I'd never stop you from doing what you truly want. If writing and traveling are what you want, it's your life. I'll find something to do with myself while you're gone."

"Gone? Who said anything about going anywhere? I'm submitting an article, one article. I don't even believe they'll publish it. Competition is fierce in the field of journalism."

"Not satisfied with our life, with being my wife. I am not even so concerned about the job as I am about where it will lead. One assignment after another, late nights, missed dinners."

"You don't understand. It's lovely here in Mexico. I was overwhelmed by the romance between us and I wanted to weave that into a story about travel. But, even more than that, I'm not fulfilled. I want to be worthy of you, to make you proud." He saw the hurt welling up in her eyes. It towered over the resentment he felt in his heart.

"Not fulfilled?"

She hesitated, not certain he wasn't mocking her. "Fulfilled. I have had no children. Writing is my child. Every woman has needs. Some, children. Some, a career. Some, perhaps both."

"I never heard anything so stupid in all my life. Fulfilled? We have money, a great farm, wonderful horses, our own trail system. We travel. We dine at fine restaurants. You have more jewelry that any two women. What the hell more do you want?" He was angry, but not so angry he wouldn't listen. She knew his moods; knew when his anger tuned out all reason. This time, he was angry, but he was listening.

"I want to achieve something, to create something. Writing is something I enjoy, but it's also like having my own child." She sipped her drink and stared out at the water. It had turned black as the light receded from the sky. It did not have the salt tang of other oceans, but the moon seemed to hover just above the waterline and the light reflected from its coal-black surface.

"Stay home and write books. Lots of writers work from home. I don't ask you for help around the farm."

"But, I do help though. You can't say I don't help." She blurted the words, hurt by the insinuation. Pierce had managed to twist the topic and distract her from her argument. He was skilled at that. He was an insecure man, and he saw only the negative in anything that threatened him emotionally. In many respects Maya felt sympathy for him and she often relented to avoid hurting Pierce.

"Yes, you help. Until some guy comes around and then you're all attentive to him."

"When? When did I do that?" Maya couldn't believe the direction their conversation was taking.

"Maya, some grubby little kid falls and you're right there to pick him up. Some guy comes around with a sad story and you pay more attention to him than to me. How about Jerry's party? I turned around and you were holding this grubby, filthy little kid and talking to its lumberjack father like the two of you were husband and wife."

"Someone had to clean the child. Its mother wouldn't budge off her behind." Tears watered up and streaked down her cheek. She always cried when she was angry, but her tears were more for Pierce's insecurities than for the accusation.

"I realize you really aren't mine. You belong to everyone else and now you're hung up on this writing thing. Are you sure writing is your real interest?"

She flung her napkin on the table and shot upward. "That's it. I want to leave. I never had any intention of leaving you. All I want to do is write. You're so caught up with insecurity and jealousy you have to own me like property." She spun on her heals and nearly tripped in her haste. "I have no intention of leaving you. I never have. I just want some other kind of work."

Pierce didn't think so. Didn't think it was just routine work. His gut told him Maya was talented enough to succeed and, in that success were the seeds of a new and different life, a life where he lived retired while his younger wife found a career. He resented the distance between them, but he knew better than to oppose her when she really wanted something. Besides, if she loved something else more than she loved him, what value did she have to him? He needed a love that was voluntary.

Perhaps it was time they separated, he thought. *He and Maya were so different. His ideas were of a past generation, a generation of nobility, respect for womanhood, protectionism, morality. He opened doors for women, took their arms to assist them, kept his language civil, considered their feelings and coddled them. But Maya believed, despite her background and culture, that a woman was independent. Women wanted to be recognized as women. They shunned a door-opening man. They shunned the protectionism that marked the earlier relationships of men and women. They wanted the right to be free, and yet, to be understood.*

And sometimes when he thought like this, he convinced himself that he had been wrong to resent Maya's dreams and needs. He wouldn't admit it, but he saw the rightness in her argument. He just didn't want to lose her.

The evening ended in silence. They did not make love; rather, they rolled to separate ends of the bed. When morning came, Pierce was sitting in a lounge chair on the veranda and Maya dressed without saying good morning.

They flew home in silence, to the farm. Things did not improve at home either. Maya wrote her article on Valladolid. She submitted it to a national magazine. Pierce recalled how she raced up the stairs, check in hand, showing him the acceptance letter. She was bright, radiantly so and her triumph overshadowed his hurt. That was the beginning. That was the end. The lives that had twined together because of love were riven by ambition and doubt.

Several months later Maya won an award for her reporting on a local drug ring. The award specified that she had worked undercover, pretending to purchase drugs from suspected dealers, gaining their trust while funneling information to her editor. It applauded her for channeling information to the Drug Enforcement Agency as well. Pierce was shocked. He had had no idea she was working on such dangerous assignments.

They attended the awards dinner. Never did Pierce feel more isolated and insecure. It was another evening that ended in gloom. They did not speak the entire trip home. When they settled in bed, he propped the pillows between them and avoided her touch. Although he could see the hurt in her eyes before the light dimmed, he was fighting for his emotional life and resented her ambitions. It was destroying what they had. Or, what he *thought* they had.

PIERCE STIRRED FROM HIS REVERIE AND RETURNED to reality. The drug was wearing off. The blood had stopped draining. It was late and a hush settled over the hospital corridors as if death itself had descended upon them. It hurt him to think. As he slipped into sleep again, his thoughts were of the great red horse. He fantasized about riding Red through the woods and on ridges surrounding his home. But he was less sure now that this would ever happen. And he was less sure that Maya would return. Or that succeeding with Red would have any affect on Maya's career plans.

He was not better in the morning. The painkillers had worn off and he was suffering. He awakened that morning as they were inserting a fresh drain to inflate his lung. He heard Donnie just outside the door, and his eyes glowed painfully with excitement as the man entered the room.

"Hi." He shifted himself higher and winced, stabbed with pain.

"I was in the area," Donnie smiled.

"Been to the farm?"

"Twice on Sunday."

"The animals?" Pierce shifted uneasily and moved the rolling table nearer to him.

"The dogs haven't come back. The horses are fine. Doctor says you can probably leave end of the week if the lung stays inflated, but they'd rather you stay for more testing. Your blood count is low."

"What blood? They drained half of it out of me. Just trying to keep me here. Pad the bill, " he bellowed, hoping the medical staff would hear him.

"Surely not. They just want to be thorough. And you say the same thing about me."

"Nine dollars for a shot of painkiller. Can you believe that? Two Tylenol in a cup, four dollars and fifty cents. I can buy the whole bottle for two bucks."

"You haven't had a check-up in years. High time. Get the testing done and I'll keep minding the horses...for free."

"Well...for that, maybe." Pierce smiled. "Has Maya called?" He wanted her back. Loved her more than she imagined.

The vet shook his head. "We can talk about Maya later."

Pierce looked away at the dingy window through which little light flowed. "Probably called and couldn't reach me."

"What about the testing?" Donnie pressed. "Will you stay?"

He nodded with a grumble. "Could use the rest. Okay."

Donnie turned his head away and stared at the blank television set. "What the hell happened? You're really busted up."

Pierce sighed in exasperation, his face registering disappointment. "Had Red by the old barn...some squirrels spooked him. Bolted."

Donnie noted his breathlessness and cut him off. "So what convinced you that you were hurt?" The vet's face remained placid.

"Bad hurt. Hard time breathing. Couldn't climb stairs." He was gasping again, fighting for each breath.

"You're wheezing. Shall I get the doctor?"

"No."

"Sure!" he mocked. "What did you do after that? Catch Red and ride him again?"

"Yes. If I didn't do it then…couldn't do it later."

"Surely not. You didn't really remount. He damn near killed you and it's not like you to get thrown. This is crazy, just letting go over… "

For a time, Pierce said nothing. Then, he wheezed a hoarse answer. "Got me on oxygen. Breathing better now. "

"I'll come tomorrow. If you need me sooner, just call."

"Sure," he wheezed. "Thanks for everything."

"I'm just repaying an old debt. Remember when my head was in a basket because of marital problems? I recall a guy who didn't have to help me, but he was there. Not just as a guy giving legal advice, but a friend talking me through a bad time. We rednecks just don't forget that kind of thing." He looked away and Pierce laid his hand on the man's forearm.

"Tired now. See you tomorrow, maybe?" He gasped slightly. Donnie left and the room hushed into silence.

I DO NOT KNOW WHERE THE MAN IS. I know he was hurt. Something on the barn roof clattered and scraped making a frightening noise. I had been grazing calmly when it sounded and I bolted as fast as I could. I wanted to escape with the man as fast as I could. It was a while before I realized the man was not on my back. I turned and looked back and he was lying on the ground. It seemed odd not to have him guiding me. I felt lost, frightened. He moved and called to me so I walked back to him, still wary of the sounds that had scared me. But whatever it was that made the noise was gone.

I moved nearer to him and touched him with my nose. I was sorry I hurt him. I did not mean to. He reached up and grasped the stirrup and began pulling himself up from the ground. He moaned as he laid against me. His breath was raspy and hollow. It seemed so strange. For a long time he lay against me, breathing hard. I did not move. But I nuzzled him from time to time to show him I was sorry.

It took a long time before he mounted and he screeched when he pulled himself into the saddle. He guided me back along the trail, then turned me toward the old barn. We returned to where I had thrown him and he made me stand. We stood a long time and I could hear his pain as he groaned. I think he must be very brave this man.

This morning I was communicating with Diablo and he told me many things about Pierce. That he is much older than Maya. Diablo says she greets the man with smiling eyes and they walk casually, slowly along the gravel road, aiming in no particular direction or at any particular speed. A flaming, golden array of fall leaves floats lazily down from trees, but they do not notice. Nor do they notice the bare spaces on the hillsides where the leaves have fallen first. Diablo says they began to argue and then she went away and did not return. He doesn't think she'll come home. He also told me that Pierce went to a hospital. It's where the vet cares for people instead of animals. And he told me that Pierce misses his wife, but he may never see her again.

I think that is why the man is so sad. I saw him when they brought him home from the hospital. He glanced at me as the vehicle went by and our eyes met. He did not look well. He was pale and somber. They drove him up to the house. I could not see what happened then. Perhaps he will visit me tomorrow.

I like the man who takes care of us while Pierce recovers. He is kind too, but I want my friend. I trust him. When the storms came and lightening crackled across the sky, Pierce came and stayed with me, calming me, telling me everything would be all right. I would not like the woman though. I have never met her, but I do not like her. She was not here when Pierce came home from the hospital. She should want to be here to take care of the man she loves. He is not a stallion that goes from mare to mare. Diablo says the man only has one woman. That is also strange to me. But if my friend wants only one woman, I will not tell him he is wrong to mate with only one human.

I am puzzled, too, about why he lost his balance when I bolted. It just wasn't like him to be so unsteady. There were other times I startled and he *did not fall. So it was unlike him not to stay in the saddle. But I am happy he is home. Perhaps he will ride me again when he is better. I will do better then. I am prepared now about the squirrels in the old barn and they will not frighten me again. I wish I could tell him that. He is like no other man I have known. I trust him. It's as though he knows my thoughts and understands me. I look into his eyes and I see many things. Most of all I see a sadness deep in his heart. I wonder what it is that makes him so sad. Horses do not get sad. We do not feel anything but fear and contentment. But the man feels hurt and pain and loneliness. I wish I could help him. I wish I could help my friend.*

How frail are humans.

The testing took six days. Each day, a different series. Each day, Dr. Hassid visited, examined his lungs, read his chart and said nothing definitive. On the sixth day a middle-aged doctor visited Pierce. He was so broad his shoulder sloped into his neck and so tall that his lab coat did not reach his knees. Pierce didn't like the way the doctor averted his eyes when he entered the room. That meant bad news.

"I'm Dr. Barry." He seemed affable enough and Pierce liked the way the doctor exuded a straight-forward attitude. "How are you feeling today?"

"Like a man who wants to get back to living." He grabbed a plastic cup and drank as if there were whiskey in it. His food lay untouched. But the man didn't smile at the comment and Pierce felt uneasy about the doctor's reservation. It was almost as if a smile from the doctor meant everything was going to be all right.

"I'd like to go over the tests with you and ask some questions, Mr. Bernard."

"Call me Pierce."

"Fine. I'm Dayton."

"Had this stiffness long?"

"A while."

"Can't grip things?"

"Not much."

"Losing your balance?"

"Some, especially drunk."

"And you suffer muscle weakness, sudden jabs of pain."

The statement surprised him. He'd had stiffness that worsened, but he had paid it no mind. "Haven't really noticed. It's not so much stiffness as dropping things. Clumsy, I guess."

"Difficulty breathing sometimes?"

"Touch of asthma. Punctured lung."

"Trouble working your limbs? Fingers. That kind of thing?"

"Yeah. Arthritis, I guess." Pierce searched the doctor's eyes for a reaction to his answers. He knew something was coming, but it wasn't definable.

The doctor wrote on a small pad. "Appetite?"

"I don't eat all that much. My sinal drip irritates my throat and makes it hard to swallow."

"Difficulty swallowing?

"Sometimes."

"Take anything for the asthma?"

"Antihistamines. Inhalers."

"They help?"

"Some."

"Let's have a look." Pierce opened his mouth and the doctor examined his throat, taking a good deal of time.

"What kind of doctor are you, anyway?" Pierce asked when the doctor sat back. But Dayton didn't answer. He felt the wrists, the fingers, the arms, underneath his armpits, squeezing, pressing, noting any sign of pain or discomfort on Pierce's face. He asked Pierce to squeeze his hands. Examined his eyes. Felt under his throat.

"A neurologist," he said, finally, still writing on the chart.

"I see."

"Tell me about the muscle cramps."

"Mostly in the lower legs. I lift hay bales, ride, train horses. How'd you know I get leg cramps?"

"Just a wild guess."

"Some guess, Dayton."

"Are you married?"

"Yes."

"Is your wife home?"

"Actually we're apart right now."

"Separated?"

"No.

The doctor's face inherited a puzzled look. "I don't understand."

"Look, Doc, my wife wrote a book about the Mayan culture. She came from there and had a lot of in-depth information. So she wrote a book and she's been on a tour to sell it."

"So she's not in the area."

"She calls when she can get to a phone. And we're hoping the tour will give us both some space, some time to think. " Pierce looked away for the first time since the doctor addressed him.

"If you and your wife weren't separated, would you still have the urge to make love?"

"No, not like a few years ago—I'm older now, I guess. Doc, can we talk about something else?"

"I see from your charts you're on Albuterol, Serevent and Flovent for asthma. No other medication than for pain from this accident?"

"No. I passed out and they brought me in here. I still don't know who it was."

"A pneumothorax is nothing to ignore. A lot of blood in that right lung."

The doctor shifted his stance and sat in the cushioned chair to Pierce's right. Pierce noticed that the man's nose had been broken. *Probably a football accident*, he thought.

"Why all the questions?" Pierce asked.

"You're a pretty active man?" The doctor continued, ignoring Pierce.

"Never sit still. Always working on the farm. It's what I love."

"Good, that's good, you're active. I want you to grip my hands and squeeze as hard as you can."

"I did that before."

"Just grip as hard as you can."

Pierce grasped the doctor's extended hands and tried squeezing. He felt suddenly weak, powerless.

"Good," the doctor said, releasing Pierces hands and then writing on the chart.

"You didn't do all those tests and ask all those questions to tell me it's good I'm active. Let's have it!"

"We did an EMG, muscle biopsy, blood test, CT scan, MRI. The results, coupled with your complaints, loss of muscle tone and flexibility, poor gripping power, difficulty swallowing...well, the short of it is, you have amyotrophic lateral sclerosis, Lou Gehrig's disease. Your inability to grasp very hard tells me it's pretty advanced."

Pierce was stunned. One moment he was ready to bolt out of bed and the next, tears were streaming down his face. He turned toward the window and stared at a pale blue sky littered with strains of ash gray clouds. "Oh God, poor Maya. Who'll take care of her?"

"The question is who will take care of you."

"Any cure? They must have made some strides since Gehrig's time."

"It's a progressive disease. There is no cure. However, there are a lot of things we can do to delay the onset of disability. I'll recommend a complete work-up. Light aerobic exercises to keep the muscles flexible and reduce fatigue. Physical therapy helps. There are dozens of medications to relieve symptoms and make you more comfortable. And we can keep you pain-free."

"In other words, it just gets worse if you don't take care of it."

"Not exactly." The doctor's tone was didactic. "There isn't any *taking care of* it. The disease worsens with time. How much time, we can't say. Some people suffer the onset and are functional for years. Others, a few months. We've no way of telling and we still know very little about A.L.S."

"So you're telling me it's incurable, right?"

"We can make you feel better. And perhaps we can prolong your life. But, no, we can't cure you. Not yet, anyway." This was a talk the doctor had made before and it was obvious he didn't relish the thought of doing it. His eyes grew into somber, pale, blue orbs that twitched from side-to-side, trying to avoid the patient's stare.

"And you can't say how long it will take before I'm dead, right?"

"What I can say is that the average is three to six years. Some people function for years with the disease. Others don't reach the national average."

"And how will it be as the disease worsens? What happens then?"

"You're already manifesting symptoms. Sexual function is one of the first to go. Muscle weakness, difficulty swallowing usually follow. And…" he hesitated, "I suspect the horse accident wasn't because you were thrown. Loss of equilibrium is another symptom of A.L.S. You couldn't grip hard enough to stay on the horse."

"And down the road…?"

"You'll function less and less. Eventually, bedridden."

"I see."

"My advice would be that you live it up for as long as you can. Take that vacation you always wanted. That hunting trip you've always dreamed about. If there is anything you have always wanted to do, I'd do it. We have no way of knowing how fast or slowly the symptoms will progress. Try to make amends with your wife. You'll need her care. Perhaps we could contact her. Advise her of the situation. She might re-consider and come home." He hesitated. "It's not an easy disease."

"Not much of a life, is that? Not the kind of thing you saddle a wife with."

"It's a bum break, Pierce. Believe it or not, the risk of A.L.S is one in one-million. There are about five thousand new cases each year but not enough to justify research. But we are making progress. They're making genetic studies in France. We just don't know when a breakthrough will come. You have time. If something breaks, your name will be on a list for immediate treatment."

"Thanks for being straight. Now, when can I go home?"

"I'd like to do a few more tests…"

"No more tests!" Pierce turned his head to the far window and stared at the grey sky beyond. It had become a dull day that threatened showers.

How appropriate, he thought, *that the day should be so miserable.* "I've heard everything I need to hear. I just want to go home."

"Don't you want some idea of how advanced the disease is? Or a second opinion? I can recommend several specialists."

"I don't need any more false hopes." Pierce hesitated for a moment then turned his gaze back to the doctor. "This conversation is between you and me? Private, right?"

"Absolutely!"

"Even Maya can't be told unless I say so?"

"Not unless you authorize it."

"She's not to know anything. I'm releasing myself from hospital care and I don't want her to know a thing. If she calls you, no one is to tell her about my medical condition. She must think my lung is healed, my stiffness just an aftermath of having no oxygen in my system."

"I think you're making a mistake. What happens down the road when she finds out? You can't hide this kind of thing."

"I'll face that when I come to it."

"She's bound to notice sooner or later. She's got to come home to care for you. What will you tell her then?"

"Trust me, Doc. I'll work that out. Maya's a fine woman and I've given her a hard time. She doesn't deserve a break like this. I'll not let her foul up her career when I'm as good as dead. If she has to care for an invalid, she doesn't need to know about it right now."

"Don't you owe her the truth?"

"I owe her the gift of freedom. As far as being taken care of, it's not a problem, Doc. Got a sister in New Jersey. She's divorced, got three kids. I'll move in with her and pay rent. She can use the money. When I get so bad I can't handle myself, I'll admit myself into some kind of home health program. But not a word to Maya...not *ever*."

"I am legally obligated to protect your privacy. But I still think you're making a mistake."

Pierce shook his head. "I'm probably doing the finest thing I've ever done for her. Now, sign an order and get me out of here. She could be calling home right now."

Dr. Barry nodded, still staring at the man who had just received a death sentence. The man seemed too sure of himself, too certain, but it was not a doctor's task to understand motives. That was for the psychology department or a support group. He hesitated by the door, spoke a few words to a nurse, then disappeared into the great chasm beyond the room.

The nurse came in and injected something into the intravenous tube, mumbling about the doctor ordering a sedative right at the end of her shift. It was the last thing Pierce needed, but he accepted it. In a short time he drifted off, hearing the phone ring and carrying on a mythical conversation with Maya that he knew was only a dreamy mist.

"How are you Pierce?" She sounded so distant, cool. Yet, she was talking to him and, in his dream-world, it was what held him together.

"Not as bad as they make me out to be. It's good to hear from you."

"I've missed you. Funny, I never thought I would."

"No?"

"I just thought I'd go on writing, not even thinking about you. I find myself wandering back to you in my idle moments or when I've suffered writer's block."

"That's nice to know because I miss you terribly."

"You had an accident with the horse?"

Pierce knew it was just a dream. He really didn't have to answer. "I had Red up by the old barn today," he croaked, something intangibly different about his voice.

"You don't sound good. How hurt are you?"

He didn't reply.

"Pier. I asked how badly you're hurt."

He hesitated before answering. "Some."

"Some? What's that mean?"

"Collapsed lung. A few broken bones. Nothing I can't handle."

"You don't sound good. I can hear you wheezing."

"I'll be okay. Sore, but all right."

"Sure!" she mocked. "Mr. Macho."

For a time, he said nothing. Then, he uttered a hoarse answer.

"Tomorrow. I'll go home tomorrow."

"I'll call tomorrow night."

"Sure," he said. "I'm really tired now. I'll go."

"If you need anything, write it down and tell me tomorrow when I call."

"I'll be better in the morning. Maya?" he gasped slightly. "I'm glad you called. I love you." But the phone in his dream had already clicked and there was only silence then. He knew it had been a dream. There was no way Maya could know he had been hurt, no way she could know he was in a hospital. He was certain she'd come home once she knew.

She didn't come, though. Didn't even call. Pierced kept hoping she would call, tell him she was coming home. But she did not. Instead the hospital arranged transportation and help by having an emergency vehicle transport him home. He was able to walk, to care for himself. It wasn't necessary for them to remain and he told them to go. He was fine. He appreciated their help. They wouldn't accept a gratuity from him so he wrote out a check for two-hundred-fifty dollars as a donation to their service.

Donnie telephoned him and made sure the neighbors dropped in on him. Good people, just up the road. People who cared about others. People with the same pioneer spirit that had settled the West. The women brought him food. The men cared for the animals, worked his land, cut and baled his hay. A young girl, Tori, who he had once taken riding, came to call on him, to run errands to the store. Pierce liked her. She was bright and energetic and she had a nice way with the horses. But they were all mere ghosts; invisible spirits who nodded a "hello" then plunged into the work to be done. They brought him food, picked up his mail, shopped for his groceries, but when they had done, they left. And he was left to wait for Maya.

But the days passed and Maya did not come, nor did she call. His heart sank as each day ended. Could she be so cruel as not to care, even when he was injured, even when he needed her? No, that wasn't his Maya. Something was wrong. He'd ride the red horse along the farm trails, away from the barn, away from its familiar haunts. Then Maya would respect him again, love him again and she'd come home. He had failed too often at other things and that was why she had gone away. It wasn't the writing. She needed a husband who was strong and capable.

As the time passed, he grew stronger. He hobbled down to the paddock and spoke to Red. They had to ride the trails, to succeed. The red horse had to trust him because in that trust was the key to Maya's return. He believed that. He lived that. It became his credo and his faith. And the faith would have sustained him, though even the strongest faith can be shaken.

He arose one morning and said, "Happy birthday, Maya." She was sure to call that day. She never missed her birthday. He recalled how bright she would be on her own birthday, said that it was a very special day when a new star was born. Everyone had a star. Everyone had a special day. She'd search for her birthday gift and Pierce always took pride in hiding it so she couldn't find it. He loved the sparkle in her eye when she unraveled his clumsy wrappings, loved her excitement when she saw the gift. Yes, she would call…today of all days.

He walked out onto the porch and surveyed the land. The tall grass no longer blew in the gentle wind because it had been slashed at the base and fluffed by whirling teeters. When it lay in neat rows, the wind dried it and the sun cured it. Tractor-drawn balers moved along the rows and packed the loose hay into square bales. Then friends gathered the bales and stacked them in barns. Pierce recalled the fresh smell of that hay, the steaming heat it produced as it was stored in the barns. But it was cropped now and the fields lay flat and lush.

He spotted Donnie driving up the road and sat on the porch until the man was standing before him. For some reason he thought of Maya again, how she'd rise early in the morning, have coffee perking when he came down to breakfast, had bread in the toaster. But she was not there and he had to face the vet. Donnie puffed up the final stair and signaled to the older man.

"Take a seat," Pierce offered.

"Ahhhhh, I'm bushed," the vet replied. "Been working the thoroughbred farm, fifty-two horses and not a one with a kind disposition."

"You love it." Pierce wondered why the vet stopped that particular morning. Donnie spied the whiskey glass in front of Pierce.

"It's Maya's birthday. I'm having a drink in her honor." He tipped the bottle toward the vet who shook his head and declined. Pierce poured another for himself. It was obvious he'd been drinking the night before. His hair was still sleep-ruffled, his eyes filled with red fire, bloodshot and puffy. "I need for her to come home. She should at least come home for her birthday."

"Surely not, Pierce. Not after all this time."

Pierce did not reply. He stared straight ahead at the fields, listened to the mourning doves as they cooed in the trees.

Donnie cleared his throat and emitted a deep sigh. "I told you we needed to talk...about Maya."

"You've heard from her?"

The vet frowned and hunkered down into his chair. "It's time to let go, Pierce. Jesus, I hate being the one to tell you. Maya isn't coming back."

"What do you mean, she's not coming back? Who the hell are you to say that?" The vet's head jerked as the angry man rose suddenly and stood before him glowering. He backed away, turned, looked out at the dewy grass, glistening with the night moisture. Out beyond the copse where Challenge was buried, tiny rays of sunlight were coursing through grayish clouds as if sent from heaven. "Don't tell me she's not coming back. She calls me. Hear now? She calls me. Sometimes she even whispers as I am sleeping, but she slips out before I wake. That's Maya. She won't let me see her because she's peeved about this reporting thing, but she comes here."

Donnie waited a moment before continuing. "I'm your friend, Pierce. That's who. Someone has to make you see. Maya's gone. She can't telephone because she's dead. She can't whisper in your ear because she's not here. Oh, she may be just over the line and you may feel her from time to time. A scent of perfume. An article of her clothing. But it's not Maya."

Pierce sat down again. He suddenly felt weary, as though all the energy had drained through a tiny hole in reality. "I'm sorry. Everyone keeps asking about Maya. What's between us is our business. We'll work things out."

"You've kept Maya alive...in your mind...in your heart. Held on to her so desperately, you've invented someone who just isn't there. And I'm worried about you, Pierce. I mean you're going a little crazy perpetuating her memory. You need to let go."

The vet stared into the man's eyes and, in them, he saw the rising doubt, the recognition of a reality the man had always known. "Maya's not coming back, Pierce. Inside, you know that. I thought at some point everything would be clear to you...and because...because I'm your friend, I didn't want to be the one to tell you. She's not coming back. She wrote that undercover story about the drug dealers. She was with the F.B.I. the night she died, giving them names, locations, pay-off times. On her way home, someone ran her off the road, forcing her car into the river. She was a witness they couldn't afford. They never did find out who leaked the information about her. For my money it was that fancy editor she worked for. Creating his own headline."

Pierce's face reddened. Tears streaked down his cheeks, falling to his chest where his heart lay. Quietly he sobbed, shaking his head in disbelief. "But no," he whined, "she got out of the car. She's just hiding. Afraid they'll find her. When the time is right, she'll contact me. We'll get away from here."

"Surely not. You don't really believe that? The police searched for days. They never found her body."

"She telephones me. Every night, Donnie. I need to tell her something. Something important." His voice slipped into a whisper and he glanced around as if making certain no one was listening. "That back field. The one near the old barn? We had a heavy rain the other day and when I went back there, the grass was full of diamonds. I couldn't believe it. Diamonds all over the place. I could have filled my pockets with a fortune." His laugh was a tantalizing laugh, full of elation and deviltry, but his face was calm and serious. "I could have picked a fortune but I'm waiting for Maya. She should see this. That's what I have to tell her."

"I know you believe that, but it's just not so. There are no diamonds. There isn't any Maya, at least, not anymore, not here, not alive. She's only in your mind and heart now. I wish she could come back. I don't like to see you hurting this way. Death is part of life. We accept it or we perish."

"But we spent that night in Lexington. I didn't imagine that."

"No, Pierce, you didn't. It's where you celebrated an anniversary. You wanted to go back to Tahiti, but Maya just wanted something simple. It happened. It just didn't happen when you think it did."

"We had a wonderful time there. She was the kind of woman you could be happy with no matter where you took her."

"I know, Pierce. But Maya's gone and she wouldn't want you doing this to yourself."

Donnie looked away. He could not face the man. The boyish look in his eyes faded into a dull realization that perhaps he had gone too far.

"She did get away, didn't she, Donnie?"

"No, Pierce, she didn't. There were blood stains in the car. Damage to the left rear of her car. The police know that some vehicle, probably a truck, came up behind her, pushed the rear of her car until she lost control and plunged into the river. It's no good what you're doing. Surely not. You just have to accept some things and then move forward."

"And you're saying there were no telephone calls? It was all my imagination?"

"Sometimes when we can't accept something, when we love too deeply... Well, surely things must seem a certain way, but they really aren't. I think you needed to keep Maya alive because you couldn't bear to let her go and it clouded your judgment."

Pierce nodded. He respected Donnie. Knew the man was incapable of lying. He choked out the next words.

"I guess I've always known. She was a wonderful woman, warm, compassionate, vibrant. We had such a good thing until she started writing. She was so good, so lovely. How could they do that to her?"

He paced nervously across the porch and back. "I had to keep her alive. It was too painful to think of how frightened she had to have been when they rammed her car. I can hear the crash, hear her scream as she went off the bridge. I think of the water rushing into the vehicle, of her struggling to unfasten the seatbelt and swim up out of the car. I wonder what her last thoughts were. I wonder if she and I will meet on the other side."

"It's no good guessing. You don't know how the end came. She could have been gone before she ever hit the water. The whole thing happened in a matter of seconds. Surely she never knew what hit her. All I know is that you felt guilty because you let her go to that meeting, but it wasn't your fault. She was determined to find her own destiny. We can't rail against that, Pierce."

"God, I can't live without her. I'll go crazy if she doesn't come home soon."

"I know," Donnie sympathized. "But you've got to start living again. You've got your animals. And that red horse loves you. There's even a chance you'll find someone else. It happens, you know."

At that, Pierce burst into laughter. Not a sedate laughter, but a laughter provoked by the irony of the man's statement. He laughed so hard he coughed until his face reddened beyond the whiskey. Then the tears stopped and hung on his cheeks like glistening dew drops. His composure slowly returned. A smile creased his face.

The vet took this as a sign that Pierce was enjoying a private joke with himself and he felt inwardly good about himself that he had precipitated it. Perhaps his friend had finally ended a delusion that plagued him, finally accepted his wife's death. Thus armed, Pierce could go on, perhaps find someone else, find happiness again. Still, there was something in the laugh that bothered him.

"What's the joke, Pierce?"

"Donnie, I don't have much time to do any of those things."

"Surely not."

"They didn't keep me in the hospital because of my horse injuries. They were testing for something else."

"They wouldn't tell me much. That privacy thing."

"Can't blame them. Death is kind of a private thing."

"Death?"

"Himself."

"Surely not. It's can't be that bad, Pierce. It just can't."

"I've got Lou Gehrig's disease. It's the reason I got hurt on Red."

"Well, they've got all kinds of stuff for that."

"Not as much as you think."

"What have they got you on?"

"I don't know the names. They just gave me two prescriptions. If it's my time, it's not my place to cheat God."

"You can't just sit back and do nothing."

"I agree. But I need your help before I start following the doctor's regimen. Do I have it?"

"Sure you do. As long as I have your word, you'll fight this thing, not give in to it."

"I promise you Donnie, I'll fight in my own way, but I need my full strength. I can't be pitching hay and caring for horses while I'm on medication. Doctor says for me to stay off the tractor and leave the machinery alone."

"You've no need to worry about the horses. I'll take care of them until you're well."

"I'd like to still ride Red. Doc says I can do that as long as I feel confident about it. I think the horse is ready."

"Let me go out with you."

"Not hardly. I worked a long time to get him on the trail alone. Want to spoil it for me now?"

"Just the first time, then."

"Stop being an old mother hen. I'm not dead yet. Remember, I was riding before they discovered I was sick. All I ask is that when I am gone, you care for my horses. Can you drop by tomorrow, around supper?"

"I'll make it my business to."

"I'll give you a packet of papers. My Will, the farm papers, instructions on the equipment and what to do with some of it. My guns. There's a special provision for them. I'll hang on to them until I'm gone, though. Nobody's getting my guns while I'm alive."

"I don't understand why you're doing this now. You've got plenty of time. I had an uncle with A.L.S. He lived for twenty years and had two kids after they found his illness."

"Sure you did."

"Swear on my Bible."

"Donnie, I just want to have all this over and done. Off my mind. Then I can get on with the business of living. It's only just in case."

"Just in case?"

"Well, suppose I had a heart attack instead of this Gehrig's disease? What then? Maya's...she's...gone. Who else do I have?"

"Pierce, I'll do whatever you need. I'll come by at supper. Take you out to the Mexican grille in town. Just opened."

"Just what I need. Spicy, hot Mexican food. You're on."

The vet stayed for a while longer and, when he felt certain that Pierce was settled, excused himself and stood up. They shook hands and Pierce held the younger's man's hand until he was certain the vet would return for the papers.

Pierce watched the pickup motor down the long, gravel road. Now that the vet was gone, he knew he might never see him again. But he felt confident his instructions would be carried out. His animals would be cared for. Perhaps even the dogs might return and Donnie would take them in.

So Donnie finally had the courage to tell me the truth, he mused.

And Pierce knew that truth. He knew when Maya left, he might never see her again. Over and over, he cursed himself for letting her go. And yet, he had always believed in destiny, that it would take a person where it willed him to go. *There are always forks in the roads we take.* He had taken his when he gave up law and bought the farm. He wanted to come home, to something he and Maya could share. But her dream had been different and he knew when she left, that he might never see her again. He recalled the lateness of the hour and the desperation of waiting for her telephone call. Well into the night hours, he waited and, when the hour was too late to expect her, then the phone call came. He did not recall the blur that followed. He never recalled it. She was on her way home, but he did not remember everything she said. All he did was wait...for Maya to return. She never did.

When he was certain the vet had gone, Pierce tottered down the stairs. He took a long pull from the whiskey bottle he had selected, took another and walked down to Red's paddock. He put the horse through its paces in the round pen. Today would be the day. He'd ride the red horse on the trail.

He'd show Maya he could be capable and strong again. She'd feel secure, love him again, come back home. Donnie didn't know. He didn't understand. Maya was there. She was real. All he had to do was wait and then, he could reach and touch her, smell the fragrance of her hair, feel the warmth of her satin skin.

Pierce led the horse out, soothing him with sweet words. He took many pulls from the bottle as he groomed and saddled the animal. It took him a long time to bridle the horse, for the stiffness was coming sooner and sooner. He did not take the medication. He had always known that the end was inevitable. What point was there to medication?

At times, he laid his head against the great animal and wept. The horse seemed to understand and remained still. This was his friend and he would do nothing to injure him again.

When he had recovered from his sorrow, Pierce inhaled deeply, checked the cinch once more and, using a mounting block, swung himself into the saddle. They moved quietly out of the barn and into the sunlight. The early morning mist had lifted above the grasslands as the sun seared through it. Steam rose up as the legumes were heated and warmed. Light-streams shafted through the treetops and lit the ground. It would be a nice day…the kind of day he and Maya would have loved to ride together. But Maya was waiting elsewhere and, now, it was just Pierce and the horse with the golden mane.

THE MAN IS SAD TODAY. I CAN TELL IN THE WAY HE WORKS me on the ground. He is listless and inattentive. Twice, I almost stepped on his foot. He didn't seem to mind. He worked me longer than usual as if his mind were elsewhere and his thoughts not on me at all. That saddens me because today I am very calm and I am ready to take him on the trail.

I have not seen the woman since I came here, but I know when a man is near death. Death is something every horse knows. I knew when racehorses were going to die. And the man has the same smell. He forgot the carrots, too. He always brings carrots into the round pen to reward me, but he has not done that today. I forgive him, though, because I know my friend is not himself. I wish I could make him smile. He walks me to the barn and I am perfect for him. Then he saddles and bridles me, not too tightly either. He always has trouble with the bridle because he is so short. So I bow my head, and he feeds the bit gently into my mouth and places the bridle over one ear. Then he skirts to the other side and pulls the rest of the bridle over my other ear. Sometimes the bridle hangs on my ear and makes me look silly, but I am patient with him because he is short and cannot help what he does. There is the smell of grain on his breath, too, as he had when he staggered into my stall and slept.

He mounts me in the round pen as he always does. I walk at his command, back when he asks, even side step which has always been hard for me to do. He is satisfied with my performance. I follow his lead left and right, back again for him, go to the far end of the road that has always spooked me. I am excited now. I think he means to try the trails. If I am good, perhaps, he will not be so sad. Perhaps, if I act well, the smell of Death will go away.

But he does not take me on the trail. Instead we return to the round pen and he dismounts. He rubs me hard because he is pleased. He tightens the cinch again and puts a bottle to his lips. The bottle is near full when he begins and he drinks a third of it before he stops. He checks my bridle to make certain it is not too tight. Then he pushes on the saddle until I am standing balanced on all four feet.

He mounts and I stand instead of moving off as I usually do. He is pleased with this and rubs my withers as a reward. We continue jogging around the round pen. I am calm now. Something in the man has changed and I feel no fear. The goblins behind the round pen that always spooked me have no meaning for me now. I trust the man. I want to please him. We have come so far, this man and I. I did not trust him. Now I find confidence in him because he is dominant in a different way. He does not nip my hind or my flanks. But he is strong and protective. I only wish I could make him happy.

He dismounts now, opens the gate and secures it so it does not swing shut. Beyond is the small paddock and beyond that the road and still further the trail head to Swamp Trail. He mounts again and instead of walking off right away, I stand again and await his command. He urges me forward in his kind, easy way, and we saunter to the paddock gate. He does not tense. He is very calm. I move through the paddock opening onto the road. I know where he is headed, and I go there without trepidation. I do not spook at the tractor or the farm implements as I ordinarily would because I know the man is sad. I do not refuse to go forward toward the trail head. He praises me and I am pleased, proud to be his mount.

We enter the trail head. The leaves are brown and crisp and mount a deafening sound as we head uphill. Somehow, the sounds do not bother me. I have heard them before. I know what they are. Even when the wind scatters them before me, I do not spook. This day is different. It is special. Even the man's touch is soft and loving. He gives me direction with his whole body, not just his hands.

We traipse up Sassy Slope to Lonesome Trail, then to Swamp Trail. I approach the point where I have always refused. He tenses slightly, then relaxes, and I go forward. Ten feet, twenty, fifty. We are in free fall. The woods are losing their leaves, and I can see the barrenness around me. A deer starts off in the woods. Only I hear the sound, but I am not rattled. The man and I are one now, one heart, one mind, one courage, one spirit. He speaks to me as we ride. There is a melancholy tone to his voice. I am focused on his voice, on the touch of the reins.

We are far past the smaller trails and entering the main trail which stretches for miles. His touch on the rein is still light, almost as if he is letting me take him where I will, yet guiding me when I falter from lack of experience. There is something different about this time. I do not know what, but I know it is different.

The wind picks up a little and the sky clouds up. A mist forms in the air, but it is a pleasant mist. It is not rain. My friend settles deeper into the saddle. He is relaxed. Sometimes he talks, but mostly he is silent. Frequently he slips the bottle from his jacket and drinks from it. When he does, he permits me to graze where the grass is lush and the shoots are tender.

We turn from the main trail onto the branch trails that fork and loop around. A squirrel chatters through the leaves and races up a shaggy-bark hickory. The man stares quizzically as though not really seeing the animal at all, and I simply plod on as if it had never been there. Occasionally I stop to sniff the air or listen to another animal crashing off ahead of us, but today, I want to please the man and I am tranquil and patient. I have always been frightened when he took me away from the herd, but today everything is restful and slow.

Time trots by. A half hour, an hour. We've have never ridden this long. We stretch into the mist and the mist becomes fog. The fog envelopes us, but it is a kind fog, and it dampens sound. I do not mind it. Neither does the man. I glance behind, and the fog closes round us. It's like walking into nothingness and finding there is something there. I no longer feel the man on my back, but I know he is there. Perhaps something is happening that will never again happen.

More time stretches on. We ride for two hours, then three, covering all the trails, even forging some new ones. The man and I are one. The trails blend into our consciousness and fade into memory. Then suddenly, I realize we are headed for home. The mist has become light rain, and we are headed home. The man and I become individuals again. I am the horse with the golden mane, and he is the man with the sadness. He is unsteady in the saddle. His words are slurred and sluggish. For some reason I wish this ride would never end, for the man and I have come far. I have learned the meaning of love and I know I love this man.

He reins me to a stop and turns around to view the trail we have just traversed. He stares for a long time. The rain strikes the ground with a restful strumming. The leaves underfoot become supple and soft. Then he assumes command again and we are moving home.

I amble into the barn. It's the first time I wish we were not home again. He removes the bridle, letting me spit out the metal piece so it does not rattle my teeth. He has to stand on his mounting block to pull the saddle off. I turn my head to laugh as he does so, but he is not laughing. He has never looked as old as he looks now.

Gently he rubs me down with a warm towel and praises me for my excellence. He rubs my joints with alcohol to remove the stiffness and massages my back with short, circular motions. I stand for a moment and he scratches my forehead where my sweet spot is. I love when he does this, but this time, something is different, for he whispers a goodbye.

He puts his arms around my neck and hugs me for a long time. There is the water flowing from his eyes. Diablo has told me about this strange phenomenon. Humans call it crying. It comes when they are sad. Then he takes the bottle from his jacket and drinks. It makes him speak funny words and lose his balance. He is silly when he stumbles and there is no one to correct him with the bit. His face is grim, his eyes dull and empty. He strokes my withers softly and lays his head against my face. I nuzzle him and his eyes light again with happiness. But only for a moment and then the light dims. I watch him for a time. I do not understand his sadness. He mutters words I do not comprehend, but the tone is kind and sweet.

He leads me out of the barn and to my paddock. He turns and, of a sudden, the whole man seems to wilt. He has always stood straight, but he is sunken now and shriveled like a dead leaf. He trudges down the homeward bound road, toward his house. His shoulders sag, his pace is methodical and deliberate. He is going home to sleep now, tired and beaten by life. Somehow I know I will not see him again. It is then that I know sadness too. No, I will not see him again. And we will not ride the quiet trail again. The man is going home to sleep. And from this sleep, he will not awaken. I know what lies beyond. It is a place where he will find his Maya... a place where they will love again. The place where she has been waiting all along.

AFTERWORD

Many years ago, I stopped in a small, obscure confectionery store to purchase cigarettes. When one is addicted to smoking—a habit I discarded years ago—he is apt to stop at any likely location to purchase the "weed". I had never seen the store before, although I had passed there many times. It was housed in an ancient, yellow stone building, vintage 1910 or thereabouts, a corner store with apartments above it, to the right and left as high as the fifth floor. The outside read *Sol's Confectionery/Grocery,* but the sign was dilapidated and faded and the white lettering was black with soot. The interior was no better. The dusty windows were cold, unwelcoming, and admitted little light. Sol, the owner, was a German Jew, slightly built, cordial, European and in his fifties, although he appeared considerably older. My impression, then, was that he was a lonely man. I say this because he procrastinated my leaving by raising new topics of conversation. Once, he actually grasped me by the arm to restrain me from leaving.

That first time, we spoke long enough for me to comprehend that Sol could open new worlds for me. He was mature beyond his years, fawning, docile almost obsequious, and I detected the European culture from which he had birthed. One of those worlds emerged from behind the counter in the form of a massive, arthritic Doberman pinscher. The white hair on his muzzle told me he was at the far end of his years. What daunted me were the long scars across his snout, the stitched bulge where an eye had been, and the shorn ear that had healed in a flopped position. He was formidable, but not menacing. Instead, he sauntered across the floor, his nails tapping on the linoleum as he did so. He ambled up to me and poked his snout up to be petted.

"Is he friendly?" I asked, not wishing to find myself on the wrong end of a savage dog.

"Yah, yah! He issssss a goot dawk...unless dey go behind der register, yah." Sol hissed like a snake when he said this.

I surmised Sol said this in the event I was not what I appeared to be, for his store was in a high-crime area where robberies were common. Cautiously, I reached for Eric's neck. Patting a dog on the head is an aggressive sign that some dogs resent. What they resent, they sink their fangs into and while he was scarred and ugly, his fangs were all intact.

"What's his name again?" I inquired, still petting the dog.

"Eric. Der nomin issssss Eric. He issssss mien...how you zay, guards mien body." His accent was laden with ancestry and conjured up a vision of palaces, banquets and extravagant balls, mirrored halls and winding staircases as well as long, tree-lined drives.

"Bodyguard?" I volunteered, again noting that Sol was not completely secure with strangers.

"Yah," he smiled, "guards der body."

"How did Eric get all those scars?"

In that musty store, with sullied windows and faded curtains, the old man proceeded to tell me of his walk in the deserted marshlands near the highway and the wild dog pack that attacked him and Eric. I was young and twenty then. I had never met a European before, much less one who had been a prisoner in a Nazi concentration camp. For the next two years, I stopped in Sol's store, purchased cigarettes and other sundries, petted Eric and listened to the spellbinding stories of a man who had lived. He spoke of pre-war Germany, band concerts with brass blaring the jolly songs of a happy nation, people whirling on the grass that surrounded latticed gazebos, strolling couples daring to hold hands out of the sight of their parents, others rowing their boats in slow time around the lake. Sol was lonely and thus he offered payment by regaling me with stories of cabarets, beer gardens, horses drawing elaborate, glittering coaches behind them as they trotted up to magnificent mansions afire with candlelight and music.

Women were revered and respected. Children spoke only when addressed. Dresses touched the floor and were never pulled so high as to expose an ankle. Men waxed their mustaches to prevent them from drooping and slicked down their hair with greasy concoctions. He spoke of a Germany with new technology. The dirigible that could make the transatlantic flight. He even spoke of the Hindenberg disaster at the Lakewood Naval Base. He dwelled on the airplane, Wagner's music, mechanized devices to make life easier and faster. And as he spoke his clouded, grey eyes glistened with rapture as he relived the happy days of his native land.

He remembered "der" Keiser (Keiser Wilhelm) and the Great War. Sol had met some American soldiers, dough boys they were called though he did not know why. He did not find them to be conquerors but noble and compassionate, and he liked them. Germany was a defeated nation, but the Americans he met never treated the individual German as such. They were especially kind to children and women. From his back room, he brought a photograph of himself and a Yank Sergeant. Sol was a teen then but mature enough to have adult friends.

"Zargeant Villis Burks, yah. Zat vas hissss nomin. Und he spoke Deutch." Sol and Sergeant Willis Burks had become friends and for a number of years corresponded until the advent of the Second World War. Mail between Germany and America was suspended during the war. They lost touch.

Like so many other Jews, Sol suffered arrest and incarceration in a concentration camp. He survived. Others did not. He was seldom able to speak to me of the atrocities, the people, the killing. I did not press the matter. The pained expression in his eyes signaled that I should avoid the topic.

Sometimes, he spoke of individual men. Some seemed to stay long enough for Sol to recognize them. Others, he saw for such a short time he did not need to memorize their faces. What did it matter? They all had that frightened, haunted, ghastly look. They were hungry, filthy, and under-clothed. He watched skeletons drifting around the camp like ghosts. He heard rumors. Stories of mass burials. Experiments by the doctors using humans for subjects. Showers that were not showers. He heard bulldozers in the far end of camp. He wondered how the human spirit could survive. He believed some of what he heard because he had to believe it and because his logic could not deny it. He wondered how he would behave when his turn came. It was difficult to believe all of it, that men could commit these atrocities upon other men. After all, were they not all members of the human race?

And then he was free. Germany was war-torn. What remained of his shattered landsmen organized and sought their native land, the country from which they had come. The old Germany was dead and the new nation had no place for them. He sailed to Israel. The Jewish organizations tracked down his wife, Ida. She and Sol were reunited. Because they loved, they mended the tattered remnants of their lives. Mended them until a fanatic tossed a bomb into a crowded café and blew Ida and other patrons into death. Sol remained but there were too many memories in Israel. He traced a relative living in New York, and eventually gained admittance into the United States. He was proud of his citizenship. He was proud to be an American. I was proud to know him.

So now, Sol lives again, here among these pages, and in this place, no harm can come to him. His spirit can never be imprisoned again. Was it him the woman saw? Did it really happen?

I am old now and I harbor the fading memory of an aging man. Perhaps, I imagined the woman. Perhaps, she was a dream. But if she was real, then someone did help her. I choose to believe that someone was my friend, Sol and his "dawk," Eric. There is more to the story, perhaps, stranger still. Not long after the incident with the stranded woman I visited the place where Sol was buried. It was a Jewish Cemetery near Clifton, New Jersey. The area is heavily industrial and probably the last place on earth there should be a cemetery. The traffic din shattered and smothered any respectful quiet that should have been there. The soil was soft and wet from rain and squished underfoot as I searched for his marker.

It took me a while to locate his gravesite because there was no caretaker and I could find no listing of the persons buried there. When I did locate it, it was as simple in composure as Sol had been, quiet, undefined, unattended.

I said a prayer and lingered, thinking about the marvelous stories and histories Sol had filled me with. To my right I heard a sound. I thought it was another person. I glanced quickly only to confirm my hearing and standing there was a glimpse of a man and a dog. A glimpse that is not easily defined. In the movies it is always a ghostly apparition or an actual person. It stands. It has dimension. It can be seen, even conversed with. It can be friendly or hostile. But this was just a peek, a fleeting image. It could have been a brush of hair or something tangled on the eyelid and not an apparition at all.

I should have been content to leave it at that, but I did not. I walked to where I saw the supposed apparition. When I looked down at the earth, there was the clear imprint of a dog's paw. And it was fresh and newly made, but what was most remarkable is that it was a large paw print and what is even more remarkable is that along side it was the print of a man's foot.

Sol? Eric? I like to think so. I like to think my friend is waiting for me just beyond and with many more stories to tell.

I always knew that one day I would write Eric's story. I hope I have done justice to both. Perhaps I have added a touch or two, but then as Charles Dickens wrote in A Christmas Carol: *Are these the spirits that will be? Assure me that I may change these shadows you have shown me, by an altered life.*

Russell A. Vassallo

ALSO BY
RUSSELL A. VASSALLO

Tears and Tales

STORIES OF ANIMAL
AND HUMAN RESCUE

"Best Book Award 2006" Finalist
Fiction/Short Stories

"*Tears And Tales* offers up a remarkable story of life, love, beauty, independence, and glorious relationships favorably acknowledging basic truths which simply make life worth living. *Tears And Tales* is especially recommended reading, particularly to cancer patients and animal lovers."
–Midwest Book Review, July 2006

"Through ten heartwarming stories of animal companionship, *Tears and Tales* is based on Vassallo's personal memories of the animals that comforted him in good and bad times."
–Seton Hall University Magazine, *Pirates in Print*

"Russell Vassallo presents these real-life stories with an attitude of respect for all living things. These are unforgettable creatures and the author has created an unforgettable book." –Vernon Tucker, Farrier, Liberty, KY

ISBN: 978-0-9776739-0-2   176 pages   paperback $16.95

Available at Amazon.com or from the publisher at www.krazyduck.com